The Boxer

POPULAR DOGS' BREED SERIES

THE BOXER

ELIZABETH SOMERFIELD

Revised by Stafford Somerfield

POPULAR DOGS
London Sydney Auckland Johannesburg

Popular Dogs Publishing Co. Ltd

An imprint of Century Hutchinson

Brookmount House, 62–65 Chandos Place
Covent Garden, London WC2N 4NW

Century Hutchinson Australia (Pty) Ltd
88–91 Albion Street, Surry Hills, NSW 2010

Century Hutchinson New Zealand Limited
191 Archers Road, PO Box 40-086, Glenfield, Auckland 10

Century Hutchinson South Africa (Pty) Ltd
PO Box 337, Bergvlei 2012, South Africa

First published as *The Popular Boxer* 1955
Revised 1956, 1959, 1961, 1963
Reissued as *The Boxer* 1968
Revised 1970, 1974, 1977, 1985, 1989

Set in Baskerville

Printed and bound in Great Britain by Mackays of Chatham

British Library Cataloguing in Publication Data
Somerfield, Elizabeth
  The boxer
  1. Boxer dogs. Care
  I. Title   II. Somerfield, Stafford
  636.7′3

ISBN 0 09 174042 8

CONTENTS

ILLUSTRATIONS

ACKNOWLEDGEMENTS

Without the help of my husband, Stafford Somerfield, former chairman of the British Boxer Club, who sub-edited my scribbled manuscript, I doubt if this book would ever have gone to the printers.

I am also indebted to the following:

The Kennel Club for permission to publish the Boxer Standard.

Mr Phil Drabble, author of *Black Country*, and the publishers, Messrs Robert Hale Ltd, for allowing me to quote an extract from that book.

Frau Stockmann, the German authority, for permission to reprint her article on her dogs.

Breeders and owners who have contributed information and pictures.

Robert McDougal for permission to use his statistics.

AUTHOR'S INTRODUCTION

Shall we take it for granted that readers of this book are already dog lovers, and now want to know something about the Boxer? That to me is very understandable, for in my estimation this breed is way ahead of anything else on four legs. I hope you will forgive me for this bias, which is partly explained because of my interest in Boxers since the early days of their popularity in this country.

But not only that. To me the Boxer has a most charming nature and it has certainly made an impression on the legion of dog lovers in Great Britain. I think it will be lasting. He is, of course, a British dog if you go back far enough (as I shall explain in a later chapter) and that may supply another reason why we have taken to him so rapidly and so widely. Again, he is very much like the British in character—essentially a great home lover and rightly jealous of his family. He is also slow to anger, and can be trusted implicitly, but if provoked he can look after himself in a big way. And take it from me, he will not start a quarrel, but may quite easily finish one. As a guard dog he can be trained to be tough, but instantly obedient, while his faithfulness is unsurpassed.

A Boxer, like the British race, takes some understanding. He doesn't stand at the front gate of his home issuing shrill threats to all and sundry. He goes quietly about his business, and gives a gruff warning when it is absolutely necessary. But don't let an intruder be deceived by this pleasant and happy exterior, for when he's called on to do his stuff the Boxer will rise brilliantly to the occasion. That has been proved time and again, especially in Kenya where a Boxer I sent out there as a guard dog died defending his master's family and home. Not even the cruel knives

13

of his attackers turned him from his duty.

As a breeder of dogs for over forty years I have always been interested in the views of members of the general public who have come to me for advice about a pet, or a companion, as distinct from a show dog (a different proposition which we shall be dealing with at length). Their views can be summed up something like this: they do not want a quarrelsome dog, nor one that is too difficult to look after, nor one that is too finicky about his food; nor one that is too big, or too small. And he must love children, be absolutely trustworthy and a good guard.

The Boxer can fulfil all these requirements. He can hop into the back of the car, curl up in the kitchen, and his short coat, though needing regular brushing, is not difficult to manage, or too time-wasting. As for children, the Boxer of correct temperament from reliable stock will practically adopt them. For all these reasons then, our breed has swept forward in popularity.

All dogs are at their best as companions in individual homes. I write that without any fear of contradiction, for I have observed this to be a fact after many years' experience. True the stud dog, or, perhaps, a show dog in certain cases, must be prevented from becoming soft, but as a general run of things the Boxer is at his happiest and gives of his best when he's one of the family. Given the chance, he'll make your hearth his home, and won't be truly happy until he's made sure of a place in your heart. The Boxer is not the sort of dog that can be ignored or pushed around if you want the best results. Not that he'll complain unduly if you do, but if you have perception you will realize that he's not his normal buoyant self.

Take my first champion, Serenade. Scold her and she would wince, but praise her and she would try and wag off that old stump of a tail. And Serenade's mother—Alma von der Frankenwarte, the daughter of Int. Ch. Lustig von Dom of Tulgey Wood—or just Liska to her friends. She had the heart of a lion in a tough corner, but I never saw her pick a quarrel. But if any other dogs took her place at my feet beside the fire she had a quiet way of speaking to them. They understood that 'Grandma' required the

respect as well as the affection of the family. She was a
great character, which is something I like in a dog. Among
other things, we never knew how it was that she could tell
the time. But she could, and every night at nine o'clock
sharp she would take herself off to bed, which was her
special place at the top of the stairs. Here she would curl
up and, believe it or not, in cold weather pull her own
blanket over her head. Yes, Boxers have character all
right.

Now Liska has gone where all good dogs go when they
leave us, and today her descendants carry on the tradition.
That is one of the pleasures of breeding dogs: to see the
succeeding generations, and note in them the characteristics of their forebears.

Boxers are quick-witted, appreciative and intelligent,
but don't expect miracles if you don't train them properly.
Like children, they must have lessons if they are to learn
the right things to do. Of course they are naughty when
pups, and find it fun to get into mischief, but give your
Boxer your love and attention and he will behave like the
brightest boy in the class. But don't expect too much, too
soon, and remember that it depends on you as much as
on the dog.

So, briefly, this is a glance at the Boxer as a pet, but he
can also be a great show dog, and it's worth while
remembering that it will cost you just as much to keep a
not very good dog as one who can give the added pleasure
of winning prizes. And so, later, I shall devote a good deal
of space to explaining how to go about the enjoyable and
satisfying task of selecting, rearing and breeding show
stock.

Today, in Great Britain, the top-class Boxer is being
recognized by both breed and all-round judges as the sort
of dog which has the style and proportions necessary to
make him into a Best in Show winner over all other breeds.
So far that has been done infrequently at championship
shows—a high honour indeed—but it will happen more
often in the future, for the quality of Boxers in this
country is improving every year. In America, where the
breed has also been a great success, he has gone right to

the top at big shows very much more frequently, and one famous dog achieved this over a hundred times—a record in any breed and an incredible performance.

Now the reason for this is that the top-show Boxer has lovely proportions and great showmanship. If you have an eye for a dog you will know what I mean. He is perfectly balanced. Leave out his distinctive head (with strong jaw and noble brow) for a moment, and look at the rest of him. To me, no other animal possesses such a clean-cut outline, and a body which expresses virility and strength, as well as speed. The Standard of the breed calls it 'substance' and 'elegance'—but don't let us be too technical.

Look at that short, straight back, the clean arched neck, the gay well set-on tail, the turn of stifle, the depth of brisket, strong quarters, the straight front legs on tight feet like a cat's. Give this body a true Boxer's head, an attractive colour with a flash of white, and any dog lover will catch his breath. This really is something.

But we must be frank. Not all Boxers present such a dream picture, but given the true temperament of the breed, there isn't one that can't give you a warm feeling because he's your dog. To me he's the canine aristocrat: the tough chap, who can be gentle, the gay fellow who likes a joke, to run, play, have a game at any time. And the comforting, insinuating beast who, knowing that it's a winter's night and that you are lonely, perhaps, will put a cold nose in your hand, and say: 'It's all right, I'm here. I'll never leave you.'

But not all champions prove themselves as outstanding sires or dams, and in the end only a handful of dogs and bitches can be shown to have had any influence on the breed. As with the dogs so with the owners. It is astonishing that only a few of us have bred five or more champions. Unhappily some of these are no longer with us, for time takes a heavy toll.

I've tried to make it clear that though it falls to few to breed and show champions, thousands of others keep a Boxer as a guard and a companion. It is for these owners also that I have written this book in the hope that it will give them an added interest in the breed and assist them

MAZELAINE'S TEXAS RANGER

A sire with a lasting influence on British Boxers. A gift to the author from Mr and Mrs J.P. Wagner of the famous Mazelaine Kennels in America. A monorchid, he sired six champions in Britain and many other certificate winners

BULL BAITING

The Boxer's early ancestors were English Bulldogs. This old print, from *The Bulldog*, by Edgar Farman, shows bull baiting in progress

BOXER ANCESTOR
Sixpence, a Bulldog born 1872.
The likeness to a Boxer is unmistakable

INT. CH. SIGURD VON DOM OF BARMERE
The first of the great modern Boxers

CH. PANFIELD SERENADE
Britain's first Boxer bitch champion

to get the best out of their dogs.

Many countries assisted us to produce the British Boxer, and it is an error to regard the various strains in Britain today as German, Dutch or American. They are all Boxers, with a common ancestry which goes back in most instances to the famous dogs I have called The Immortals. No matter where they began their careers, they have combined to produce the genuine British article combining the best characteristics.

We are natural dog breeders in these islands, and the Boxer has made rapid strides. But I was pleased to see that from 1957 onwards the rate of numerical progress steadied down, for this reason: to get the best dogs, breeding must be discriminate. Good ones are more likely to produce good ones than indifferent specimens which may be delightful pets, but are not themselves likely to improve the breed. This makes it extremely important that the best breeding material is sought out and used. Information within these pages should help newcomers in making these important decisions.

I cannot emphasize too highly the desirability of breeding from dogs and bitches of good temperament. Nothing lets down a breed so much as nervous or bad-tempered ones. Fortunately there are not a great number in our breed, but those that do suffer in this respect should be studiously avoided.

Allow me, then, to welcome new Boxer owners. They say that the best advice comes from personal experience, and I've tried to put down my thoughts, ideas and information collected over the years in the hope that time taken up in reading will be worthwhile. I think it will be.

The dog it is said is man's best friend, but let us go a step further and say the Boxer is the most true and lasting friend of all.

It says a lot for the popularity of the Boxer that in 1968 and again in 1970, 1974 and 1976 I was asked to bring this book up to date. I did so with pleasure, for after so many years I still remain a fan of the breed.

Taking a quick look at the list of champions I note with enthusiasm that of the new Boxers to achieve the title several come from smaller kennels. This is important for the Boxer thrives where he is treated as an individual.

Of course the bigger kennels have a greater chance of achieving fame for they have a greater selection. But such is the art of breeding that the owner with just one bitch can go to the top providing the best blood-lines are followed.

I have one word of warning to offer as I survey the scene more than forty years after the first Boxer was registered in Britain. Care must be taken about temperament. Nothing lets down a breed more than faulty character.

Read the Standard again. Our beautiful breed must be alert, intelligent, friendly and bold when necessary. And I've seen too many winners who do not measure up.

In breeding the true Boxer, character is just as important as shape and colour and probably more so. Study the pedigrees in this book by all means, but that is not the only guide. Get to know what sort of animals these dogs really were. I've said it all before, and risk repeating myself when I write that the true Boxer must not only look the part, he must behave without fear, with good manners and with sufficient boldness to look you straight in the eye with sincerity and friendship.

E.S.

REVISER'S NOTE

Elizabeth Somerfield, one of the great British Boxer breeders, died in the spring of 1977, and it was her wish that I should carry on with this book.

Many animals and their owners to whom Dibbie referred in earlier editions have now died, but there seems no reason to change the text for this twelfth edition except to bring records up to date and to add the years from 1977 to 1987.

I am proud to continue her work.

S.S.

Ivychurch, Romney Marsh, Kent
1989

I

How It All Started

It's a common and understandable weakness of humans to find pleasure in tracing their ancestors back to the distant ages when even to have had a name was a mark of distinction. So it is with dogs. There is an urge to know where they came from; how they came to exist at all.

In an effort to satisfy the curiosity of the Boxer owner it is not proposed to extend this exercise back to the Ark when, as we are reliably informed, two of each kind of animal were preserved from the Flood. Let us be content with noting the fact that more than 2,000 years before the birth of Christ the Assyrians used packs of dogs in their battles.

You can say if you like (and no one can contradict you) that these were the first Boxers though, of course, they were the first of scores of other breeds as well, and it would be simpler and save argument if we just accepted them as the very early dogs. One thing is pretty certain: these ancient fighting dogs possessed many of the characteristics of the Boxer. They could run, they were virile, and they had immense courage. In ancient times, of course, breeding was indiscriminate, and survival went to the swift, the strong and I suppose the lucky.

Later some attempt was made to breed dogs which were outstanding hunters and workers with the idea of improving their skill and intelligence. But this had nothing to do with physical appearance. The object was purely to breed dogs for specific duties. That is the key to all selective breeding in ancient times.

As far as the Boxer was concerned he was the sort of dog required to hunt animals like the bison, the bear and the boar. Many of the needed characteristics were the same as for the ancient fighting dog: speed to keep up with the chase, daring to attack the quarry, and the strength to hang on till the hunters arrived. Much-needed characteristics were a strong jaw to retain the grip, the set-back nose to enable the dog to breathe while holding on, and the well-developed muscles to withstand the strain. These characteristics are retained till this day in the Boxer.

But all this was before the day of any particular breed. They were merely the sort of dogs which could do this kind of job better than any others. They were simply called the beissers, or the biters, and to these words were much later affixed others like buffal, baren, or bullen, meaning buffalo-biter, bear-biter, or bull-biter, to indicate how the dog was used.

Let us accept it, then, that dogs were helpful to man from the very earliest days. They assisted him in the hunt; they were trained to guard his property, and in return they secured his protection. They lived with him and were no longer wild.

These barenbeissers, or bullenbeissers, can be traced back to the primitive Celtic and Teutonic tribes, and later they were found in the British Isles. It is an amusing thought that we have been exporting dogs since the Romans first came to these shores and took back with them some of our bullenbeissers. Evidently they found them more useful than those at home. We have always had ability to produce excellent livestock, and we retain the same skill today.

By the Middle Ages another step forward had been made, and dogs had become roughly divided into three kinds. It was a simple division, and had been based broadly on the work that was required of them. There was the heavy bullenbeisser (the English type and the ancestors of the Mastiff), the large hound (which led to the Great Dane) and the small bullenbeissers, the forerunner of the English Bulldog and the Boxer. It is with the development of the last named with which we are concerned.

*   *   *

Man, as we have seen, had begun to breed dogs to suit the jobs he wanted them to do, and a change was bound to come in development when it was no longer necessary for man to hunt to live. Typical of this country, sport then took a hand, and we find dogs used for bull baiting. There was also a practical side to it, as we shall see. The demands of this 'sport' again affected the characteristics of the dog, this time to make him smaller, quicker and better able to fight the bull in a confined space. For a description of the scene I have gone to a book named *Black Country* by Phil Drabble.

'Wherever you go in the Black Country you will find bull-rings and bull-stakes . . .' he writes. 'At one time it had been illegal to kill a bull that had not been baited, for two reasons. Partly that everyone should be aware that a bull was about to be killed. Then their butcher could not easily palm tough old bull on them instead of prime beef. In addition to this, it was believed that any animal dying immediately after very violent exertion became more tender . . . [Hence the practical side.]

'Initially this rite had been performed by the butcher, who kept special dogs for the purpose. But the general public soon took an interest, and it became profitable to allow them to pay for the privilege of baiting a bull with their own dogs. This became popular all over the country, but nowhere was it loved more than amongst the tough brawny ironworkers and colliers of the Black Country.

'It was still practised here ten years after it became illegal in 1825, and besides well known places like the Bull Stakes at Darlaston and Sedgley, there was at that time a recognized place in almost every village . . . .

'The rules of the game were simple enough. The bull was tethered by a rope to his horns and a stake, or iron ring, in the village square or on a fair ground. This rope was about twenty-five yards long so that the bull had about a fifty-yard circle in which to manœuvre. And he quickly got enough experience to stay in the middle of his circle where he had freedom to move about. In those days it was literally dangerous to be "at the end of one's tether".

'When the "bullot", or owner of the bull, was ready he

charged anything from 10p. to 50p. "a run". That is to say, he got a fee from everyone who fancied the chance of his dog. Believe me, the bulldogs of those times were not only game but cunning as well. When they were let go, or slipped, they didn't just rush in where angels fear to tread. They crept stealthily forward, keeping themselves as flattened on the ground as possible. The bull waited for them, head down, front legs close together.

'Then the duel began. The bull's aim was to slip a horn under, not through the dog, and flick him as high into the air as possible. If he succeeded the dog's owner would be waiting for him to try to break his fall. Some men tried to catch their dogs in their leather aprons, whilst others became extraordinarily adroit at slipping a stiff bamboo pole under their dog's flying form so that he slid harmlessly to the ground. If they failed, the dog landed with a thud enough to wind him if he escaped broken bones. And however much he was damaged, he was expected to crawl back and tackle the bull again.

'If the bull failed to toss the dog away then the dog had a chance of victory. He tried to grip his quarry by the nose, or cheek, or eye piece, or tongue so firmly that the poor brute would fall to the ground "pinned" in his agonies as he tried to shake himself free. And the dog that first pinned the bull won the contest.

'Of course, the sort of animals that masquerade as bulldogs today wouldn't have stood a chance. Real bulldogs were much taller on the leg, barrel-chested for heart-room and power, and had muzzles about half-way between the modern bulldogs and a stocky Stafford bull-terrier.'

Notice particularly Mr Drabble's description of the dogs bred to fight the bull: 'Real bulldogs were much taller on the leg [than the modern bulldog], barrel-chested for heart-room and power, and had muzzles about half-way between the modern bulldogs and a stocky Stafford bull-terrier.'

That, surely, is a good description of our breed, and there can be no doubt at all that the Boxer owes its start as a registered and recognized breed to the mating of an

English Bulldog, named Tom, belonging to a Dr Toenniessen who lived in Munich, to German bitches of a similar type.

It wasn't until I looked closely into the history of the Boxer that I realized that he is in fact one of the old English breeds. It so happens that he was nurtured in Germany, but the line stretches way back beyond that to the days when Englishmen bred the best kind of dog to bait the bull. What clearly happened was that in this country the development of the Bulldog was towards the stocky, short-legged type, with rounder heads and more pronounced chins, while in Germany an effort was made (and it was successful) to produce a more elegant dog possessing longer, straight front legs, and with the ability to act as an escort dog (as the Standard of the breed puts it) 'with horse, bicycle or carriage'.

It is interesting to re-read an article which appeared in the *News Chronicle* on 4 May, 1937. It was written by John Woodward. He said:

'Another foreign breed! Yes; but not so foreign when you know him. Look at an old print of a Bulldog and a modern photograph of a Boxer and the likeness will astonish you.

'It is as though Nature, in spite of us, had preserved the old British breed, emblematic of the national character. No disrespect to the present-day Bulldog; but he is not the bulldog of tradition. The Boxer is that.

'For centuries used for bear and boar-hunting, he has a fine heredity both in physique and intelligence. Courage, loyalty, obedience are in the blood, and it is doubtful if any dog makes a better escort or protector.

'But like all good guards, the Boxer is restrained. Alert to every strange sound, watchful of every suspicious movement, he knows when to keep quiet and is never stupidly aggressive. The British Boxer Dog Club gives us a nice description: "It should carry itself with calm self-assurance, and the frown on its face is no more than a warning to pay regard to its self-respect." Well-named the Boxer!

'He is a strong but graceful dog, built on good satisfying

lines; a noble head, powerful jaw, fine neck, wide chest, straight legs, docked tail, short coat, brindle or red colour.

'A dog easy to groom, hardy to rear, and of manageable size—weighing about sixty pounds. Abroad his ears are cropped, and certainly it makes for smartness, but not much is lost by leaving the ears as God made them and English law decrees.

'Many foreign dogs have become such established English breeds that we get a shock when we remember their origin. The Spaniel and Labrador, for instance. The Boxer, most decidedly, is a dog we should also make our own, and I prophesy that we will. He's like an old friend returning home.'

This was an article of tremendous truth and value. And how right Mr Woodward was!

For more evidence that the Boxer is an 'old friend returning home' I go to an eminent authority, the late A. Croxton-Smith, a former Chairman of the Kennel Club who had this to say in the *Sporting and Dramatic* in November 1935:

'It will be noticed that Boxers are reminiscent of the Bulldog, *from which they sprang*. They are longer in the body, however, higher on the leg, and altogether more active, nor have they the exaggerated turn-up, heavy wrinkle, and abnormally short nose, though their jaws are bluntish. They give the impression of being good natured dogs, and in formation a combination of power and activity, and, as far as one can learn, their dispositions are delightful. They have courage without aggressiveness.'

Even the great German Boxer breeder, Herr Philip Stockmann, was a little unhappy about the name of the breed—Boxer. For quite obviously that is an English word. Writing on this subject many years ago in his book *Der Boxer* he says:

'The Boxer's original name was bull-biter or bear-biter .... By interbreeding lighter, more agile dogs with the heavy Bulldogs in the course of time there arrived the breeding of a strong but fast dog. Thereby the ground stock of the Boxer was laid. The Bulldogs of England and Boxers of Germany have the same ancestors. The name bull-biter means exactly the same as Bulldog, but the name was also often used for the Boxer up to the last quarter of the nineteenth century.

'The English, as born breeding geniuses,' (continues Stockmann with a touch of irony) 'conceived the over-typical and grotesque, and so produced the present-day Bulldog. The practical Germans, however, did not wish to sacrifice the value of the use of his bull-biters to a monstrous external appearance. But there were breeders who readily followed the English aim, at least in some points. Through that arose a confusion, that no one knew what to do about. Boxers, Bulldogs, Pugs, were all lumped together. Soon Bulldogs, which came from England, were bred in, *and with them the English name "Boxer"*. We have since expunged the English Bulldog from our Boxer. Why did the English name prosper with us? Surely the translation into German "Kampfer" would not have been worse!'

So much for Stockmann on this point. One appreciates his difficulty about the word 'Boxer', but personally I'm very glad it persisted rather than 'Kampfer', which he suggested.

Where exactly the word 'Boxer' came from I cannot discover, but one suggestion is that the breed took its name from the way Boxers use their front feet when at play. They cuff each other with their paws in the manner of the old bare-knuckle fighters.

Be that as it may, I think we can fairly claim that our breed is English in origin, but at the same time no one wishes to deny that the Germans played an important part in its development, and it was from their land that the Boxer returned home to England after a long sojourn in a far country.

2

Thanks to Tom!

So much for the ancient history. Now let us attempt to get a picture of the early Boxers, remembering (and this is very important) that the development of the breed has all occurred in less than 100 years. If Boxer breeders kept this more firmly in mind they would avoid some of the disappointment they feel when a litter on which they had placed great hopes does not turn out as expected.

One hundred years is not long in this context and is too short a period to have bred out many major faults. No one is surprised when all-white puppies appear in a Boxer litter because we now realize that as white Bulldogs were extensively used in the early days (which explains the attractive white markings we all hope to see), by the very nature of things they must reappear from time to time.

Why then must there be astonishment when there pops up a roach back or loose shoulders, for example, or even an untypical head? They are all there in the background. All that we can do about it now is to avoid these faults as best we can by breeding away from them. Gradually they will be eliminated.

Back now to the 1890s when Dr Toenniessen, living in Munich, had an English bulldog, named Tom (what a good old English name!). Unfortunately, as far as I can discover, no one has a picture of Tom, but one thing is certain: he was as white as the driven snow. It is also safe to assume that he looked very much like the Bulldogs of the last century. They had straight front legs, good length of neck, and not an exaggerated body, in fact far more like a Boxer than the Bulldog seen in the show-rings today.

Like the Boxer they were agile, alert and swift-moving dogs.

No. I in the old *German Boxer Stud Book* was Flocki, a male brindle whelped 26 February, 1895. His sire was Tom who had been mated to George Muhlbauer's Alt's Schecken, the breeder being Andrew Nerf. Flocki not only had the distinction of being No. I in the stud book, but was also the first Boxer ever to be shown.

There is a story behind the appearance of Flocki in the Munich show-ring. In 1895 a Viennese named Friedrich Roberth had come to the city, and had taken notice of the Boxers. From all accounts he was a sincere dog lover, and had previously been interested in Airedales, but he was now to become enamoured of the short-coated breed. He soon found two more fanciers with a similar passion, named Elard Konig and R. Hopner, and after their first meeting they persuaded the St Bernard Club, with which one of them had some association, to include a class for Boxers at the club's next show. Four entries, including Flocki, was the result.

In the following January the Deutscher Boxer Club was formed, and on 29 March of the same year held their first show at the home of Joseph Himmelreich. There were 20 entries and Elard Konig was the judge. By present-day Boxer standards the collection of dogs at Mr Himmel-reich's house that day were an odd-looking lot. Several were white, some were white with patches of brindle or fawn (the Germans called it yellow). Others were black.

Philip Stockmann says in *Der Boxer* that the dogs displayed a middling uniformity. 'Only one dog had a cleft nose, and one bitch was too much like a Bulldog.' He adds: 'The Boxer of that time was mostly white or parti-coloured; small to the ground, without much nobility, and often very poor hindquarters, but with really fine typical heads.'

Undoubtedly the breed developed a great deal in the first half of this century, and today we are reaching a uniformity which must be recognized. In the early days, however, it is obvious that all sorts of types were exhibited, and this made it tremendously difficult for us to breed good, sound dogs. Still, today, patience and hard work has had its reward.

It was after the show of 1896 that the Germans got down to the task of producing a Standard of the breed, and to this Standard and the ones that have followed, we shall devote some attention. It took the Munich Club six years to get it settled, which doesn't surprise me, for it has taken just about as long to get one or two minor alterations to the present-day Standard discussed, much less adopted. The Standard of any breed of dogs is as revered as the Tablets of Stone on which were written the Ten Commandments, and very wisely, too, for there are many pitfalls to be avoided. At the same time, this should not rule out thoughtful revision from time to time.

Anyway, the first German Standard was adopted on 14 January, 1902. History relates that there were many arguments, and one result was that the new club was split with dissension. British readers who sometimes wonder why it is there are so many Boxer clubs in these small islands can console themselves with the thought that at least Boxer lovers are in this respect being consistent. From the very beginning there have been differences of opinion.

By 1905, however, all the German fanciers had combined again, and the Standard of the Munich Club was generally accepted. There were to be other splits and rejoinings, but this did not prevent the Boxer from gaining strength till World War I when breeding was much curtailed.

One of the highlights of the preceding years had been publication of the first stud book in July 1904. It came out with the first issue of *Boxer Blätter*, the first magazine devoted entirely to our breed. It is to the *Boxer Blätter* that we owe much of the information about the early Boxers.

3

The Early Boxers

Though the Germans claim the Boxer as their breed, we have seen that the first sire came from England. Now notice that the first important dam came from France. She was a dark brindle bitch named Flora, imported by the same George Alt, of Munich, already mentioned. George Alt mated her to the Munich dog known as 'Boxer', and they produced a fawn and white male who took the name of his subsequent owner, George Lechner, and was entered in the stud book as Lechner's Boxer.

From Lechner's Boxer we shall see that these early German breeders were well aware that to establish a type it was necessary to breed closely. We find that Boxer went back to his mother and produced Flora 2nd and Alt's Schecken (who was mated to Tom, and produced Flocki). Alt's Schecken (a brindle and white) also produced a white bitch, Ch. Blanka von Angertor.

Blanka gets a mention because she was mated to Piccolo von Angertor, a son of Maier's Lord who was by Lechner's Boxer out of Flora 2nd (another white, by the way) and produced Meta von der Passage who proved herself to be the first great producing bitch of the breed. Her photograph shows her to possess all the characteristics which keep reappearing today, and cause us to raise our hands to the heavens. First, she was nearly all white (there was a patch of brindle on her head and another spot on her left side). Then she had a long sway back, fell off in croup, had short stumpy front legs and, to cap all, was down-faced. Today she wouldn't reach the show-ring, much less get a prize. But don't let us be too rough on Meta. Without her the whole history of Boxers would have taken a different shape.

Another of the very early ones we must notice is Flock St Salvator, who was used as the model when first attempts were made to write a Standard. He was a stylish dog compared with many of his period, but his very light fawn colouring detracted from his appearance. Nevertheless he is a key dog in the early history, for he was mated to Meta and between them they produced two dogs who were also destined to have a great influence. These were Ch. Schani von der Passage and Hugo von Pfalzgau. Meta at another time was bred to a brindle dog named Wotan, yet another successful mating, for it was to lead to the brindle male Ch. Gigerl, who was to play his part both by reason of his virtues and his faulty roach back which reappears to this day.

It is my intention in this chapter to name only the key animals of the early history in an effort to give a clear picture, and I shall leave out many who may have been good ones themselves, but did not, probably through no fault of their own, have any marked influence on the breed.

Also it is simpler to deal principally with males. There is another reason for this. The male, with a few outstanding exceptions, must have a greater influence than the female. A popular dog at stud can sire a great number of puppies, whereas the number of any bitch's children is strictly limited.

Meta, then, produced Schani and Hugo, and they in turn gave us Boxers who were also to have an influence. Schani sired Ch. Rigo von Angertor, the outstanding show dog of his day, and Hugo produced Ch. Curt von Pfalzgau. Rigo was a deep red in colour, and he passed this richness on to his offspring. We still keep it today. The first of the great fawn show Boxers, he was an outstanding sire, and at a time when champions were not easy to make he produced thirteen.

Despite that, it was Curt who was to do most for the breed, and he also beat Rigo on one occasion in the show-ring, an event which was to shake the German Boxer world. Curt had a beautifully constructed body, but it was

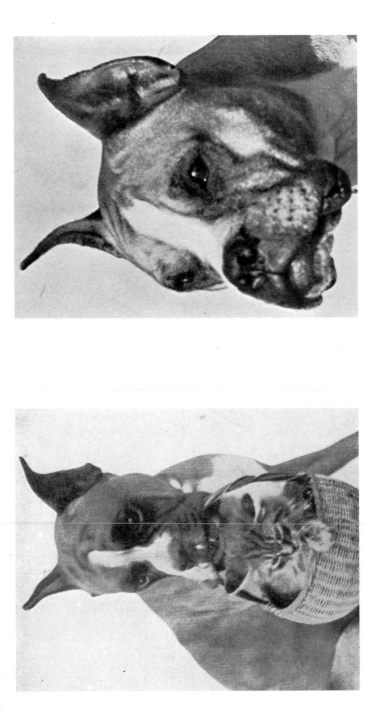

ALMA VON DER FRANKENWARTE
The Lustig daughter who had a great influence on the breed in Britain

INT. CH. LUSTIG VON DOM OF TULGEY WOOD
One of the greatest Boxers of all time

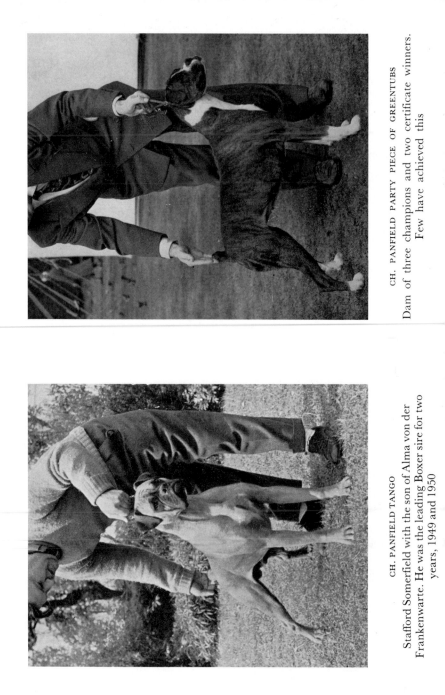

CH. PANFIELD TANGO

Stafford Somerfield with the son of Alma von der Frankenwarte. He was the leading Boxer sire for two years, 1949 and 1950

CH. PANFIELD PARTY PIECE OF GREENTUBS

Dam of three champions and two certificate winners. Few have achieved this

CH. GREMLIN SUMMER STORM
Record breaker in his day

INT. CH. SEEFELD PICASSO
Winner of twenty-four challenge certificates, sire of eighteen
champions and sixteen champion grandchildren

CH. STEYNMERE NIGHT RIDER
Proved to be a fine sire

CH. MARBELTON DESPERATE DAN
A top winning male with twenty-nine
certificates

CH. WINUWUK MILRAY'S RED BARON O'
VALVAY
Baron at 9 years old

generally felt that Rigo could beat him on head quality.

Curt's greatest son was Rolf von Vogelsberg, a brindle, but as the Germans had divided the colours into separate classes by this time he did not meet another great show dog of his day—a fawn—except once. This was Ch. Milo von Eigelstein, who like Rolf himself was out of a Ch. Rigo daughter. Milo was better in body than Rolf, but failed to him in head. On the one occasion they met for the challenge trophy Milo won. He did not live long, and had no outstanding sons, but through his daughters he wins for himself an honourable place. Among his descendants was the Siegerin Uni von der Würm who became the grandmother of Lustig and Utz von Dom.

Rolf was to become the property of a couple whose names will always be linked with the Boxer, and their kennels will be remembered as long as the breed exists. I refer, of course, to Herr Stockmann, his wife Frau Friederun Stockmann, and their world-famous von Dom strain.

Frau Stockmann owned her first Boxer in 1909 when an art student in Munich before she was married. Though she had noticed pictures of the breed much earlier, and had vowed one day to have one, it was not until she met her husband that her wish became reality.

Frau Stockmann has described this Boxer, how she and Herr Stockmann acquired Rolf, and how the von Dom Kennels got its name, in a charming article which appeared in the August 1951 issue of the *Boxer Blätter*. It is so refreshingly frank and so full of interest that we reprint it. She wrote:

'I saw my first Boxer—or perhaps it was some type of Bulldog—in a book of popular breeds which my brother gave me for Christmas. Looking back through the years, it seems to me that my life has been inseparably connected with the Boxer ever since, for as soon as I saw it, I was determined to own such a dog.

'Ordinarily, my parents were very generous in fulfilling my desires. But I was unable to convince them that I needed a dog. And that's when I began looking forward to college. I knew I was going to Munich in 1909 to study sculpture under Professor Baerman. The independence I envisioned had a special meaning to me. Unlike the young ladies who dreamt of dances and theatre parties, I could think only of the beautiful Munich I wanted to see. In my imagination, I took long walks down its lovely avenues in the company of a good friend, not a two-legged friend, but a four-legged one—a Boxer.

'It was in Munich, while I was attending night classes in drawing, that I met my future husband. For some time I paid no attention to him or the other young men. But one day he told me how his dog had knocked over a lamp while bounding to meet him. My interest suddenly wakened. What kind of a dog was this? I asked. "Oh," said my future husband, "he's like a tiger—with a big head and a great black muzzle!" A Boxer I thought. And from then on my interest in Mr Boxer-owner increased. Soon I became better acquainted with him, and, of course, with Pluto, his dog. In a way, Pluto was the best-mannered Boxer I have ever seen, but he had acquired some undesirable habits during the times when my husband found it necessary to leave him with other people. He had developed into a scrapper and poacher, for instance, having killed a buck of considerable size and broken the spine of a dog much larger than he.

'By the time I'd known Herr Stockmann six months I owned Pluto, the first Boxer of my life. Even though his bad habits caused me much trouble and grief, for a long while he was to me the dearest and most beautiful of dogs. Owning him awakened in me a desire to learn more of his breed, too. From Herr Albert Schmoeger I got some Boxer literature, a booklet and issues of *Boxer Blätter* which contained the judges' reports. I studied them eagerly and compared my Pluto with the champions they pictured and described. What a disappointment! First I noticed Pluto's wet neck, then his straight stifle, and—although I didn't see it at first—I realized later that his back was much too long. As if these shortcomings weren't enough, I had no pedigree of Pluto. I didn't give up hope, though. There was a chance that Pluto's offspring would be of better quality.

'Perhaps it was bold of me to ask Herr Schmoeger whether Pluto could be registered and used for breeding. But he answered "yes", to my great delight, and managed to find a six-month-old female for me. And so—though I'd never thought seriously of buying a female—Laska became my property just eight days later.

'Once the transaction was completed, I began to worry about breaking the news to my parents, who unknowingly were financing the dogs along with my college expenses. Besides that, my days as an undergraduate were nearing their end, and I had to decide what I intended doing in the future.

'When school closed, though, I had no choice. I took my dogs and started the long trip to Luebeck in Northern Germany. From there we went by boat to Riga, Latvia, and I hoped all the way that my parents would pay the extra expenses which travelling with animals involves.

'It was all right; the two dogs immediately won my parents' affections. My father especially loved Laska.

'I had shown Laska, incidentally, to Herr Schmoeger, just before leaving Munich. He liked her very much—so much that he thought it would be a pity to breed her to a poor specimen like Pluto.

'Meanwhile, I had become a member of the Boxer Club and an eager reader of *Boxer Blätter* and a magazine called *Dog Sport and Hunting*. At that time a male, Rolf Vogelsberg, was a rising star among brindles. I preferred brindles, even though Laska was fawn with a white blaze, and this Champion Rolf Vogelsberg completely captured my interest.

'The year 1911 brought a great event in my life. Herr Stockmann came to Riga and we were married there. Shortly after the ceremony we decided to attend our first dog show, which was to be held in Munich. We left Riga eleven days prior to the show and the dogs were to follow by train, since the train was faster and the dogs wouldn't need to be crated so long. But when we reached the border, the dogs had not yet arrived. What could we do? Today I'd know how to handle the situation; I would stay at the station until the dogs came. But in those days occurrences of this kind were common on Russian rail-roads. If the dogs became nervous during the trip they were removed and left until another train crew decided to pick them up and take them on to their destination. My husband suggested I send a telegram tracing the dogs. It seemed a good idea, so I did. Slightly relieved, we continued our trip.

'Two days later we arrived at our new home in Fuerstenfeldbruck near Munich. The dogs, of course, had not arrived. Day after day we went to the train station in vain. I was relinquishing the last desperate glimmer of hope when, on the eighth day, the dogs finally showed up. They looked a little lean and in need of grooming, but they were happy to see us. At the show three days later, Laska went Reserve Winner.

'Both Laska and Pluto were registered under the von Dom name, but neither of them contributed much to the breed. Pluto died without even having been used at stud, and Laska's offspring were of poor quality.

'At the Munich show, I saw Rolf von Vogelsberg and learned he was for sale. The price was rather high, but I had some money tucked away which had been earmarked for the purchase of my trousseau. As was always the case, dogs took precedence. A friend took over Pluto, and Rolf von Vogelsberg moved into the von Dom Kennels.

'Even today, I feel I was disloyal to Pluto. I loved him dearly. He brought my husband and me together. What's more, he gave our kennel its name. He lived with my mother-in-law in Mainz when he was young, across the street from the Dom (Cathedral). Since it was from there he began his roaming and adventuring, we called him Pluto von Dom. When I used von Dom as a kennel name later on, I was informed (particularly by foreign breeders) that von Dom meant "outstanding" and that it was quite presumptuous of me, a beginner, to apply this name to my kennel.

'Laska and Rolf von Vogelsberg were not the only dogs I owned at this time. A happy incident led to the purchase of Traudel von Steinhausen, Laska's mother. She was a somewhat old female, but a much better producer than her daughter. Unfortunately, I had some bad luck with her litters. Of the five males and three females in the first litter, only three males and one female lived. I picked one of the males and dreamt of raising my own champion. But Traudel accidentally killed him eight days later. Her other two puppy dogs had been spoken for. They developed beautifully and became outstanding males. By today's rating standard, they were V-dogs—"Excellent". These two, Wotan and Racker von Dom, received several first prizes, and on one occasion Wotan beat his half-brother Ch. Rolf Walhall. That was at least a small success for a beginning breeder.

'My next litter was out of Laska—all mediocre puppies. Then Traudel had another litter by a repeat breeding to Rolf von Vogelsberg. She had nine males—four of them white—and only two lived. Of these two, only Credo von Dom was shown successfully.

'The fourth litter brought the long-awaited winner. At that time, Herr Schmoeger had a small, but very typey, bitch—Bilma. He'd had bad luck in breeding her and had never been able to raise any of her pups. So it was agreed that he would lease Bilma to me for two puppies. Bilma delivered the largest litter I had for a long time. Of the six males and five females, I left five pups with her while Laska nursed the other six.

'This litter contained my first Sieger (champion), Dampf von Dom. He won his title at Hamburg against tough competition from six other "certain" prospects. I was unable to be there because my daughter had been born only two weeks earlier, and it was at this Hamburg show that my husband received such an irresistible offer for Dampf that he sold him to America. (To Herbert H. Lehman, later Governor of the State of New York.)

'We didn't learn until twenty years later that Dampf had become the first Boxer to finish his American championship. His litter mates were of some significance to the breed, too, although Herr Schmoeger had his usual bad luck. He picked a male and female, both fawns. The bitch—after Dampf, the best of the litter—he gave to one of our old friends, Josef Widman. The male he kept for

himself he named Debes (the best), but Debes turned out
to be the poorest dog in the litter.

'Gradually I obtained several more females; some of
them good, some rather odd. Looking through my kennel
books today, I shake my head, though, at the ignorance I
displayed. The best of the bitches I got during this period
was Siegerin Urschi von Hiltensberg, a really delightful
three-year-old brindle that won forty first prizes. I had
three litters out of her, but only one good bitch, Morna
von Dom, which for a long time was called "the pride of
Leipzig".

'I was not too well satisfied with the results of my
breeding. I owned a number of females, but felt they were
not the right ones. To correct this situation, I was in the
process of obtaining a very typey and powerfully-built
bitch I had seen in a show at Ulm, when the first
indications of approaching bad times were felt. We
learned of the assassination of the Archduke Francis
Ferdinand at Sarajevo. World War I had started.

'I realized I wouldn't be able to feed all my dogs, so I
began selling off most of them. My husband was drafted
and placed in charge of a unit of war dogs. The
government had put out a call for dogs, and the Boxer
Club had been the first organization to respond, supplying
a number of good dogs for training.

'Meanwhile I was completely cut off from my family in
Riga and was left to take care of a small child and a large,
rather expensive house. The government provided no
means of support for us; but, in spite of financial
difficulties, I was able to keep most of my remaining
dogs—three bitches and my old Rolf von Vogelsberg.
Finally, it came to the point where I could no longer feed
Rolf, and my husband had to take him into his canine field
unit.

'One of the most beautiful females then in Germany was
Zilli von der Elbe, a large red fawn with a white blaze. Zilli
was not bred for a long time because of her show career,
and when she finally did produce a litter consisting of
several males and one female, the event caused great
excitement among Boxer breeders. This first daughter of

the large and beautiful mother remained small and of no importance; but later in the war Zilli had another litter and I was given Bella von der Erftal-Elbe, a large golden fawn bitch with an excellent body and a head that was slightly long.

'Bella introduced herself to my family group by killing a goat and a valuable hen. I bred her to Rolf von Vogelsberg, and the resulting litter produced Raudi von Dom, who later produced the champions Priska and Pierette of Brunswiga Kennels. I kept a brindle bitch, Ch. Rassel von Dom. I now owned two females—Rassel and Derby, a sister of Dampf. When Derby died shortly afterwards, I wasn't able to bury her in the frozen ground. So I tied her body in a heavy sack and put it in the garden. Little Rassel, only six months, would sit next to her dead playmate and grieve for hours. That decided it. Rassel was not a good-looking female, but I made up my mind to keep her because of her loyalty.

'Black Boxers existed then. Their first breeder was a disagreeable man. Rumour had it that the first black Boxers were produced by a Bulldog-Schnauzer mating. Actually, the ancestry was not too important since few dogs were registered then and many unregistered dogs were used for breeding. But this story, and the somewhat distasteful behaviour of their owner, caused strong opposition to build up against black Boxers.

'Among his dogs was a small, insignificant female which was bred to a Rolf von Vogelsberg son. From this mating came Flock von der Adelegg, a male with many good characteristics. I used him in an experiment. Even though there was some public demand for black Boxers, they remained the stepchildren of the breed. That was a challenge, so I decided to try my luck. I bred Rassel, a Rolf daughter, to Flock, a Rolf grandson. The result was about what I had figured—one black female, one brindle male, and one black male with a lot of white. All three were of good quality.

'In 1918 I showed Uter von Dom, the black and white male, at the Munich show. He was far superior to the competing dogs and would have won without question—

had not the judge refused to put up a black and white Boxer. Today I realize that he was influenced by that group of breeders opposed to blacks. Soon after, the black colour was prohibited, even though it did not constitute any disadvantage to the breed, and the black Boxer became extinct.

'The end of the war brought a big change in my life. My large house was sold and the farm "Reichschmitt" purchased. From then on I had many disappointments and losses. Rolf, who won his last champion title at the age of eleven, died suddenly. My other dogs were suffering from all sorts of skin diseases, and food and medicine were hardly available. A nice litter out of Rassel by Ch. Alexander von Deutenkofen died at the age of four months.

'The move to the farm turned out to be a catastrophe. There were not enough kennels and no material to build them with. We were lacking food and other necessities during a period when money lost more of its value every day. However, one man's poison is another man's meat, to turn an old parable hindside to. A disease broke out among cattle which made the meat inedible for human beings. I bought beef by the carload and fed it to my dogs. They ate and ate. This providential incident saved Rassel's last litter which contained Zwibel von Dom, a large, well-built golden fawn bitch.

'From Zwibel stemmed all the von Dom dogs that were to earn the kennel its reputation and popularity. In ten years she had ten litters. However, she was a murderess, a trait she probably inherited along with size and colour from her grandmother, Bella von der Erftal. She killed two of my best females, one of which was Belinde Hassia, mother of the great Sigurd von Dom.

'Zwibel's most important offspring was Iwein von Dom, by Ch. Buko von Biederstein. Buko was a great grandson of Rolf Vogelsberg; Zwibel, a Rolf granddaughter. Everyone recognized Iwein as an outstandingly beautiful dog, but he couldn't be shown because of his aggressive temperament. His best son was Sigurd von Dom.

'Sigurd soon influenced the whole breed. I got Lustig—

by Zorn von Dom, a Sigurd son—out of Esta von der Würm, a Sigurd daughter. And a return breeding of Zorn and Esta produced Utz. Although Zorn did a great deal for the breed, he was surpassed by his son Lustig.

'It would make too long a story if I were to tell all the details of my tribulations or list the names of all my dogs which won top honours. But I can say this: the success I have had has not come easily.'

I make no excuse for printing this article in full for it is of absorbing interest to all who love the Boxer. We are fortunate to have Frau Stockmann's personal account.

It is an appropriate point to add here that Herr Stockmann died at the end of World War II, but that Frau Stockmann went on to breed many more fine dogs. She judged Boxers both in the United States and England (twice). She died in 1974. We learnt much from her visits.

4

The Immortals

Sigurd

This account of the von Dom Kennels has put us a little in front of our history, so let us return briefly to Rolf von Vogelsberg. A brindle son of Curt von Pfalzgau, he was the great grandson of Ch. Gigerl to whom we have already referred.

Gigerl had passed to him his great qualities, but also that bugbear of the roach back. The wise German judges, however, did not allow this fault to blind them to the dog's great qualities. In the various critiques upon him he is described as a male of 24 inches, possessing an ideal head and neck, perfectly placed shoulders, excellent front and hindquarters. His show record is astounding. He started at the age of two (notice that the Germans were in no hurry to bring out a show dog), and won all along the line until World War I. After hostilities he returned at the age of eleven to take the Sieger title for the fifth time at Munich. One doubts whether such a remarkable record will ever be equalled.

Rolf also stamped his great quality on his progeny, though the war cut down the number, and there was also a reluctance on the part of some breeders to use him. They were inclined to see only the dog's back—not as straight as they would have liked—and missed his all-over value. There is a lesson there for breeders today.

Rolf kept his name alive particularly through his son Ch. Rolf Walhall, another fine, upstanding brindle male who in turn sired Ch. Moritz von Goldrain, the brindle sire of Ch. Caesar von Deutenkofen. All of these are key dogs in our Boxer history. From Caesar came Sieger Check von Hunnenstein and Dudel von Pfarrhaus who were to put the Boxer into the international field. Check was sold to the United States, and there he went best in show under Alva Rosenberg in 1932, the first Boxer to achieve the distinction. Mr Rosenberg was an all-rounder with a world-wide reputation. It was my privilege to see him judge the American Boxer Club's great show in New York in 1952.

He recalled Check with great relish. He was not a big dog, but he was beautifully balanced and sound, possessing great elegance. He did a tremendous lot for the breed in the States. But not only there, even though just one of his daughters, Anitra of Mazelaine, became the mother of six American champions. Perhaps his greatest feat was performed in Germany before he was sent across the broad Atlantic to the New World. He sired Saxonia's Andl, the mother of the great Int. Ch. Dorian von Marienhof of Mazelaine.

So Caesar sired Check, who sired Andl, who was the mother of Dorian. But that was not all. Caesar's son, Ch. Buko von Biederstein, was the father of Iwein von Dom who in his turn gave the world the immortal Int. Ch. Sigurd von Dom of Barmere.

Sigurd was exported from Germany in 1934, but at that time he was five, and before he left he had produced sons and daughters destined to make him one of the most important—if not *the* most important—Boxer of all time. Jack Wagner,[1] the great American breeder, in his brilliant book on the Boxer has declared that 'to Sigurd, more than to any other individual dog, we owe the tremendous advance in consistent perfected balance of power and excellence'.

A great winner both at home and in the States, Sigurd made his impact on the breed through his two sons Xerxes and Zorn. Xerxes, mated to a daughter of Ch. Check von Hunnenstein, produced the brindle dog, Int. Ch. Dorian von Marienhof, who was destined to become world famous, while Zorn, mated to Esta von der Würm, a Sigurd daughter, sired Lustig, whom Frau Stockmann has

[1]Died 1974.

described to us as the greatest dog she ever bred. Lustig, a fawn with white markings, never defeated in the show-ring (nor was Dorian), also became an International Champion and spread his influence throughout the globe.

To these great dogs, Lustig and Dorian, through their common grandsire Sigurd, Boxer breeders the world over owe practically everything. They in all truth were the really great ones of the past, and we shall see how they dominated the breed on both sides of the Atlantic.

Thus the German breeders set their seal on the breed. Studying their methods one is immediately struck by the fact that they were well aware of genetic principles and produced their top-class dogs by careful selection and line and in-breeding. The Germans also had rigid rules about breeding dogs which members of the clubs were bound to follow. Both brood bitches and stud dogs had to be approved and permission given for matings to take place. Even the puppies were subject to close scrutiny and, if the local warden so decided, certain ones had to be put down. In any case, no more than six were allowed to be kept in any one litter. By these methods the Boxer Club kept the whole breeding system under strict control. For non-compliance penalties were severe. Certainly the puppies could not be registered. (It should be noticed here that the German Boxer Club had far greater authority than its counterpart in this country, where control is vested in the Kennel Club.)

The Germans claimed that by their methods they ensured the purity and progress of their dogs, but such a system would not work here. Germans are much more submissive to authority. We like our freedom, and it will be a bad day for us when someone has the right to walk in and tell us how to breed, or how not to breed, our dogs. There is no likelihood of it happening. Maybe the other way is better for the Boxer (though such a system is obviously open to abuse), but in any case we should never permit it, so there is little point in taking it further. Let the Germans please themselves; we shall stick to the right to breed when and to whom we like. We shall also decide for ourselves which pups we shall keep and which, if any, we shall discard. Though our way may appear haphazard to other eyes we are convinced that it is right *for us*, and that's what matters.

The scene now switches to the United States where Boxers were first imported about 1903. Among those to have shown a keen interest were the Lehmans, a distinguished New York family. Irving Lehman was a Chief Judge of the Court of Appeal of New York, and his brother, Herbert H. Lehman, became Governor of that city. The latter brought to the States Sieger Dampf von Dom who became the first American Boxer Champion in 1915.

Governor Lehman's son was serving with the United States Forces in this country during World War II, and came out to see the Boxers in my kennel. It was a most interesting link with Boxer lovers in the States.

The breed progressed only slowly in America at first with the 1914–18 World War particularly cutting down interest, and it was not until 1932 that Check von Hunnenstein arrived and really put Boxers on the map in the New World. Check was the first to win Best in Show all breeds. He became a US Champion the same year as he arrived and won many converts to the breed by his great personality.

Dampf started a further stream of importations which climaxed in 1934 with the arrival of the great Sigurd. As we have seen, Sigurd had all the best German blood behind him—Caesar von Deutenkofen, Rolf von Walhall, back to the Stockmanns' famous Rolf von Vogelsberg and beyond to Hugo von Pfalzgau. He arrived when five, and died in 1942 when nearly thirteen. In that time he proved himself one of the greatest sires in Boxer history, even though there was a shortage of outstanding bitches in the States.

His greatest feats as a sire were in fact performed in Germany before he left for the States. There he sired Zorn von Dom and Xerxes von Dom who produced respectively Lustig and Dorian von Marienhof. Sigurd, Utz, Lustig and Dorian became the Big Four of American Boxers, dominating their day and generation. And Sigurd was not only one of this select band himself, but the other three were his grandsons. Thus the name of Stockmann triumphed across the seas.

For those who like facts and figures, Sigurd not only took top show honours in both Germany and the States but produced 25 champions.

This book is not intended as a history of the breed in the United States (there are already several volumes devoted to that subject) but we must pay some attention to the Big Four because their influence was also strongly felt in Britain. In two ways. In a line stemming straight from Germany to these islands, and by the longer route from Germany to America and then across the Atlantic again to the United Kingdom. The former of these grew faint with the passing of time, but the latter has become even stronger during the past few years.

We must not leave Check too hurriedly, for he was responsible for Dorian through the latter's dam Saxonia's Andl. Check was not a big dog, being about 23 at the shoulders, but he was a brindle of great style and excellent conformation. He took the Austrian Sieger title in 1929 and the German and Czechoslovakian titles the following year. His American show debut came in 1932, and in the following two years he was taken into the ring 36 times and on 35 occasions he was Best of Breed. Francis A. Bigler claims that the great popularity of Boxers in America today was started by Check because of his 'unique make-up, stylish appearance and sterling character'.

Sigurd was born on 14 July, 1929, and started his show career proper in 1931 (though he had already done well as a pup). In the next two years he swept the boards in Germany and his fame spread to America where the founder of the Barmere Kennels (Mrs William Z. Breed) was already taking a great interest in Boxers, and owned some good ones. Hearing about Stockmanns' super fawn Sieger she became determined to buy him. He was purchased for her by Charles Ludwig, and arrived in the States two days before the Morris and Essex Show. The year was 1934.

Imagine the excitement. Mrs Breed had already entered

Sigurd, but he arrived after the journey by sea looking thin and gaunt. For the next 48 hours (and indeed for ever afterwards) Sigurd was treated like a king, and then when the great day arrived Mrs Breed herself, wearing her well-known white kennel coat, the pockets stuffed with pieces of liver, stepped into the ring with him. He went Best of Breed, and the winning of his American title was only a matter of time.

We had the pleasure of meeting Mrs Breed when we were in New York, and heard first hand how greatly beloved was this wonderful dog. Apparently he greeted those who went to his bench most gravely, and invariably put up a paw to shake hands. Altogether in the States he took 54 Best of Breed wins (including Westminster in 1935 and 1936), was 51 times placed in the group, including eight Firsts, and was twice Best in Show All Breeds. A remarkable record, especially as these were early days.

Mrs Breed, whose frankness and sense of humour were renowned, tells how Sigurd gave her a most embarrassing moment during the spring of 1934. Preparing him for the ring, she used olive oil on his coat and a mixture of charcoal and vaseline on his muzzle. At one show Sigurd had not been properly cleaned off and the judge, unhappily, wore spotless white flannel trousers. After passing his hands over the dog's head and body the judge stepped back to admire him, rubbing his palms down his trousers as he did so. We draw a discreet veil over the rest of the scene, but record that Sigurd again took Best of Breed.

So it went on until a sad day in 1942 when Sigurd died aged twelve and a half. This is Mrs Breed's own comment on him:

'I realize that it was purely an accident that I acquired Sigurd von Dom, but I shall always be proud that I should have been the one to bring this great dog to America. Despite his comparatively limited opportunities at stud in this country, Sigurd sired innumerable champions in America and left behind him many more champion grandchildren, champion great-grandchildren and so on, through the fifth and sixth generations. My little Ch. Barmere's Locket is a double Sigurd great-great-granddaughter. No one can appreciate, more than I do, my good fortune in being the owner of the great Sigurd. I shall be everlastingly grateful that I was privileged to enjoy his love and companionship for upwards of seven and a half years.'

It was of this dog that Frank Bigler, the American canine historian, was moved to write:

> Now his show-day's done, and the latticed gate
>   Is for ever closed on his battered crate,
> And his show-leash hangs on the wall in state
>   'Mid the trophies of the ring.
>
> But Sigurd still roams the sweeping lawn
>   With none of the beauty of vigour gone—
> An athlete modelled in bronze and brawn,
>   And every inch a king.

Lustig

The previous pages dealt with Int. Ch. Sigurd von Dom. We must now deal with his three grandsons. Remember that all of these not only dominated the establishment of the breed in the United States, but also in Great Britain.

No useful purpose would be served by trying to prove which was the greatest; the importance of each was tremendous, but it will be convenient to deal with Lustig first because his ancestors were more prominent in the early days in England.

Lustig, like Sigurd, was bred by the Stockmanns, and he was sired by the brindle Sigurd son, Zorn von Dom, out of the Sigurd daughter, Esta von der Würm. Notice that in-breeding—a Sigurd son to a Sigurd daughter, revealing the complete faith of the world's pioneer breeders in their 'grand old man'. It was the result of years of careful planning and patience, and those who aspire to reach the top by a short cut (and we have known several) should pay heed to the way the Stockmanns went to work. And they were the early masters.

The philosopher has reminded us that by studying the past we are able more closely to forecast the future. It is worth remembering. Get out the pedigrees, then, and go over the ground with the Stockmanns. Zorn, the proposed sire, was by Sigurd out of Dudel von Pfarrhaus, a daughter of Caesar Deutenkofen who was Sigurd's great-grandsire through Ch. Buko von Biederstein and Iwein von Dom. The bitch, Esta, was by Sigurd out of Uni von der Würm, a daughter of Sieger Edler von Isarstrand out of another fine bitch, Meta von Rechenberg-Wehrspitz.

It was to be a winter litter. The mating took place at Reichsmitt in late October 1933, and on 28 December the puppies arrived—a litter carefully calculated and greatly hoped for. It was to be one that changed the whole face of Boxer breeding. Among the puppies was a sturdy fawn, with white chest and feet, a white blaze and white spilling down one side of the black muzzle. As he grew he seemed perfection, particularly in head which, in the opinion of many, has never been equalled. The Stockmanns, with very good cause, felt they had bred pretty well their ideal.

As Lustig grew and his power increased it was evident that there was no fawn in Germany to touch him. One who saw him often tells us that he was a proud dog, beautifully mannered, noble in outlook, and sheer perfection in skull, muzzle and expression. In 1935 he became Czechoslovakian Sieger, and in the following year he was the Fachschaftssieger (club champion dog, winner of First Open with rating of Excellent under three different judges), German Reichssieger (winner of the annual speciality championship show, thereby becoming dog champion of the year) and Weltsieger (World Champion). He was never beaten.

By this time his fame had reached America, and soon the offers for him began to arrive. The Stockmanns did not want to sell, but eventually they yielded to an offer made on behalf of Erwin O. Freund of the Tulgey Wood Kennels. Fortunately for the breed in Europe Lustig had been bred to 36 bitches before he went off to the States, and some of that breeding was destined for England.

He arrived in America in March 1937, round his neck

---

a collar bearing the words: 'I am the splendid Lustig.' It was indeed a triumphant entry into the New World. The same month he had started his second show career, and he completed his championship in a week. As in the land of his birth, he was never beaten in his breed. He was retired from the ring in September 1938 at the age of five and a half, having been shown 20 times, and capturing 20 Bests of Breed, 12 groups, and twice Best in Show All Breeds.

Strides had been made since Sigurd's day and there were a great number of good bitches ready for him. Altogether he was mated to 168, and sired 41 American champions. To this number must be added the German title winners which we have never seen numbered. There is little doubt that Lustig's record as a sire is the best ever in the breed. He died on 14 June, 1945, aged eleven and a half, leaving an indelible mark on the German, American and British Boxers.

Dorian

Like the Stockmanns in Germany, Mr and Mrs John P. Wagner in the United States have had great influence on the Boxer. Some years ago while on tour in America we had the good luck to spend a short holiday with them at their ranch in Texas, and while sitting in their sun-drenched garden we heard something of the Mazelaine story. Though told with modesty (and with good humour) it soon became apparent that Mazelaine (a combination of Mrs Wagner's Christian names Mazie Elaine) must rank with von Dom in Boxer history.

The story of their interest in the breed dates from 1933 when they purchased their first puppy (a bitch whom they named Landa of Mazelaine) in Milwaukee where they were then living. Again for those wishing to gain success the easy way, let it be noted that Landa was no great one. Her price, by the way, was 130 dollars, a curious figure, thought Mr Wagner, who enquired the reason. The owner's wife it appeared needed new teeth, and that was the price of them. So the great Mazelaine Kennel was begun on the price of a set of dentures!

Landa was bred to Check von Hunnenstein, with whom we are already familiar, and she produced the Wagners' first litter whelped on 11 November, 1933. In it was Anitra of Mazelaine who, bred to Dorian, gave the Wagners their first American-bred champion.

That brings Dorian into the picture. He was a golden brindle dog with white chest and toes, sired by Xerxes von Dom, the fawn son of Sigurd, in 1933. His mother, Saxonia's Andl, was a Check von Hunnenstein daughter, and the breeder was Frau Tecklaschneider of the Marienhof Kennel in Germany. She had sold him at the age of eight weeks to a local butcher.

To the Wagners' home in Milwaukee came news that Dorian was a super Boxer, possessing remarkable elegance and style as well as substance, and noted also for his perfect action. In body there had never been anything in Germany to touch him and he had easily become a Sieger. Naturally, the Wagners were interested, but how could they get him, for it was strongly believed that the owner didn't wish to sell.

They were advised to leave things until Christmas. At that time most Germans are concerned about the money available for a proper celebration of the feast, the purchase of gifts and all other seasonable expenses. The Wagners waited and then, just before Christmas Eve, put through a personal call from Milwaukee, up on the shores of Lake Michigan, to Germany. It was a shrewd stroke. The butcher, dazzled by a four-figure offer for a dog he had bought for a pet price, agreed to sell. There was jubilation in the Wagner home. But they were anxious, too, and impatient for the day on which Dorian would arrive by boat in New York.

On 5 January, 1936, they were at the pier waiting for the boat, and as soon as it tied up Mr Wagner and a friend dashed aboard. Mrs Wagner waited on the dockside watching the odd assortment of travellers one sees on those occasions. Suddenly she saw the ship's butcher come down the gangway and walk along the dock. He was leading the most beautiful Boxer she had ever seen. Yes, it was Dorian. Mazie took charge of him, and led him to the car, where she was sitting with Dorian on her lap when Jack Wagner and his friend returned, bitterly disappointed, to tell her that Dorian couldn't be found. Then they saw him. It was a glorious moment.

That night there was a celebration in Jack Dempsey's restaurant in New York for Wagner had told the ex-World Champion Heavyweight that he was meeting a Boxer arriving from Germany. 'Bring him along,' said Dempsey, 'I'd like to meet him, and, besides, he can have a steak.' Suddenly it dawned on the Wagners that Dempsey meant the other sort of boxer. They kept their secret. Imagine the scene when into the restaurant walked Dorian von Marienhof, a champion, true, but of a different kind. Dempsey was photographed with Dorian and, keeping up the joke, Wagner said the Boxer was in joint ownership and they intended to sell shares in him. This was duly reported, and for six months afterwards Mrs Wagner was kept busy writing letters, returning contributions and explaining that for reasons unforeseen at the time, the idea of a syndicate had had to be abandoned.

And, by the way, Jack Dempsey kept his word. He gave Dorian a steak. And Dorian, like your Boxer, or mine, couldn't eat it fast enough. Then he was sick.

Then next month Dorian was shown at Westminster (America's equivalent of Crufts) and went Best of Breed. In straight shows he took his championship, and went right on winning. As in Germany, he was never beaten in the show-ring. In 1937 he was again Best of Breed at Westminster and this time the winner of the working group.

He looked magnificent on that day. Approaching his fourth birthday he was at the peak of his condition and power, and as his long stride took him up and down the great hall at Madison Square there was a great roar of applause. Fortunately for British breeders Mr Wagner presented the British Boxer Club with a film of Dorian in action and many have seen his phenomenal movement. It is sheer poetry. In Boxer classes he was never anywhere but at the top of the line, and altogether he scored 22 Best in Show wins.

Dorian died on 24 March, 1941, aged nearly eight, and in the Wagners' gardens at Milwaukee a stone was raised to his memory. He had not been used at stud to the same extent as Lustig, and we were surprised to learn from the Wagners that he was mated to only 20 odd bitches outside the Mazelaine Kennels, but his record of 37 American-bred champions was remarkable.

Not only was he a great producer, but so were his sons.

That was not all. The Wagners discovered the winning secret which the uninitiated call the Dorian-Lustig 'cross'. From mating Lustig daughters to Dorian, and vice versa, and continuing the process to following generations they produced scores of champions (we even found the Wagners themselves slightly vague as to the number) but it was enough to give them a world's record. But we know that this was no 'cross' at all. It was planned line-breeding, for Lustig and Dorian were first cousins. The father of each was sired by Sigurd.

Utz von Dom, Lustig's brother, the remaining member of the Big Four, also comes into the picture, but before we discuss him we must refer shortly to some of Dorian's great successors. I shall only select a few highlights, though scores deserve mention.

In 1947 his grandson (through the dam's side) Ch. Warlord of Mazelaine went Best in Show All Breeds at Westminster, the first Boxer to achieve this supreme award in the States. Warlord had previously won the group in 1945 and '46. Warlord's dam was Ch. Symphony of Mazelaine, and she was one of eight by Dorian out of Ch. Crona von Zwergeck, seven of whom became champions. His sire was Utz.

Later the Wagners bred their greatest Boxer, Ch. Mazelaine's Zazarac Brandy, a golden brindle whom we were very proud to meet in New York. Not only did he emulate Warlord and go Best in Show All Breeds at 'The Garden' (as Americans call the Westminster Show because it is held at Madison Square Garden) but set up a record unmatched in his day by any other dog of any breed. He was Best in Show over 60 times—an incredible figure. Later the figure was to be beaten by Ch. Bang Away of Sirrah Crest, also a Dorian descendant.

Brandy was not only a beautifully constructed Boxer with a superlative head, but was a charming dog. We saw him lording it on the most comfortable chair in a sitting-room, and also in the show-ring. In both circumstances he was superb.

We were astonished to hear it said in England by people who had never seen him that he had a poor backline. That is absurd. He was a dog most difficult to fault, though he had, very definitely, a mind of his own. He was not always prepared to show himself to his best advantage. But in my estimation he was a truly great Boxer.

Brandy was, of course, a direct descendant of Dorian through his sire Ch. Merry Monarch (another great producer) who was by the Dorian son, Mahderf's El Chico. Brandy sired many U.S. champions.

Another of his sons was the Reichssieger Mazelaine's Czardas. Czardas came to England via Frau Stockmann who selected him as a puppy when she went to the States to judge the breed in 1949. Frau Stockmann took Czardas home with her and made him the first non-German-bred Boxer to win the Sieger title. That strikes me as an interesting and significant event. The Americans, after taking the cream of the German Boxers between the two wars, were eventually able to send one back to the land of their birth—and win a top award. Czardas was much travelled, for eventually he was purchased by an American family living in England, and they took him back to the States.

No chapter on the American dogs, no matter how brief, can be completed without reference to the fabulous Ch. Bang Away of Sirrah Crest, the fawn and white marked bombshell who took away Brandy's record as the greatest winning dog of all time in any breed. In 1955 he topped 121 Best in Show wins. I doubt if the world will ever see a greater show record than this.

Bang Away, bred by Dr and Mrs R. C. Harris of California, is another descendant of Dorian on both sides of his pedigree. His sire was Int. Ch. Ursa Major of Sirrah Crest, who was by Ch. Yobang of the same affix who was by Ch. Duke Cronian the Dorian son. Duke Cronian figures three times in a four-generation pedigree.

One of our most vivid experiences is to have seen Warlord, Brandy and Bang Away in the ring together. It was a non-competitive exhibition, televised and filmed, and through the kindness of the late Major Bostock, President of the British Boxer Club, I brought back to this country a permanent film record which has been enjoyed by Boxer clubs throughout Great Britain. All Boxer enthusiasts seeing this film should remember that Warlord was by then past his peak, and that Brandy had been retired from the show-ring. Bang Away, great showman that he was, behaved like a film star.

I was also fortunate, through the abounding generosity of Mr and Mrs Wagner, to bring home to England the Dorian blood through Bang Away's full brother, the brindle and white marked Mazelaine's Texas Ranger.[1] The Wagners, great breeders of Boxers as they are, thought so highly of the breeding (very largely their own in the background) that they obtained from Dr Harris Bang Away's sire and dam Ursa Major, and Verily Verily of Sirrah Crest. But they did not breed another Bang Away. That only happens once.

Utz

We must now return to the last of the Big Four who is possibly not so well known as the other three—Sigurd, Lustig and Dorian—but who also has played a significant part in the development of the modern Boxer.

To get this story right go back to 1937 when Mr and Mrs Wagner visited Germany for the Sieger show. In the junior puppy class they saw a fawn who immediately made them exclaim: 'Who's that?' Reference to the catalogue revealed that it was Utz—a pup bred exactly the same way as Lustig but in a later litter. He had been whelped on 18 April, 1936.

[1] Died 1958.

They were not able to get him until 1939 when the Stockmanns sent him over to the Mazelaine Kennels just before the outbreak of the Second World War. Utz had a particularly wonderful head (there are some who saw all the Big Four who say it was the finest of them all). He took his title with ease, winning the working group at Westminster, and then proved himself as a great producer. Again, in comparing the records of Sigurd, Lustig, Dorian and Utz it must be remembered that the circumstances were not the same for any of them. Utz was the last of them to arrive, and the number of good bitches available had by then increased.

Beginning in 1942, Utz was the leading sire of champions for five consecutive years, being particularly successful with Dorian daughters. Study of the old pedigrees will reveal that the interplay of progeny of the Big Four undoubtedly placed American Boxers on top of the world for a long time. In one year Utz sired nine champions out of six different bitches which in itself was a record. Altogether he sired 37 champions. The greatest was Warlord, while his granddaughter, Ch. El Wendi of Rockland, was among the finest bitches ever bred in the States.

More figures would weary the reader, so we will leave it there, though one always feels Utz has not claimed the limelight he deserves.

So much for the Big Four, and our brief glance at their history. They are important to us not only because of their supremacy in the States (and this by no means implies that there were no others) but because of their progeny which found their way to Great Britain. Over here also these four played a vital part.

5

Britain Takes a Hand

Boxer history in this country falls into two distinct phases. There was a short period before World War II (when only a handful of people were interested in the breed and only one champion dog, who had no subsequent influence, was made up) and the years up to the time of writing since the war. Altogether the period to be studied in Great Britain stretches over 60 odd years, but only the last 50 are significant.

In the second phase, which from the show-going point of view is the more important, the popularity of the breed has so grown that today there are not many more numerous breeds registered.

Up to the end of 1987 there have been 368 champions in Great Britain, and I have compiled a list of them all (see Appendix A) showing how they were bred, colour, owners and breeders.

Study of this list reveals that they also fall into distinct sections. These may be termed the early German, British, Dutch and American influences. The UK has now come into its own.

Of the early German importations two stand out above all others. These were a son and a daughter of the famous Lustig von Dom named Zunftig von Dom and Alma von der Frankenwarte.

Zunftig von Dom, a most promising fawn, bred by the Stockmanns, was imported by Mr Dawson in 1939. With the war in progress, Mr Dawson sent Zunftig to the United States to be sold for the International Red Cross Fund. This was a great loss to British breeders. Zunftig sired two litters in this country and one, from Mr Dawson's

imported bitch Bessi von Trauntal, was important because
it contained a brindle dog, Stainburndorf Zulu, of whom
we shall have more to relate. Zunftig became an American
champion in 1941.

Directly from Alma von der Frankenwarte stemmed my
two sires Ch. Panfield Tango and Ch. Panfield Ringleader
who were together responsible for 11 English champions.
These two dogs can be said to have dominated the scene
immediately after the war. Ringleader had a remarkable
record of winning progeny.

From Holland, where they were bred by Mr Peter
Zimmerman, came Dutch Ch. Faust vom Haus Germania
and his brother Helios of the same prefix. Both of these
came in the ownership of the late Mrs Dunkels and Mrs
Gamble of the Breakstones Kennels. These two dogs also
had a great influence, and between them sired seven
champions. Another dog to whom the breed owes much
is Holger von Germania, bred in Germany, but a son of
Mr Zimmerman's Favoriet vom Haus Germania who spent
some of her life both at home in Holland, in Germany and
in England. Holger, owned here by Miss Bing, sired four
champions and was himself the first dog to get his title
here after the war.

Though males, obviously, have a greater opportunity to
make their influence felt, there were three bitches in
addition to Alma who played a considerable part. These
were my Ch. Panfield Serenade, Alma's daughter by her
own grandson; Ch. Orburn Kekeri, Holger's famous
daughter owned by Mrs Hullock, and Britta van Gerdas
Hoeve, a cropped bitch bred in Holland, and owned over
here by Mr Vandenberg.

Serenade achieved fame by becoming the country's first
bitch champion, and then by producing Ringleader and
his sister Ch. Panfield Rhythm. Kekeri's high spot was to
be the first Boxer to win Best in Show All Breeds at a
championship show. She was also a great brood bitch, for
mated to Helios she became the dam of two Winkinglight
champion brothers, Viking and Venturer. Viking, in the
ownership of Mrs Anson, became the country's greatest
show male in the Boxer breed up to 1955.

In subsequent chapters I shall dwell on the achievements of these animals, for between them they have been
responsible for a large number of our champion and
certificate-winning dogs and bitches. There were others,
but these can be said to have laid the foundation.

Later, for example, there was to come from Germany
Axel von Bad Oeyn, who sired four champions, while
from the United States arrived USA Ch. Awldogg Southdown's Rector who sired an outstanding show-winning
bitch, Ch. Geronimo Carissima. But this is another chapter
recounting the American influence. For the moment let
us salute these stalwarts of the old brigade of whom I have
spoken here, and then turn to the year 1911 when Britain
saw its very first Boxer.

The very first Boxer of which we know in this country was
a bitch named Jondy, a daughter of Remos von Pfalzgau.
Remos had a brilliant championship career in Germany
way back, and was himself a son of Hugo von Pfalzgau,
one of the Flock and Meta progeny. Meta von der Passage
(to give her her full name) you will recall was practically
the mother of all Boxers. But what happened to Jondy,
who was born in 1911, we have never discovered. Like
many others she possibly was kept as somebody's pet.
There is no record that she had any sons or daughters.

After this start, which unfortunately came to nothing as
far as we know, there is a record that Dr McMaster of
Ballymena, Northern Ireland, brought in two Boxers in
1919. Again, little is known about them. The late Mr Allon
Dawson said they were good specimens, but did not
produce any offspring. Mr Dawson, who owned in
Yorkshire the well-known Stainburndorf Kennels, was
himself one of the earliest to be interested in the breed,
and the part he played in its development was of the
utmost importance. He was one of the pioneers in Britain
to whom all Boxer breeders owe a great deal.

There was another boxer male in the country in the
1930s that we knew nothing about until much later. His
name was Bouboule, and was owned by Mrs Eirene Miller.

She bought him in Paris, and brought him to England in
1933. Mrs Miller made exhaustive enquiries about other
Boxers, but found none. So Bouboule also, I'm afraid, left
no descendants. His pedigree shows he was born on 15
June, 1927, and was bred by Herr Steinacher. Mrs Miller
tells me her Boxer was 'unbelievably intelligent. He was
also tremendously strong and wiry, though not very
heavily built, would only fight if deliberately set on, and
was more than a match for most.' Definitely of correct
Boxer temperament.

Finding that little was known about the breed in
England at that time Mrs Miller wrote to the Boxer Club
of France, and the reply she received from Strasbourg in
1933 declares: 'I am happy to hear that you are owner of
a Boxer as I was the opinion to find not any Boxers in
England. From 18 months we consider the Boxer ripe for
the breed; for the bitch her third heat. It is the same for
the brindle Boxers as for the yellow dogs. I know that it
is forbidden in England to cut the ears, the only obstacles
for our race. Please dispose of my services for any further
information.'

Which goes to show that the breed was still in its infancy
in England in 1933.

There was in fact yet another English Boxer owner in
the early twenties. Before her marriage she was Miss Rose
William-Powlett who had a pet Boxer which was never
registered or bred from. Her daughter, the former Mrs
Dulanty, was to become an enthusiast of the breed. But
none of these dogs, as far as we can discover, did anything
to establish the great Boxer family in these islands.

In 1932 Miss P. M. Rogers imported a bitch named Cilly
von Rothenberg in whelp to Drill von Kurland. The result
was the first entry for Boxers in the *Kennel Gazette* of
February 1933. It reads: Rothenberg, Cilly von, bitch, Miss
P. M. Rogers; sire Asso von Zenith, dam Evis von
Niederhof; breeder Herr G. Fhlow, whelped Feb. 7, 1930.
With it went another entry: Riverhill Racketeer, dog;
Misses P. M. and F. M. Rogers, sire Drill von Kurland, dam
Cilly von Rothenberg; breeder Miss P. M. Rogers, whelped
June, 16th 1932. Racketeer, therefore, was one of Cilly's

pups, and the Misses Rogers became the first Boxer breeders in Great Britain. Later they were to breed Racketeer back to his dam, producing another litter.

So the Boxer gradually began to make an appearance in the British Isles from whence came Tom, the Bulldog, the father of them all. In 1933 Mrs Cecil Sprigge of Abinger Common, Surrey, imported from Paris a red dog sired by Armin von der Haake, who was a first prizewinner at Hamburg in 1929. She called him Fritz of Leith Hill (her own prefix). The following year she brought over a young Dutch brindle bitch, Kralingen's Liesel, daughter of Champion Armin Edelblut. In the same year these two produced a litter, and Mrs Sprigge interested that great dog showman Charles Cruft.

Alert as always to encourage a 'new' breed, he gave the Boxer wide publicity, and at his Jubilee Show in 1936 put on the first Boxer class ever to be held at a British dog show. Mrs Sprigge guaranteed the class which was won by Willi von Brandenburg, owned by Mrs I. M. Graham. Willi was one of the puppies born in 1932 to Cilly von Rothenberg. Altogether nine Boxers were shown, the other eight being the puppies of the Fritz and Liesel litter.

It was in 1936, also, that Mr F. W. Burman, of Berkshire, bred a litter, having imported two bitches, Birka von Emilienhorst and Quitta von Biederstein. Another Boxer to appear was Grief of Kahlgrund, owned by Mrs Sneyd. About the same time Mrs Sprigge obtained from Germany Gretl von der Boxerstadt in whelp to Hansl von Biederstein, who was a descendant of Caesar von Deutenkofen. Gretl, a lightly marked golden brindle, was a well-constructed bitch of good temperament. Her litter produced the first British-bred champion Boxer, a brindle dog of great substance named Horsa of Leith Hill, who got his title in 1939. His owner was Mrs Caro.

This was the only champion Boxer in the country until after World War II. Unlike in America, practically all dog showing came to an end here during the war. There were shows of a restricted kind, but the Kennel Club gave no certificates. Before this close-down Mr Dawson obtained certificates with two bitches, the Lustig daughters, Stainburndorf Vanda (one) and Stainburndorf Wendy (two), and with a dog, Stainburndorf Asdor (one).

Mr Dawson's interest had been aroused about 1934, and in 1935 he bought a bitch from Mrs Sprigge, named Sally. Sally's charming disposition appealed to him very much, and Mr Dawson became a great Boxer enthusiast. He made enquiries about the good dogs in Germany, and as a result imported Rex von Durrenberg (a son of Alarm von Brabant and Ora von Durrenberg), Bessi von Traun-tal, Hella von der Eibe, Klasse von der Humboldtshöhe and, as he puts it, 'by a considerable stroke of fortune', Burga von Twiel, in whelp to Lustig. From this litter he obtained his certificate winners, Vanda and Wendy. Asdor was the son of Hella von der Eibe by Rex von Durrenberg.

About 1936 Mrs Siggers imported Anita von Konrads-höhe who was mated to Arras von Neibsheim. This dog was a son of Arras von der Magdalenenquelle in turn by Hansl von Biederstein. Arras von Neibsheim was owned by a Mr Rankin. This mating produced the certificate winners Cuckmere Kora and Cuckmere Krin. Krin was, in fact, the first Boxer ever to be awarded a certificate in Great Britain. Mrs Pacey gave it to him at the L.K.A. championship show, on 14 March, 1939. Cuckmere Krin sired for Mrs Siggers the bitch Ch. Cuckmere Krinetta, who was the fourth champion in the breed in Great Britain, and the first fawn to be a champion.

Others that come into this early background were a bitch named Gunda von Hohenneuffen, imported by Messrs Russell and Rhodes, in whelp to Batto de la Bruche D'Alsace, and a dog, Tell von der Magdalenenquelle. This one mated to Quitta von Biederstein sired Sigurd of Luckings owned by Mr Betteridge, one of the founders of the British Boxer Club.

Another breeder to come forward in 1937 was Miss D. Birrell who made history by bringing over the first Boxer from the United States. This was a bitch, So Se Sumbula, who had been mated in America to Champion Corsa von Uracher Wasserfall.

This same year Mr Charles Cruft put on his great Coronation Show, and this time there were 14 Boxer entries, of which four, with cropped ears, were not for competition. (If I am not mistaken, it was at this show that Mr Dawson put his first Boxer in the show-ring, namely Ortrud of Leith Hill.) Also in 1937 he purchased Quitta von Biederstein, and registered five litters. At the 1938 Cruft's Show Boxer entries totalled 24. (When I judged the breed there in 1957 the record entry was 421.)

In December 1936, a number of the early breeders founded the British Boxer Dog Club, and held its first meeting at the R.A.C., Pall Mall. The first president was W. L. McCandlish, and Mrs Sprigge was the first secretary and treasurer. Mr McCandlish was followed as president by Mrs Caro, from whom Major D. F. Bostock took over. On his death the honour fell to me. Now it has passed on to Ferelith Somerfield. The first executive committee consisted of Mr Dawson, Mr G. Betteridge and Miss Birrell. In 1937 the Club was affiliated to the Kennel Club, and in 1939 it guaranteed Boxer classes at Crufts, Harrogate, Birmingham and the Kennel Club shows.

When the Club was first formed there was kept a British Dog register. I have a copy for 1938 in front of me. It contains the names of 82 dogs and bitches; 18 carried the prefix of Leith Hill, belonging to Mrs Sprigge; another 18 were Stainburndorfs; 8 were from the Luckings Kennel of Mr F. W. Burman, and 8 of the Uttershill prefix of Miss D. Birrell.

No. 1 on the register was Fritz of Leith Hill, No. 2 Kralingen's Liesel and No. 3 Cilly von Rothenberg.

The first annual report stated that when the Club started there were 6 members and this number had increased to 12 in the first year. The original members were: C. Balzer, G. W. Betteridge, Miss D. Birrell, Mrs Blackham, Allon Dawson, Mrs Fawcett, A. S. Harrison, the Misses Rose and Lloyd, N. H. Russell, Mrs Cecil Sprigge and W. L. McCandlish.

That was the modest beginning. Today there are Boxer clubs in all parts of the British Isles. The growth of this breed has been remarkable, especially since World War II. The table which follows reveals the outstanding jump in registrations which followed the end of hostilities in 1945 and rocketed the Boxer from 70th position in the Kennel Club's list to 4th in 1953 and '54.

In 1955 registrations still showed an upward trend, and a year later a further remarkable increase placed the Boxer third in order of popularity. Only the Miniature Poodle and Welsh Corgi (Pembroke) were above them. This was going a little too fast, for a too rapid rise can mean that breeding has become insufficiently discriminate. In the sixties registrations settled at a more realistic figure, and in the seventies they levelled off around 4,000. In 1975, however, there was a severe drop. Increased costs were the most likely cause. A big slump followed and then came an upturn. Until now in the late eighties there are around 5,000 registrations a year.

Year	Registrations	Year	Registrations
1945	399	1967	4,421
1946	707	1968	4,374
1947	1,412	1969	4,457
1948	1,922	1970	4,230
1949	2,644	1971	3,727
1950	3,647	1972	3,984
1951	4,464	1973	4,039
1952	4,479	1974	4,162
1953	5,592	1975	3,527
1954	6,054	1976	1,431[1]
1955	6,786	1977	971[1]
1956	7,570	1978	2,669
1957	7,020	1979	3,933
1958	6,979	1980	4,430
1959	7,410	1981	3,947
1960	7,137	1982	4,070
1961	6,902	1983	4,693
1962	6,803	1984	4,759
1963	6,029	1985	5,321
1964	5,419	1986	5,185
1965	5,152	1987	4,911
1966	4,104		

[1]The 1976 and 1977 figures were affected by a change in the registration system.

CH. PANFIELD RINGLEADER
Sire of seven champions, a record for the breed in
Britain until 1962

CH. NORWATCH BROCK BUSTER
One of the leading modern males

CH. MERRIVEEN FASCINATION
A beautiful bitch and Crufts' winner, 1957

CH. WARDROBES CLAIR DE LUNE
A great winning bitch with thirty-one certificates

CH. SIMOOR STATUS SYMBOL

A young 1980 champion. His sister also became a champion. They are by Ch. Simoor Status Quo, a son of Picasso

CH. FAERDORN PHEASANT PLUCKER

One of the great modern Boxers

CH. WARDROBES WILD MINK

Sire of eleven champions

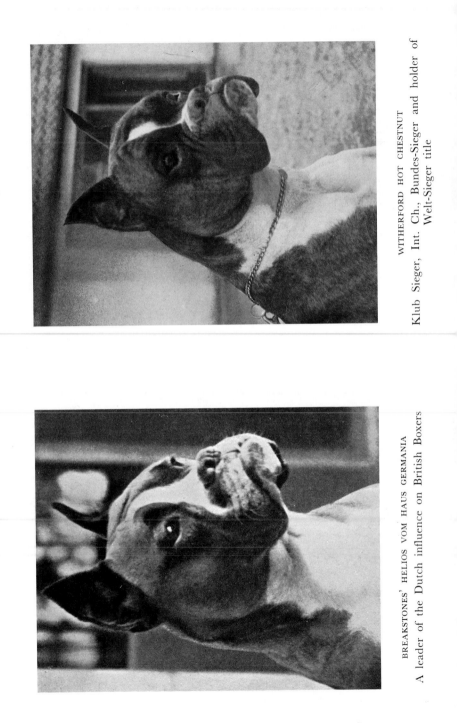

WITHERFORD HOT CHESTNUT
Klub Sieger, Int. Ch., Bundes-Sieger and holder of Welt-Sieger title

BREAKSTONES' HELIOS VOM HAUS GERMANIA
A leader of the Dutch influence on British Boxers

6

The Panfield Line

The golden brindle bitch, Gretl von der Boxerstadt, came into my possession in May 1940. She was at the time owned by Mrs Gingell who was living in the Cornish town of Perranporth.

I had first seen Gretl in 1938. Not only a well-constructed bitch of good colour, she also had a most charming temperament. In 1939 I bought one of Gretl's puppies by Fritz of Leith Hill. I named her Annaliese, and she became the first Panfield Boxer.

At that time the country was preparing for the invasion which never came. There was no market at all for dogs, and prices were down to zero. Gretl changed hands for £5, and I put up this sum in partnership with Miss Mary Davis.

When Gretl came into season the great problem was to whom to mate her. The intention was to use Zunftig, but by this time Mr Dawson had sent him to America. Like so many things in life, luck played a hand. While motoring in Hampstead I saw a good-looking Boxer being led along the pavement. In those days Boxers were still rare enough for lovers of the breed to exclaim, 'Look, there's a Boxer!' when they saw one and, if possible, make some attempt to speak to the owner. This is what I did and discovered the dog was Ajax von Mühlenberg, a Sigurd grandson. Here was a bit of luck indeed, as no one knew the dog was in England. Apparently he was owned by some Austrian refugees who had escaped to London just before the outbreak of war.

So Gretl von der Boxerstadt was mated to Ajax von Mühlenberg and in the litter of eight were two red bitches and a red dog, all of whom were destined to play a big part in the future of the breed in England. The bitch was Panfield Astra, who went to Mrs Marian Fairbrother, and became the first Boxer of the Gremlin Kennels. (Mrs Fairbrother was among the first to enter the Services in the emergency, and this alone prevented her playing a big part in the breed until after the war.)

Astra was mated to Zulu, the Zunftig son, and produced Panfield Flak, the sire of Ch. Panfield Tango (who became the leading British Boxer sire for the years 1949 and 1950, and went to Mrs Gerardy's kennels in Australia where he sired many more champions). Another in Astra's litter was Gremlin Gunner, winner of two certificates immediately they were awarded after the war. Yet another Astra-Zulu pup to gain distinction was Mutineer of Maspound who sired a brindle dog, Ch. Monarchist of Maspound. Mutineer and Monarchist were owned by the late Mrs Guthrie, of Paddock Wood, a well-known breeder who had success with Great Danes and Boxers. Monarchist won his first certificate (and Best of Breed) in 1946 when Mr J. P. Wagner of Mazelaine fame came to England from the United States to award certificates to Boxers for the first time after the war.

But we must go back to Gretl. Another of her puppies by Ajax was Panfield Adler who sired Panfield Dolla of Bramblings, a fawn bitch owned by Mrs Osborn, who bred her back to Zulu. The result was a dark brindle dog, Juniper of Bramblings, who was to sire Britain's first Boxer bitch champion, Ch. Panfield Serenade. Juniper was bought from Mrs Osborn by Mr and Mrs J. Lissenden of the Awldogg prefix. Mrs Osborn, by a coincidence, had earlier bought her first Boxer from Mrs Gingell on the same day as I bought Annaliese.

Returning a moment to the two Panfield dogs Flak and Tango, it is interesting to know that Flak, a big, strong red dog who stood 25 inches at the withers, was bought by an American Army officer and was taken by him first to Germany and then to the United States. The story of Tango is even more remarkable. On his arrival in Australia he fell down the hold of the ship in which he had travelled. The dog broke several bones in his hind legs, and his life was despaired of. Veterinary advice was that he should be destroyed. But his new owner, Mrs Gerardy, was determined that if skill and perseverance could save him it would be done. It was agreed that a delicate operation should be performed by a surgeon who first studied the skeleton of another dog. He then mended a number of Tango's fractures by using silver pins and placing the dog's hindquarters in a plaster casing. A chair on wheels was then made for Tango who used to sit in it and propel himself about by his front feet. It was a remarkable operation crowned with success. The dog recovered, and though his best showing days were over, his value at stud was unimpaired, and he sired several Australian champion sons and daughters. Mrs Gerardy was later to import several other Boxers from us and established her Park Royal Kennels in Gordon, New South Wales, where she had notable success.

Tango's dam was a bitch to whom must go much of the credit for making Panfield the leading Boxer kennels for four years running from 1947. One of the last bitches Lustig mated before he left Germany was Alfa von Wurzburger-Glockli, who was by Dux von Marienhof, a son of Ch. Xerxes von Dom and Saxonia's Andl, in other words, a full brother to the famous Dorian. This was classic line-breeding, the same in fact which hit the jackpot in the United States.

Alfa had a fawn and white marked bitch named Alma von der Frankenwarte, who found her way to London and was kept there as a pet. When the bombing started the owner advertised her for sale. I went to see Alma, and was immediately struck by her clean outline and perfectly dry head. Unlike so many other Boxers in England at this time (1941) she was not stodgy and over-wrinkled but lithe, hard and alert. Other British breeders had seen her, but were not impressed, but I thought she was the best Boxer I had ever seen.

She had her faults, including a front not absolutely true, and she had suffered a prolapse, but there was something about her, even though she was grubby and too thin. She chased a cat in the mews where she was kept and revealed her extraordinary agility and power to stride over the ground. Reluctantly I decided that the price was too much for me.

Three days later I received a message by telephone. If I would take the bitch that day I could have her at a greatly reduced figure. This was something too good to miss, so I joined a syndicate, in which my partners were Miss Mary Davis and Mrs Fairbrother. We put up £5 each.

So Alma von der Frankenwarte came to the Panfield Kennels. She was a bitch who must surely take one of the proud places in the British Boxers' roll of honour. This was made possible by a combination of luck and good judgment, two ingredients essential to success. Alma had no official papers (except her Munich Boxer Club registration), but these were obtained later through the kindness of Miss Jean Grant of the Blossomlea Boxers, though not without difficulty, for England was then at war with Germany. I also learned that Alma had been mated during four seasons with four different dogs and had never had puppies.

Within three months Alma (by this time given the pet name of Liska) came into season and it was decided to use at stud Miss Davis's Monkswood Christian of Bramblings, a son of Gretl by Fritz of Leith Hill. Again by combination of circumstances and perhaps judgment, Alma was mated very late in her season, in fact on the 19th day. With success. For the first time she had a litter, but there was nothing in it anything near as good as their mother.

The following year the same situation existed. In a very narrow field at this time, the stud dog selected was Panfield Adler, another Gretl son. Result: three puppies, among them Panfield Dolla, a red bitch. Later Dolla had a dog puppy by Zulu named Juniper of Bramblings. In the course of time Alma was mated back to her own grandson, Juniper, and they produced the famous Serenade. Line-breeding had again brought its reward.

Of Serenade, Mr Wagner wrote when awarding her the C.C. in 1946: 'A bitch with a lovely head, neck and shoulders, and pleasing body. She moved well, and her clever handler got every ounce out of her.' (The handler was Mrs Fairbrother.)

For some, Serenade lacked 'stop'—that break in the Boxer head so characteristic of the breed, but they perhaps missed an overall quality that was outstanding in her day. She not only became the country's first champion bitch, but went on to win five certificates and then produced a champion daughter and a champion son who won 17 certificates between them.

The breeding which produced this outstanding result was Serenade back to her half-brother Ch. Panfield Tango. It was carefully planned. Notice in Ringleader's pedigree (on page 214) that Alma was his grandmother on both sides. In four generations Lustig appears twice and Dux twice also. This was concentrated von Dom and von Marienhof breeding.

Ringleader was a remarkable stud force. He was not a big dog, though within the Standard (which is the important thing), but he was well balanced, sound, and possessed a good head. We have never bothered about his height because behind him there were plenty of inches, particularly in Flak. As a sire he still remains important in Great Britain. In addition to 7 champions, 6 more of his progeny won C.C.s giving his children a grand total of 40 challenge certificates. In the next generation he had 8 champion grandchildren.

The mating of Flak to Alma, which produced Tango, was one of our happier strokes which we have been often asked to relate. Flak had been Alma's companion ever since he was a pup. When she came in season and we asked him to mate the old lady he didn't fancy the job at all. But we were determined, and tried several times with no result. This was desperate. Eventually we thought of a bright idea. Living nearby was a little mongrel lady which Flak loved dearly. We brought her along and his joy was quite evident. At dusk we introduced his mongrel friend and for a moment or two they romped with abandon. Then we whisked out the girl-friend while Flak wasn't looking, and quickly brought in Alma. Swiftly he embraced her. I shall never forget the look he gave me when he discovered it was 'Gran'.

Alma (Liska as we called her) was a great character. A dutiful mother, she took the greatest care of her pups until they were eight weeks old, and then kicked them out to fend for themselves. Except one; her favourite was always given special treatment and fed while any drop of milk remained, and even long after. And oddly enough, it was always her best pup. She could always pick them.

Alma died at the age of twelve, full of years, and with a great number of descendants. Now her daughter, Serenade, has also gone, and her grandson, Ringleader, is no more.

Tango not only sired the brother and sister champions, Ringleader and Rhythm, but also Ch. Panfield Flash. This dog also went out to Mrs Gerardy in Australia and there (like Ch. Panfield Zest, a Tango grandson) took his championship.

After Ringleader his daughter, Ch. Panfield Party Piece of Greentubs, carried on for me, and produced three champion sons. They played a big part and after their time I was lucky enough to bring from the United States a brother of the great champion Bang Away of Sirrah Crest.

7

The Dutch Influence and Some Leading Breeders

There was no time and little place for dog shows in Britain during the war. The first championship event for Boxers afterwards was that judged by Mr Wagner for the British Boxer Club in 1946, and held at Coventry. It was an important show, for Wagner, the recognized American authority, was to lead British breeders away from the heavy, cloddy type towards the more clean-cut dogs we have today. We have already mentioned his dog and bitch certificate winners, Monarchist and Serenade. Another young dog present was also destined for a leading role in British Boxer history. He was Holger von Germania, which Wagner made best puppy and reserve to the best dog. Holger was to become the first post-war dog champion of the breed.

Holger is an interesting dog. He was bred on the Continent from the mating of Rex von Hohenneuffen, a Lustig grandson, to Dutch Ch. Favoriet vom Haus Germania, and was owned in England by Miss Cameron Bing. He was handled to his championship by Mr George Jakeman who had taken the greatest interest in Dutch Boxers while serving as a soldier during the war. Favoriet, a beautiful animal bred by Mr Peter Zimmerman, of vom Haus Germania Kennels in Holland, came to England for a period and was to exert a considerable influence on British Boxers, first through her son, Holger.

Directly from him came four English champions; one of these was to create Boxer history by becoming the first to go Best in Show All Breeds at a championship show. This was the bitch Ch. Orburn Kekeri, bred by Miss Rands and afterwards owned by Mrs Hullock, of the Winkinglight prefix.[1] The others were Ch. Alrakim Orburn Akaboo (litter sister to Kekeri) owned by Mrs Guthrie, Ch. Hella of Belfoyne (bred by Mr Rathbone and afterwards owned by Major Bostock) and Ch. Klesby Sparklet (owned by Mrs Hucklesby and Mrs Price) and afterwards exported to New Zealand.

While in England Favoriet was bred to Collo von Dom, imported by Mr Jakeman, and two pups from the litter produced champions. The bitch, Christine of Breakstones, owned by the late Mrs Dunkels and Mrs Gamble, was mated to Dutch Ch. Faust vom Haus Germania, and became the dam of Ch. Florizel of Breakstones and of the bitch Ch. Fenella of Breakstones, winner of seven certificates, and the holder of a remarkable record. She won the bitch certificate three years running at the British Boxer Club's Championship Show. Christine's litter brother, Immertreu Kavelier, sired Ch. Burstall Gelasma. Both the latter eventually went to Major Bostock's Burstall Kennels.

From this it will be seen that Favoriet was a most important bitch, and the circumstances in which she came to England were as remarkable as her performance. Eventually Mr Zimmerman, the breeder, came over from Holland and she returned with him to the Continent where she continued her winning career and went on producing outstanding Boxers.

Another result of this association with Holland was the introduction into the Breakstones Kennels of two Dutch stud dogs which were to leave their mark indelibly printed on the breed. These were Helios vom Haus Germania and Dutch Ch. Faust vom Haus Germania. Before examining this impact, however, we must return to Mr Jakeman's import Collo, and another dog he brought over— Champus von der Fischerhutte.

Collo, bred by Frau Stockmann, was sired by Heiner von Zwergeck out of Uschi von Dom. He was an elegant dark brindle dog who must not only take the credit with

---

[1]Best in Show All Breeds at a championship show was subsequently won by Ch. Winkinglight Viking, Ch. Panfield Beau Jinks, Ch. Wardrobes Miss Mink, Ch. Felcign Fiona, Ch. Wardrobes Thunderbird, Int. Ch. Seefeld Picasso and several others.

Favoriet for Christine, but also for Ch. Panfield Bliss who was to win Best in Show under Dr R. C. Harris, owner of Bang Away, and was three times reserve to Fenella in her British Boxer Club wins. Bliss, bred by Mr Vandenberg, passed into our ownership at eight weeks old, then went to Mrs Scott and ultimately to Mr and Mrs George Dallison.

Champus, who was by Droll von Taubenhausl, a son of Ajax von der Holderberg, was a charming brindle and white marked Boxer of immense presence. He was also police trained. As a sire he was not so outstanding as Collo, but he produced one champion daughter, Ch. Florri of Breakstones.

Return now to the influence of Helios and Faust. Both dogs achieved a great deal. Altogether Faust was the sire of five English champions. They were Ch. Bucko of Gerda's Hofstee, Ch. Florizel of Breakstones, Ch. Home-hill Faust of Gerda's Hofstee, Ch. Lustig of Gerda's Hofstee, and Ch. Fenella of Breakstones. Three of these, Bucko, Homehill Faust and Lustig, were contained in one litter born to a bitch owned by Mr G. Vandenberg—Britta van Gerda's Hoeve, who was also the dam of Ch. Panfield Bliss in another litter.

Britta, mother of four champions, was one of the country's greatest female producers.

In the next generation Faust's son, Florizel, sired two champions, Ch. Anndale Sheafdon Hooch-Mi bred by Miss Jean Haggie, later owned by Major Bostock, and Miss Miller-Thomas's Ch. Blacknowe Beau Ideal, who was the first Boxer champion to be bred in Scotland.

Faust and Favoriet were litter brother and sister by Leoncillo's Alf, ex Diva vom Haus Germania, and Helios was bred the same way but out of a later litter. Faust was a dark brindle and Helios a red with white markings. It was by concentrating on this line that the late Mrs Dunkels and Mrs Gamble produced their highly successful strain. Their great show bitch Fenella, for example, was by Faust out of Christine, who was out of Favoriet, his little sister. Florizel was bred exactly the same way. Unhappily Florizel died at a comparatively early age when the leading stud dog for 1953.

Helios was to sire two champions, Ch. Winkinglight Viking and Ch. Winkinglight Venturer. Viking and Venturer were little brothers out of Ch. Orburn Kekeri, the Holger daughter, owned by Mrs Hullock. Notice this careful line-breeding. Holger was out of Favoriet, little sister to Faust. Helios, Viking's sire, was Favoriet's full brother. Kekeri was a great producing bitch. Later she was mated to Mrs Fairbrother's Ch. Gremlin Inxpot, and in this litter there were the certificate winners Gremlin Winkinglight Vigilant and Winkinglight Vesper. Vigilant became the sire of Miss Warden's Ch. Braxburn Flush Royal. Vesper produced for Mrs Hullock Ch. Winkinglight Justice.

Viking had a remarkable show career. Up to 1955 he had won more certificates than any other Boxer male, the grand total being 13.[1] A tall, upstanding red and white marked dog, he was a consistent winner for several years, and sired four champions. Bred by Mrs Hullock, Viking was purchased as a puppy by Mrs Anson who handled him to his championship. In 1957 she took him with her to Canada.

Before leaving this very considerable Dutch influence we must mention Arco van der Blomona, a son of Dutch Ch. Fix vom Haus Germania, brother of Helios, Favoriet and Faust. Arco was imported into England by Mrs Harrild, but before leaving Holland he sired Hans van der Zaankant, who was imported by Mr Dawson and afterwards owned by Mr Cartwright. Hans was to sire Ch. Ajax of Gunholme, winner of six certificates and owned by the former chairman of the Northern Boxer Club, Mr Ian S. Greig.

Reference has already been made to the part played by Mr Dawson before the war. Fortunately for our breed he maintained his interest through the years, and after the war he made many more importations, the chief of which were Frohlich von Dom and Sieger Mazelaine's Czardas. He regarded Frohlich as one of the best dogs he had ever

[1] Passed later by Ch. Gremlin Inkling, Ch. Seefeld Picasso, Ch. Desperate Dan and others.

seen. A fine upstanding red male, he proved himself at stud by siring Ch. Stainburndorf Vanderlion.

Frohlich was bred by Frau Stockmann, and was by Austrian Sieger Heiner von Zwergeck out of Goody Goody of Sirrah Crest which she brought back from the United States.[1]

In the North of England there was established immediately after the war the Knowle Crest Kennels of Mr and Mrs Philip Dyson. It was founded on Mr Dawson's Stainburndorf stock. Zulu, the Zunftig son, sired Mr and Mrs Dyson's Stainburndorf Jaguar. Another of Zulu's progeny was Stainburndorf Minesweeper. Minesweeper sired the Dysons' brindle bitch Ch. Thornick Beta of Oidar, and Beta mated to Jaguar produced Ch. Asphodel of Knowle Crest. Asphodel became the mother of Ch. Flacius of Knowle Crest, so that these breeders were able to claim three generations of champions in direct line. The sire of Flacius was the American imported Boxer, Flip of Berolina, while the Dysons' even later champion bitch, Ch. Knowle Crest Isis, was the daughter of an American sire, USA Ch. Applause of Emefar, out of a daughter of Asphodel. In 1958 they made their fifth champion, Ch. Meteor of Knowle Crest.

No history of the breed in this country would be complete without reference to the late President of the British Boxer Club, Major D. F. Bostock, who used his considerable influence to further the cause of Boxers generally in Great Britain. He started in Boxers after wide experience with other breeds and animals of many descriptions by purchasing two puppies from me during the war. His first champion was Burstall Delight, a Ringleader daughter out of Burstall Gremlin Torni, a litter sister to Ch. Panfield Bliss. Delight won 11 certificates.

After Delight, champions were made up every year, and they included Ch. Burstall Gelasma, a daughter of Immertreu Kavelier, whose show career was ended by an unfortunate accident; Ch. Burstall King, an Axel son; Ch.

[1] Later Frohlich sired Ch. Stainburndorf Dandylion and in 1955 was sent to America.

Awldogg Jacobus, a son of the American champion, Awldogg Southdown's Rector, owned by Mr and Mrs Lissenden, who also bred Jacobus.

Major Bostock also purchased Ch. Spaldene Spruce, by Ringleader, and bred by Mr and Mrs Harvey, whom he made a champion, and Ch. Anndale Sheafdon Hooch-Mi, who not only got her title but took 11 certificates. Another Burstall champion was Ch. Hella of Belfoyne, who topped a fine career by going Best in Show under Mr Charles Spannaus, the President of the American Boxer Club, at the Festival of Britain Boxer Combined Show in 1951 — a show which holds the world's record entry for Boxers.

Burstall was top Boxer kennels in 1951 and 1953 by virtue of winning the highest number of certificates in these years. Later Major Bostock played an important part in the introduction of American blood into the breed, and throughout the country Boxer breeders and clubs had reason to be grateful for his unfailing generosity.

I must now refer to the Gremlin Boxers, owned by Mrs Fairbrother, a friend of mine from schooldays. Mrs Fairbrother, like most other serious breeders, did not gain her success easily. In 1939 when in the Services her first Boxer was sent to her by rail, and arrived dead. The second was so poor that she sent it back again. Then came better luck with Panfield Astra, the bitch bred jointly by Mary Davis and myself out of Gretl von der Boxerstadt. Astra produced Gremlin Genius and Gremlin Gangster, though you wouldn't know them by these names. At one time it was possible to change a name into something quite different. So Genius became Flak and Gangster became Mutineer.

Mrs Fairbrother went with the Forces into Germany, and while there she looked for a good dog. In Wiesbaden she met Frau Markloff, a Boxer breeder, who spoke about a red male she sold as a puppy to a laundress who kept it as a pet. In exchange for coffee, cigarettes and food which the Germans were badly needing then, and a young bitch puppy she obtained from me, Mrs Fairbrother was able to get the dog. This was Gremlin Gernot von der Herren-eichen, another great grandson of Lustig through Stolz von Friedenheim and Bär von der Rheinhohe. On release from quarantine, Gernot came to my kennels for a time and was afterwards owned by Mrs Sykes of the Jonwin Kennels and finally by Miss Anderson. Gernot sired three champions.

Another of Mrs Fairbrother's achievements was to import Gremlin Bossi von Rhona, a daughter of Bär von der Rheinhohe from a von Dom bitch named Quadriga. Shortly after coming out of quarantine Bossi was mated to Ch. Panfield Tango, and as a result there were two certificate-winning bitches—Gremlin Moonsong and Gremlin Moonbeam. The latter is better known to most as, when mated to Axel von Bad Oeyn, she produced Ch. Gremlin Inxpot who won seven challenge certificates and was many times reserve. As a sire his best achievement was to produce Ch. Gremlin Inkling who had a splendid record in the show-ring. His total of 24 certificates was the highest number won by a male for many years.

Axel, the sire of Inxpot and grandsire of Inkling, deserves special mention for he was also the father of Ch. Panfield Zick (owned by Mr and Mrs Blackham), Ch. Burstall King (Major Bostock) and Ch. Toplocks Welladay of Sheafdon (Miss Haggie). He was bred in Germany and was there purchased as a pet by Col W. Forsyth, a British officer. Later Col Forsyth brought Axel to England, and when due to serve overseas again he left him in my care. Axel was by a son of Rex von Hohenneuffen out of a daughter of the same dog. Besides siring three champion dogs, Axel was the sire of a champion bitch and three certificate-winning daughters. This was a very considerable achievement by this dog who was not used at stud until he was nearly five.

Axel's son Inxpot sired one other champion besides Inkling, namely the dark-brindled dog Ch. Gremlin Indelible, who was bred by Mrs Fairbrother, and subsequently owned by Mr W. Craggs. Another champion bred by Mrs Fairbrother was Ch. Gremlin Sungari, a Tango daughter out of Bossi von Rhona.

Other Boxers which must not be forgotten were those born in Germany and imported into this country uncropped, which meant that they could compete in the British show-rings with the home-bred dogs. Three of these became champions— Holger (already discussed), his half-brother Ch. Golf von Kunzendorf (owned by Mrs Marjorie Fearfield) and Mr and Mrs Bishton's Ch. Annelie von Eddy's Gluck.

Of the other English champions there was Ch. Max of Boxholme, owned by Mrs Fotherby, who bought him as a puppy from his breeder, Mrs Pugh. Max was by Golf who, like Holger, carried the vom Germania prefix. He stemmed from Rex von Hohenneuffen, Holger's sire.

This dog, Rex, was well known in Germany where he was extensively used in the immediate post-war period. He did quite a deal for British Boxers for, in addition to Holger, he was the sire of Axel von Bad Oeyn's mother and father.

8

The American Influence

Although I shall now write about what I call the American influence on the Boxer in Britain, it should be made clear to the newcomer that practically all Boxers had their beginnings first in Germany and then in England. But it so happened that the Americans were able to buy the leading Boxer sires from the Germans chiefly between the two wars.

These purchases included the four Boxer 'immortals' — Sigurd, Lustig, Dorian and Utz. It was natural, therefore, that British breeders requiring the blood of these dogs should look across the Atlantic to the United States where they had made their homes and had been scientifically bred to produce the best type of Boxers.

As far as I can trace, the first importation from America to Britain was Miss Birrell's So Se Sumbula who came in before the war in whelp to Corsa von Uracher Wasserfall. The best known of this litter was a bitch, Gold of Uttershill, owned by the late Miss Esme Watson. Gold won one certificate.

Next to bring a Boxer from the States was Miss Jean Grant, who in 1946 imported a Lustig daughter, Ozark Jerris of Blossomlea in whelp to Ch. Quality of Barmere, a Sigurd son. She also brought in a red dog, Robin of Three Birches, a son of Ch. Warlord of Mazelaine out of Nylon II of Tulgey Wood.

The most important of these from the point of view of our history was a brindle dog puppy in the Quality-Ozark Jerris litter, by name Andrew. He was to bear the Cuckmere prefix of Mrs Siggers. Andrew became a champion, and among the bitches mated to him was Mrs

Meg Stephens's Bomza Revelmere Lulu. In this litter was the champion bitch Ch. Cuckmere Bomza Fiesta and Bomza Fledermaus, from whom Mrs Stephens built up her well-known Bomza Kennels.

Another bitch to go to Andrew was Mr and Mrs Cooke's Alrakim Maureen who bred for them Ch. Bobbysox of Greentubs and Lisa of Greentubs. This brought into prominence the Greentubs Kennels which have produced many top-class Boxers, among them my Ch. Panfield Party Piece of Greentubs, a daughter of Lisa and Ringleader. Party Piece won six Challenge Certificates, and was herself the dam of three champions. Mrs Cooke also bred Blazer of Greentubs (2 C.C.s) out of Bobbysox by Ringleader.

Another well-known breeder of pedigree dogs, cattle and ponies, famous for his Sealyhams and Herefords, had also taken an interest in the Boxer in America. He was Capt. R. S. de Quincey who imported the first American champion to come over—USA Ch. Applause of Emefar, a fine fawn dog of Mazelaine breeding. Capt. de Quincey also purchased Fostoria's Chieftain, a brindle son of USA Ch. Merry Monarch, the sire of USA Ch. Mazelaine's Zazarac Brandy.

For a number of reasons these dogs were not used very extensively at stud, but Applause left his mark in a champion daughter—Ch. Isis of Knowle Crest – and in a very famous granddaughter, Ch. Geronimo Carissima, owned by Mrs Haslam.

Carissima was sired by another American champion, Mr and Mrs Lissenden's Ch. Awldogg Southdown's Rector, from the well-known American kennels of Mr Keith Merrill. She was out of Geronimo Chloe, an Applause daughter.

Carissima was one of the most outstanding show bitches produced here, and won 17 certificates. She was a fawn with white markings, beautifully constructed, and it was a great pleasure for me to award her one of her many certificates.

A word about Rector, a fawn dog of distinction who sired many litters for Mr and Mrs Lissenden and others. Besides Carissima, he also sired Major Bostock's Ch.

CH. TYEGARTH FAMOUS GROUSE
One of the leading sires and show dogs in the eighties

GREENWAY'S CH. RAYFOS COCKROBIN
Ch. Rayfos Cockrobin, owned and bred by Mr and Mrs P. Greenway, set
new records for a red male, taking over from Inkling, Picasso and Guy.
Best-in-Show at the BBC's Jubilee Show

CH. FELCIGN FIONA
One of few Boxers to go Best in Show All Breeds at a Championship show

CH. WARDROBES AUTUMN HAZE OF AMERGLOW
Sire of nine champions

CH. TRYWELL TWELFTH NIGHT
This beautiful bitch, owned and bred by Mrs Kennett, dominated
the Boxer ring in 1986

Mr and Mrs Hambleton were usually among the winners. This is
one of their many stars, Ch. Marbelton Dressed to Kill

CH. SEEFELD GOLDSMITH

A champion, sired by a champion and sire of champions

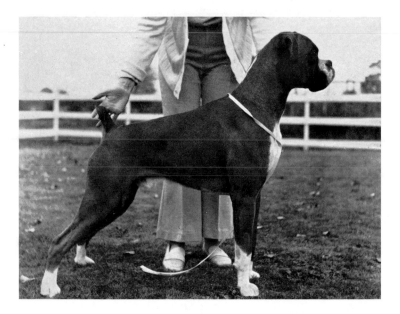

CH. STARMARK SWEET TALKIN' GUY

Top winning Boxer 1975

Awldogg Jacobus.

Capt. and Mrs Mike Jellicoe were other British breeders attracted by the American dogs, and they brought two into England from the Berolina Kennels. These were a dog, Flip, and a bitch, Tweed. Flip sired Ch. Flacius of Knowle Crest and Ch. Greatsea Masterpiece. He was a beautifully headed dog, and a great favourite at the Finemere Kennels.

In 1952 I was invited to judge the breed in America (something which I particularly appreciated as I was the first English Boxer judge so honoured) and this gave me an opportunity to see the finest Boxers in the United States both in the show-ring and at the splendidly equipped American kennels. The top male Boxers I saw there impressed me enormously, and it immediately became my ambition to bring back to England a youngster with something of the same style and personality. The three males which interested me most were: USA Ch. Mazelaine's Zazarac Brandy, USA Ch. Warwick Karneia and USA Ch. Bang Away of Sirrah Crest, and undoubtedly these were among the greatest Boxers of all time. Here are some impressions of the American Boxers which I wrote on returning to England:

'Like American judges who have come to England, I did not find that the difference between the cropped and natural ear presented any difficulty, but I did become a firm convert to the American and German style. There is no doubt (in my mind) that the crop not only gives the Boxer added attractiveness and alertness, but is the finishing touch to the harmony of the whole appearance.

'Now this opinion might get me in hot water. Cropping will never be allowed in England, so I am assured, chiefly because the view is firmly held here that it involves cruelty. On this I have no knowledge, for I have no practical experience, but I have been assured that the operation, carried out scientifically, causes no pain whatsoever to the puppies. Be that as it may, the Kennel Club is absolutely against it, and only recently strengthened the ban.

'Another comment I have heard here is that it is impudent to attempt to "improve on Nature". A moment's thought, however, reveals that most selective breeding is an attempt to improve on Nature's plan. If you are doubtful, watch your stud dogs. They would have no objection to mixing the breeding if they were allowed to do so. And for that matter what is the difference on this basis between cutting tails and ears (to which many here object)? [Later I came to turn against both cropping and docking. The former we can well do without. Docking is debatable. It has now been banned in more countries and there is a move to extend this to the UK.]

'I think most of us are looking for the same thing in our conception of the quality Boxer, though maybe we vary in the emphasis to be placed on various features. We have good head type in England, but we have possibly not paid so much attention to overall balance, hindquarters and movement as the Americans. Mind you, I saw some steep stifles and upright shoulders in America. (It would have been remarkable if I hadn't.)

'It was most interesting for me to discuss these points with American breeders, for this discussion of head versus body still continues in England. I frankly admit that I find it difficult to overlook what is to me an untypical Boxer head, even though it is carried into the ring on a sound body. But at the same time I am prepared to go a long way with those who declare that without a sound body and good movement a Boxer is useless.

'Obviously in the absence of perfect specimens (with good heads *and* sound bodies) one seeks a compromise. Is it possible to do otherwise? Anything else is like having to express a preference for one of two things, neither of which you really like. This, at best, must be unsatisfactory. In the end surely it all comes back to the dogs in the ring where all must depend on comparisons between the various competitors?

'Of one thing I feel certain, and that is on all-over quality (when the Boxer is taken altogether in one piece) is the best way to judge them. A system of judging by points leads to endless difficulty. Neither do I believe that it would be possible to reach better decisions by including more measurements in the Standard. It is impossible to measure a living thing in inches (other than the height, and that has its snags) and only the eye of the practised observer can decide.

'Because of this, there must always be differences of opinion, and that is half the fun of the dog game. For myself, I am not sorry that words like "harmony", "nobility", "substance" and "elegance" cannot be reduced to inches on a slide rule. That would only turn artists into carpenters . . . .

'I was also impressed by the way shows are organized in America. There is far more spectacle in an American dog show compared with ours, but as for our judges arriving in dinner jacket (tuxedo) or ballroom dress, well, they would feel just as much out of place as a lady in slacks at a first night at the opera.

'But I did like other details in the States, such as numbers in the rings to indicate the winning dogs; the strip of matting for the dogs to move on, and the solid enclosures (instead of a rope) for the ring itself. All these were new to me, and seemed excellent ideas. Later some were adopted in England.

'Mind you, these things are not of first importance, but desirable refinements. It is always a good thing if the spectators are able to follow exactly what is going on (which they seemed to do in the States) while at home they are often left guessing.

'I shouldn't like you to get the impression that I have gone all-American. There is much to be admired about the way many things are run in England, but because we have been doing it longer we should not shut our eyes to new ideas. Neither should any of us lose sight of the fact that the most important thing of all is the quality of the dogs.'

My own capture in the States was a 'gentleman from Texas' the brindle and white marked son of USA Ch. Ursa Major of Sirrah Crest and Verily Verily of Sirrah Crest, bred the same way as Bang Away. I first saw him at the Mazelaine Kennels at Helotes, Texas, where my husband and I spent a short holiday with Mr and Mrs Wagner. He was four and a half months old and seemed to me to be everything I had ever wished for. He was, however, far above my pocket in price, even if the Wagners would have agreed to sell him. With a sigh, we decided 'Tex' was not for us.

The brief period in the Texas sun over, we made plans for our return journey over to New York and England. Before saying 'Good-bye' we took one more look at the kennels which included a score of the Mazelaine famous champions and also 'Tex'.

'He's going to be quite a nice dog,' said Jack Wagner in his usual modest way. And then he added something which made our hearts leap: 'If you'd like him, you can take him with you. I've brought home to America some pretty nice dogs from Europe, and I'd like to think I was sending one back.'

So, just as simply as that, Mazelaine's Texas Ranger came into our possession. Such an act of generosity and friendship I shall never forget. We had also learned more about Boxers in that short visit than ever we knew before.

Mr and Mrs Wagner not only knew their breed from A to Z, they also discussed their own champions quite freely, pointing out both their virtues and their faults, eager to pass on some of their knowledge they have gained through hard experience.

I salute them as the greatest Boxer breeders I have ever known, and also as two of my greatest friends.

Now all was bustle to make arrangements for the shipping of 'Tex' by air from San Antonio airfield across America to New York and then in the *Queen Elizabeth* from New York to Southampton. At San Antonio it was found that the weight of the pup plus his crate was more than the permitted amount for one article. But fortunately they were Boxer lovers down there, and the crate was put aboard without the pup. Then the pup was placed in a cardboard box and put in the aircraft. 'Don't worry,' said the pilot, 'that will satisfy the authorities. When we are in flight you can put the dawg in the crate.' And that's just how it was done with the neatest piece of cutting through red tape that I'd ever seen. Such an incident I never expected to encounter outside my own country.

So 'Tex' came to England and as he blimped up the gangway to the *Queen Elizabeth* I thought myself the luckiest and happiest person in the world. Not only to the Wagners, but to all my other American friends I should like to express my thanks for this great dog, and especially to Mr Charles O. Spannaus (former President of the American Boxer Club) and his family who had entertained us in their New York home and made our visit to their country possible.

'Tex' was, of course, a cropped dog, and was never shown, but in one of his first litters ex Ch. Panfield Party Piece of Greentubs he produced my first supreme winner all breeds at a championship show. This was the young Ch. Panfield Beau Jinks, later owned by Mrs Dulanty. Jinks was a brindle and white marked dog like his dad. There was another certificate winner in the litter, Panfield Beau Geste, owned by Mr G. Smith.

Mated to Ch. Panfield Bliss, Texas threw the Dallisons' Miss Bang Away who won the certificate at the Three Counties Show in 1954 under Mr George Jakeman on the same day as a Texas son, Breakstone's Charlie Boy, owned by the late Mrs Dunkels and Mrs Gamble, took the dog C.C. and Best of Breed.

In his second litter out of Party Piece 'Tex' sired Ch. Panfield Texas Tycoon. It has been significant to us to notice that 'Tex', a monorchid dog, sired fewer monorchids than any of our entire sires. Nor was there an increase in monorchids in the second generation, which is something the theorists might ponder upon. Altogether he sired six champions and was top sire two years running. He died in 1958.

It is of interest that 'Tex' was bred by the Wagners, but that 'Tex's' brother, the great Ch. Bang Away, was bred and was owned by Dr and Mrs R. C. Harris. The reason was that Mr Wagner bought the sire and dam (Ursa Major and Verily Verily) after the birth of Bang Away. All these dogs go back repeatedly to the Wagner's superlative Dorian von Marienhof.

'Tex' had a very considerable effect on the breed in this country. He threw his own outstanding qualities which, allied to British bitches, produced many splendid Boxers.

So the Panfield Boxers brought about the same fusion of strains which has always had success in this breed—the classic Lustig-Dorian combination carried forward to the tenth generation.

The American influence was further extended by importations made by Major Bostock who brought in two daughters of USA Ch. Bang Away of Sirrah Crest. These were Beaulaine's Bonadea, a beautiful red and white bitch in whelp to USA Ch. Mazelaine's Gallantry, and a brindle bitch, Kirsten of Tomira, in whelp to USA Ch. Avi's Independent Watchman. Two of Bonadea's pups became champions, these being Burstall Zipaway and Burstall Fireaway. Later Major Bostock imported from the United States Rob Roy of Tomira who soon sired three champions—Ch. Kelfrey Merry Monarch, who went to New Zealand, Ch. Burstall Little Caesar, and Ch. Burstall Icecapade.

Two others which came over were Fireball of Emefar, a Bang Away grandson, imported by myself and sold to Mrs Gerardy in Australia, and Mr and Mrs Barden's Felmoor Rainey Lane's Raffles, a son of USA Ch. Dion of Rainey Lane. Raffles sired Mrs Scheja's Ch. Tinkazan Merriveen Speculation and was then taken by his owners to Australia.

Raffles, in England a comparatively short time, had a striking influence. For Mrs F. M. Price, a most successful breeder, he sired Felcign Faro, who was the top British sire in 1958. Faro's daughter, Ch. Felcign Fiona, also owned by Mrs Price, not only won seven certificates, but took Best in Show All Breeds at Leicester the same year.

For Mrs Dellar, Raffles sired two champions, one of whom, Ch. Merriveen Fascination, was my Best of Breed winner at Crufts in 1957.

9

The Standard

The Standard of the breed is extremely important and my advice to the beginner, for whom this book is meant, is to study it carefully. There is, as I have so frequently said, no disadvantage in knowing it thoroughly, and there is no real substitute for knowledge.

But having said this, I would like it to be thoroughly understood that I am not saying that the task of understanding and appreciating Boxers finishes on thoroughly knowing the Standard. That is only the start. Afterwards comes the job of interpretation, and applying the Standard to the dogs.

So, then, start by purchasing from the Kennel Club the official Breed Standards (Working Group) and turn to the Boxer. The older, fuller version is reproduced here. The current (1986) version is reproduced on page 105.

Characteristics

The character of the Boxer is of the greatest importance and demands the most careful attention. He is renowned from olden times for his great love and faithfulness to his master and household, his alertness and fearless courage as a defender and protector. The Boxer is docile but distrustful of strangers. He is bright and friendly in play but brave and determined when roused. His intelligence and willing tractability, his modesty and cleanliness make him a highly desirable family dog and cheerful companion. He is the soul of honesty and loyalty. He is never false or treacherous even in his old age.

General Appearance

The Boxer is a medium-sized, sturdy, smooth-haired dog of short square figure and strong limb. The musculation is clean and powerfully developed, and should stand out plastically from under the skin. Movement of the Boxer should be alive with energy. His gait, although firm, is elastic. The stride free and roomy; carriage proud and noble. As a service and guard dog he must combine a considerable degree of elegance with the substance and power essential to his duties; those of an enduring escort dog whether with horse, bicycle or carriage and as a splendid jumper. Only a body whose individual limbs are built to withstand the most strenuous 'mechanical' effort and assembled as a complete and harmonious whole can respond to such demands. Therefore to be at its highest efficiency the Boxer must never be plump or heavy. Whilst equipped for great speed, it must not be racy. When judging the Boxer the first thing to be considered is general appearance, the relation of substance to elegance and the desired relationship of the individual parts of the body to each other. Consideration, too, must be given to colour. After these, the individual parts should be examined for their correct construction and their functions. Special attention should be devoted to the head.

Head and Skull

The head imparts to the Boxer a unique individual stamp peculiar to the breed. It must be in perfect proportion to his body; above all it must never be too light. The muzzle is the most distinctive feature. The greatest value is to be placed on its being of correct form and in absolute proportion to the skull. The beauty of the head depends upon the harmonious proportion between the muzzle and the skull. From whatever direction the head is viewed, whether from the front, from the top or from the side, the muzzle should always appear in correct relationship to the skull. That means that the head should never appear too small or too large. The length of the muzzle to the whole of the head should be as 1 is to 3. The head should

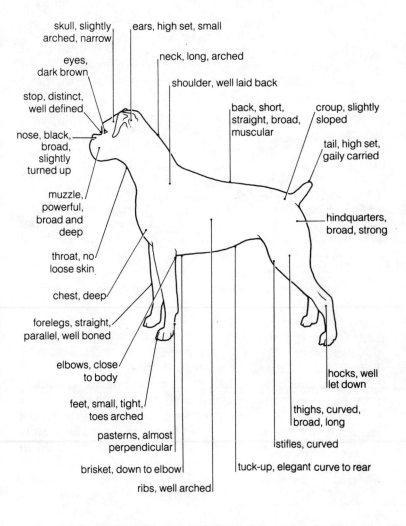

skull, slightly arched, narrow

ears, high set, small

eyes, dark brown

neck, long, arched

stop, distinct, well defined

shoulder, well laid back

nose, black, broad, slightly turned up

back, short, straight, broad, muscular

croup, slightly sloped

tail, high set, gaily carried

muzzle, powerful, broad and deep

hindquarters, broad, strong

throat, no loose skin

chest, deep

forelegs, straight, parallel, well boned

elbows, close to body

hocks, well let down

feet, small, tight, toes arched

thighs, curved, broad, long

pasterns, almost perpendicular

stifles, curved

brisket, down to elbow

tuck-up, elegant curve to rear

ribs, well arched

Colour : Fawn, red, brindled, mask black; white markings permitted

Coat : Short, shiny, smooth, tight to body

Height : Dogs 22½″ – 25″ at shoulder
Bitches 21″ – 23″ at shoulder

not show deep wrinkles. Normally wrinkles will spring up on the top of the skull when the dog is alert. Folds are always indicated from the root of the nose running downwards on both sides of the muzzle. The dark mask is confined to the muzzle. It must be in distinct relief to the colour of the head so that the face will not have a 'sombre' expression. The muzzle must be powerfully developed in length, in breadth and in height. It must not be pointed or narrow, short or shallow. Its shape is influenced through the formation of both jaw-bones, the placement of teeth in the jaw-bones, and through the quality of the lips. The top of the skull should be slightly arched. It should not be so short that it is rotund, too flat, or too broad. The occiput should not be too pronounced. The forehead should form a distinct stop with the top line of the muzzle, which should not be forced back into the forehead like that of a Bulldog. Neither should it slope away (downfaced). The tip of the nose should lie somewhat higher than the root of the muzzle. The forehead should show a suggestion of furrow which, however, should never be too deep, especially between the eyes. Corresponding with the powerful set of teeth, the cheeks accordingly should be well developed without protruding from the head with 'too bulgy' an appearance. For preference they should taper into the muzzle in a slight, graceful curve. The nose should be broad and black, very slightly turned up. The nostrils should be broad with a naso-labial line between them. The two jaw-bones should not terminate in a normal perpendicular level in the front but the lower jaw should protrude beyond the upper jaw and bend slightly upwards. The Boxer is normally undershot. The upper jaw should be broad where attached to the skull, and maintain this breadth except for a very slight tapering to the front.

Eyes

The eyes should be dark brown; not too small or protruding; not deep set. They should disclose an expression of energy and intelligence, but should never appear gloomy, threatening or piercing. The eyes must have a dark rim.

Ears

Some American and Continental Boxers are cropped and are ineligible for competition under Kennel Club Regulations. The Boxer's natural ears are defined as: moderate in size (small rather than large), thin to the touch, set on wide apart at the highest points of the sides of the skull and lying flat and close to the cheek when in repose. When the dog is alert the ears should fall forward with a definite crease.

Mouth

The canine teeth should be as widely separated as possible. The incisors (6) should all be in one row, with no projection of the middle teeth. In the upper jaw they should be slightly concave. In the lower they should be in a straight line. Both jaws should be very wide in front; bite powerful and sound, the teeth set in the most normal possible arrangement. The lips complete the formation of the muzzle. The upper lip should be thick and padded and fill out the hollow space in front formed by the projection of the lower jaw and be supported by the fangs of the jaw. These fangs must stand as far apart as possible and be of good length so that the front surface of the muzzle becomes broad and almost square; to form an obtuse (rounded) angle with the top line of the muzzle. The lower edge of the upper lip should rest on the edge of the lower lip. The repandous (bent upward) part of the under-jaw with the lower lip (sometimes called the chin) must not rise above the front of the upper lip. On the other hand it should not disappear under it. It must, however, be plainly perceptible when viewed from the front as well as the side, without protruding and bending upward as in the English Bulldog. The teeth of the under-jaw should not be seen when the mouth is closed, neither should the tongue show when the mouth is closed.

Neck

The neck should be not too thick and short but of ample length, yet strong, round, muscular and clean-cut throughout. There should be a distinctly marked nape and an elegant arch down to the back.

Forequarters

The chest should be deep and reach down to the elbows. The depth of the chest should be half the height of the dog at the withers. The ribs should be well arched but not barrel-shaped. They should extend far to the rear. The loins should be short, close and taut and slightly tucked up. The lower stomach line should blend into an elegant curve to the rear. The shoulders should be long and sloping, close lying but not excessively covered with muscle. The upper arm should be long and form a right-angle to the shoulder-blade. The forelegs when seen from the front should be straight, parallel to each other and have strong, firmly articulated (joined) bones. The elbows should not press too closely to the chest-wall or stand off too far from it. The underarm should be perpendicular, long and firmly muscled. The pastern joint of the foreleg should be clearly defined, but not distended. The pastern should be short, slightly slanting and almost perpendicular to the ground.

Body

The body viewed in profile should be of square appearance. The length of the body from the front of the chest to the rear of the body should equal the height from the ground to the top of the shoulder, giving the Boxer a short-coupled, square profile. The torso rests on trunk-like straight legs with strong bones. The withers should be clearly defined. The whole back should be short, straight, broad, and very muscular.

Hindquarters

The hindquarters should be strongly muscled. The musculation should be hard and stand out plastically through the skin. The thighs should not be narrow and flat but broad and curved. The breech musculation should also be strongly developed. The croup should be slightly sloped, flat arched and broad. The pelvis should be long and, in females especially, broad. The upper and lower thighs should be long. The hip and knee joints should have as much angle as possible. In a standing position the knee should reach so far forward that it would meet a vertical line drawn from the hip protuberance to the floor. The hock angle should be about 140 degrees; the lower part of the foot at a slight slope of about 95 to 100 degrees from the hock joint to the floor; that is, not completely vertical. Seen from behind, the hind legs should be straight. The hocks should be clean and not distended, supported by powerful rear pads.

Feet

The feet should be small with tightly-arched toes (cat feet) and hard soles. The rear toes should be just a little longer than the front toes, but similar in all other respects.

Tail

The tail attachment should be high. The tail should be docked and carried upwards and should be not more than 2 inches long.

Coat

The coat should be short and shiny, lying smooth and tight to the body.

Colour

The permissible colours are fawn, brindle and fawn in

various shades from light yellow to dark deer red. The brindle variety should have black stripes on a golden-yellow or red-brown background. The stripes should be clearly defined and above all should not be grey or dirty. Stripes that do not cover the whole top of the body are not desirable. White markings are not undesirable; in fact they are often very attractive in appearance. The black mask is essential but when white stretches over the muzzle naturally that portion of the black mask disappears. It is not possible to get black toe-nails with white feet. It is desirable, however, to have an even distribution of head markings.

Weight and Size

Dogs: 22½–25 inches at the withers. Bitches: 21 to 23 inches at the withers. Heights above or below these figures not to be encouraged. Dogs around 23 inches should weigh about 66 lb. and bitches of about 22 inches should weigh about 62 lb.

Faults

Viciousness; treachery; unreliability; lack of temperament; cowardice. Head: a head that is not typical. A plump, bulldoggy appearance. Light bone. Lack of proportion. Bad physical condition. Lack of nobility and expression. 'Sombre' face. Unserviceable bite whether due to disease or to faulty tooth placement. Pinscher or Bulldog head. Showing the teeth or the tongue. A sloping top line of the muzzle. Too pointed or too light a bite (snipy). Eyes: visible conjunctiva (Haw). Light eyes. Ears: flying ears; rose ears; semi-erect or erect ears. Neck: dewlap. Front: too broad and low in front; loose shoulders; chest hanging between the shoulders; hare feet; turned legs and toes. Body: carp (roach) back; sway back; thin, lean back; long, narrow, sharp sunken-in loins. Weak union with the croup, hollow flanks; hanging stomach. Hindquarters: falling off, too arched or narrow croup. A low-set tail; higher in back than in front; steep, stiff or too little angulation of the hindquarters; light thighs; cow-hocks; bow-legs; hind dewclaws; soft hocks, narrow heel, tottering, waddling gait; hare's feet; hindquarters too far under or too far behind. Colour: Boxers with white or black ground colour, or entirely white or black or any other colour than fawn or brindle. (White markings are allowed but must not exceed one-third (1/3) of the ground colour.)

10

The Standard Under Review

If the beginner has waded through this he will need to draw a deep breath. Let's admit from the start that this version was one of the longest and most complicated of all the Standards.

Now it should be appreciated that this Standard was approved by the Kennel Club after the Boxer clubs had discussed it, and made their recommendations, but although it should be approached with the necessary respect, there is no good reason for taking the view that here are the Tablets of Stone and nothing should be added to or taken away therefrom, though naturally any proposed change should be treated with the utmost care, and in the true interest of the breed.

Personally, I have always advocated making the Standard clearer in certain respects, but one of the difficulties one always faces is the criticism of those who fear that a change is advocated to suit the purposes of the advocate. But such is the fate of the reformer and such reactions must be brushed on one side.

Way back, for instance, Stafford Somerfield wrote:

'It is said that fools rush in where angels fear to tread. The danger is probably not so great in the dog world, for I have yet to come across any angels in this sport. Most of those who take part in it have both feet firmly on the ground. However, I will invite brickbats by discussing the Standard of the Boxer breed—a subject which is more inflammable than a firework on a November night.

'The reason is clear. Experienced breeders will tell you there is sufficient confusion already. Don't add to it. Besides, it invites the criticism that one is embarking on that old custom of making the Standard fit the dog. And, above all, one would appear to be insufficiently grateful to those sportsmen who did so much to obtain general agreement while keeping as close as possible to the original, which was, of course, written in German.

'Not a bit of it. Even a greater Book than this has its Revised Version. Suggestions made now are not intended to be critical. The writer has an abiding respect for tradition and the past. They aim at clearing up one or two points which leave the beginner in some doubt.

'First a sentence about that old chestnut the black mask, which is still causing beginners to raise their hands in despair. The Standard says: "The black mask is *essential*, but when white stretches over the muzzle, naturally that portion of the black mask disappears.' How can one interpret that contradiction? If a black mask is *essential* that is the end of it. But we know also that white is permitted, and that many famous dogs (Lustig was one) certainly had white on their muzzles.

'Obviously, the word "essential" is the one we quarrel with. The Americans, you may be interested to know, don't use it. But their formula, I suggest, is no clearer than ours. Their Standard says: "The black mask is *absolutely required*. When white stretches over the muzzle naturally that portion of the black mask disappears."

'Now, I suggest it would be far better for everybody if a change were made to this simple and, I think, clear statement: "When there is no white on the muzzle a black mask is essential, but when white stretches over the muzzle naturally that portion of the black mask disappears."

'My second point concerns the incisors in the upper jaw. The Standard says: "In the upper jaw they should be slightly concave." Now this, really, is looking at the dog backwards. Obviously the word should be convex. For my own satisfaction I went back to the original German in Stockmann's *Der Boxer* on this point and my efficient and enthusiastic translator provides this version of the phrase: "*in einer leicht nach worn ausgebogenen*"—"bending out slightly to the front". Obviously, this was a case where the original was clear and the newer version confused.

'Another phrase which has worried me has been that describing the "musculation" (meaning muscles, of course). They should stand out plastically from the skin, says the Standard. The Germans used the word *plastisch*, which can mean pliant and mouldable. Now it becomes perfectly clear. Muscles which are pliant (hard, but flexible) are just as we thought they should be. Perhaps you will be asking: does all this matter? I think it does.'

Some time afterwards (in 1954) an attempt was made by the Northern Club to get the Standard reviewed, but they failed to get agreement. I hope their suggestion on the question of the black mask will eventually be adopted. It reads:

'When white appears on the muzzle the outline of the white must reveal the dark mask, which is otherwise essential.' This at any rate makes the position clear.

In answer to those whom I know will hold up their hands in horror to any attempt to tamper with the Standard I must point out that considerable changes have already been made from that adopted by the British Boxer Club in 1936. This reads as follows:

General Appearance

The Boxer is a medium-sized dog of sturdy build, combining power with activity. Its expression should suggest benign self-sufficiency, and any indication of a temperamental tendency to bark or show ill-temper should be sternly discouraged; but it should carry itself with calm self-assurance, and the frown on its face is no more than a warning to pay regard to its self-respect.

Head

The head should be of medium length and with the forehead wide and the cheeks clean; the head at all angles of sight giving a sharp-cut appearance. At some three-fifths of the length from occiput to nose there should be a definite break or stop. The nose should be neither turned up nor turned down. The stop enables the eyes to set under the eyebrows without being sunken. They are dark in colour, of medium size and neither round nor bulging. The muzzle is filled in below the eye and somewhat square in appearance with no loose flesh. The teeth must be undershot but only very slightly. The ears should resemble the ears of a Great Dane in shape, but be of a proportionately smaller size well in keeping with the general lines of the head. They should fall slightly forward.

Forequarters

The head is carried on a graceful muscular neck, the flesh on the neck loose but without throatiness. The chest has width with a good brisket, while the shoulders are flat and well laid back, and the elbows placed firmly at the side of the chest and move parallel to one another. The legs are straight with good bone and strong pasterns on good-sized feet with well-arched toes.

Body

The ribs are wide sprung and carried well back, and the chest has good depth. The loins should be short, coupling the hindquarters strongly to the body. The top line of the body should be straight but may have the semblance of a curve from withers to set-on of tail.

Hindquarters

The buttocks are broad enough to give strength, but not so massive as the forehand and body. The upper thigh is muscularly developed, the second thighs strong, and there is a distinct bend at the stifle; the hock is set fairly low and directly under the tail end of the dog, while the leg has good bone and the feet are firm. The tail is docked and carried upward while in motion.

Size

The height may vary from 20 to 24 inches, and the weight from 56 lb. to 64 lb.; the lesser of these measurements are more applicable to a bitch and the greater to a dog.

Colours

Brindled or red, the nose and lips must be black. White markings are permitted on the chest and paws, but never on back, legs or head, unless it be a thin line between the eyes, though that should be discouraged. In brindles the markings should be fairly distinct and definitely black or dark brown, the background may be dark brown, red, fawn or pale gold. In reds, the colour may vary from pale gold and fawn to red or deepish red-brown, and there must be no brindle hairs.

Coat and Skin

The coat is short-haired and silky. The skin is loose at the neck and on the back, but the muscles must show clearly through.

Movement

The action should be that of a dog of strength rather than of pace, but easy and true and light upon the feet.

Mr Allon Dawson subsequently wrote in the press:
 'This meeting (which approved the Standard) took place in London, attended by about nine people, including Mrs Caro, Mrs Sprigge, Mrs Rhodes, Mr Betteridge, Mr Burman, Mr McCandlish and me. Prior to the meeting the German Standard had been translated into English by two bi-lingual (German and English) interested Boxer fanciers.
 'All went smoothly with the Standard until 1946, when early in the year I was asked by the chairman of the British Boxer Club to prepare an illustrated booklet of the Standard for the benefit of members. At very considerable

cost to myself I prepared a booklet which many fanciers still possess.

'At a committee meeting early in 1946, held in London, only three members attended. Much to my surprise the other two members refused to accept this booklet. Their objection was that I had altered the word "bicycle" to "cycle" and had included reproductions of German and American champion Boxers.

'All prominent fanciers in 1946 saw the booklet and signed in the circulated book that they considered it entirely satisfactory.

'The 1946 annual general meeting held in June (while I was in America and therefore unable to be present) turned down the German Standard and went all American.

'There are people who will never be satisfied with a Standard which does not suit their idea of a Boxer. I, for one, am absolutely satisfied with our Standard, which the Northern Boxer Club worked hard to uphold, and I am strenuously opposed to any alteration.'

That is, of course, another view, and quite rightly the reader should hear all sides. I would also point out to the reader that we are all agreed on essentials, and that the points on which there has been discussion are, after all, not in this category.

In my opinion there is something to be said for the view that there is a great deal of verbiage in the German version which is characteristic of the Continental judges who concern themselves with an enormous amount of detail and place themselves in the position of not seeing the wood for the trees.

How, for instance, is it possible when judging Boxers to consider the number of degrees in the hock angle or test the capabilities of the animals with 'horse, bicycle or carriage'?

Essentials—these are the concern of the newcomer, who surely wants to grasp quickly and with some degree of certainty that he is right in the important points of the breed.

With this in mind I have taken it on myself to produce

here my own notes on the Standard, which are purely unofficial, but which leave out no essentials, and will enable the novice to acquire a sound basic knowledge from which to progress.

Notes on the Standard

The first thing to be considered is general appearance, followed by colour as more than one-third white of the whole is not allowed. After this, the individual parts should be examined for correct construction, paying special attention to the head.

Character: Alert, intelligent, friendly, bold when necessary. Faults: viciousness, lack of spirit, cowardice.

General Appearance: A balanced, well-constructed dog of square muscular figure, combining substance with elegance, and of noble bearing. Height: dogs 22½ to 25 inches at the withers, bitches 21 to 23.

Colour: All shades of fawn and brindle. White markings are allowed. When white appears on the muzzle the outline of the white should reveal the dark mask which is otherwise essential.

Movement: Alive with energy and true. The Boxer should stride out freely and cover the ground. Faults: stiff, stilted or waddling gait, plaiting.

Head (General): Never too light, with the muzzle one-third of the whole in length. No wrinkles (except on top of the head when the dog is alert, and from the root of the nose running downwards on both sides of the muzzle). Lively expression, with the mask confined to the muzzle. Faults: over-wrinkled; Bull-doggy, or Dane-ish, down-faced, sombre.

Muzzle: Powerful, broad and deep. Faults: pointed, narrow, short, shallow.

Stop: Distinct, clearly defined. Faults: forced back into forehead like a Bulldog, lack of stop.

Forehead: Showing slight furrow, which should not be too deep, especially between the eyes.

Cheeks: Well developed, but tapering into muzzle in a graceful curve. Faults: too bulgy, 'cheeky'.

Nose: Broad and black, with tip slightly higher than root.

Fault: butterfly nose.

Jaws: Powerful and wide, slightly undershot, the chin plainly seen from front and sides. Faults: too undershot like a Bulldog, showing teeth or tongue, lack of chin, wry, too pointed or light (snipy).

Eyes: dark with dark rim, medium size. Faults: light, too small and deep set, protruding, haw showing.

Ears: Moderate in size, high set, lying flat and close to the cheeks. Faults: flying, rose, erect.

Teeth: White and strong. In top jaw set in a line slightly curving outwards, and in bottom jaw in a straight line. Fault: unserviceable bite.

Lips: Thick and padded, covering teeth, the top lip resting on the lower. Fault: lippiness.

Neck: Long, arched and strong. Faults: loose skin, throaty, short.

Chest: Deep, reaching down to elbows. Faults: too broad and low in front, hanging between shoulders, 'hollow'.

Ribs: Well arched. Faults: barrel-shaped or slab-sided.

Loins: Short, with lower stomach line blending in elegant curve to the rear. Faults: long, narrow, sunken-in, weak union with croup, hanging stomach.

Shoulders: Long, close-lying and well laid back. Faults: upright, loose, loaded.

Front Legs: Straight with good bone. Elbows close to the body. Faults: not straight, short front legs.

Pasterns: Short, slightly slanting. Fault: weak pasterns.

Back: Short, straight, broad and very muscular. Faults: roach, long, sway, lean.

Hindquarters: Strongly muscled, powerful thighs, long and broad, the croup only slightly sloped, stifles curved, giving good angulation, hocks well let down. Faults: steep in stifle, falling off in croup, overbuilt behind, light thighs, cow-hocks, bow-legs, hindquarters set under or too far back.

Feet: Small, tight, toes arched. Faults: spread out, thin, flat.

Tail: Docked, high set, carried upwards. In length harmonious to the dog. Faults: low set, carried in a dejected manner.

Coat: Short, shiny, lying close to body. Faults: rough and in poor condition.

Note: Male animals should have two apparently normal testicles fully descended into the scrotum.

I am still very conscious that this is long, especially when compared with that for the Poodle, for instance, and one must admit that the Poodle breeders have reached an extremely high level. Maybe we Boxerites are still confused with detail, even when we think we have cut the points down to the bare bones. Still, this is an effort to avoid confusion, and in writing and rewriting it I have learned a lot.

The real enthusiast might spend a little time trying to do better, bearing in mind that we are catering for those who are coming into dogs for the first time and not the experts who automatically know the correct shape of a dog. For them the head is, perhaps, the most difficult to master. The only way that I know to become efficient here is to spend a lot of time looking at a good head. If there are no good ones available, study the photographs of ones acknowledged on all sides to have been first class.

In the next chapter I shall deal with the application of the Standard and judging, but before doing so I again want to draw your attention to those vital and all important words in the first paragraph of my notes. I have made them the first paragraph because that is where I think they belong!

'The first thing to be considered is general appearance . . . after this the individual parts should be examined . . . .'

Read that paragraph again. I didn't invent it. Read it again in slightly different words buried away in the second paragraph of the official Standard. 'The first thing is general appearance.'

In other words, is the animal correctly constructed, is he well balanced, is he pleasing to the eye all over? Is he characteristic of the breed? In fact: is he a Boxer? *After that*, and again read those two words, *after that*, consideration should be given to the individual parts, paying special attention to the head.

If those points are always kept in mind the beginner will avoid pitfalls into which many have fallen and at any rate he will be looking for a smart, stylish, well-balanced, lively, correctly constructed dog. Add to this a correct head and the dog before you will be without equal in the canine race.

Revised Standard (1986)

Some minor changes are made from time to time. The Standard remains the same except for the height which has been slightly increased. The new figures are: dogs 22½ to 25 inches, bitches 21 to 23 inches at the shoulder. The dog figure is increased by half an inch. That for the bitch remains the same.

General Appearance

Great nobility, smooth coated, medium sized, square build, strong bone and evident, well developed muscles.

Characteristics

Lively, strong, loyal to owner and family, but distrustful of strangers. Obedient, friendly at play, but with guarding instinct.

Temperament

Equable, biddable, fearless, self-assured.

Head and Skull

Head imparts its unique individual stamp and is in proportion to body, appearing neither light nor too heavy. Skull lean without exaggerated cheek muscles. Muzzle broad, deep and powerful, never narrow, pointed, short or shallow. Balance of skull and muzzle essential, with muzzle never appearing small, viewed from any angle. Skull cleanly covered, showing no wrinkle, except when alerted. Creases present from root of nose running down sides of muzzle. Dark mask confined to muzzle, distinctly contrasting with colour of head, even when white is present. Lower jaw undershot, curving slightly upward. Upper jaw broad where attached to skull, tapering very slightly to front. Muzzle shape completed by upper lips, thick and well padded, supported by well separated canine teeth of lower jaw. Lower edge of upper lip rests on edge of lower lip, so that chin is clearly perceptible when viewed from front or side. Lower jaw never to obscure front of upper lip, neither should teeth nor tongue be visible when mouth closed. Top of skull slightly arched, not rounded, nor too flat and broad. Occiput not too pronounced. Distinct stop, bridge of nose never forced back into forehead, nor should it be downfaced. Length of muzzle measured from tip of nose to inside corner of eye is one third length of head measured from tip of nose to occiput. Nose broad, black, slightly turned up, wide nostrils with well defined line between. Tip of nose set slightly higher than root of muzzle. Cheeks powerfully developed, never bulging.

Eyes

Dark brown, forward looking, not too small, protruding or deeply set. Showing lively intelligent expression. Dark rims with good pigmentation showing no haw.

Ears

Moderate size, thin, set wide apart on highest part of skull lying flat and close to cheek in repose, but falling forward with definite crease when alert.

Mouth

Undershot jaw, canines set wide apart with incisors (6) in straight line in lower jaw. In upper jaw set in line curving slightly forward. Bite powerful and sound, with teeth set in normal arrangement.

Neck

Round, of ample length, strong, muscular, clean cut, no dewlap. Distinctly marked nape and elegant arch down to withers.

Forequarters

Shoulders long and sloping, close lying, not excessively covered with muscle. Upper arm long, making right angle to shoulder blade. Forelegs seen from front, straight, parallel, with strong bone. Elbows not too close or standing too far from chest wall. Forearms perpendicular, long and firmly muscled. Pasterns short, clearly defined, but not distended, slightly slanted.

Body

In profile square, length from forechest to rear of upper thigh equal to height at withers. Chest deep, reaching to elbows. Depth of chest half height at withers. Ribs well arched, not barrel shaped, extending well to rear. Withers clearly defined. Back short, straight, slightly sloping, broad and strongly muscled. Loin short, well tucked up and taut. Lower abdominal line blends into curve to rear.

Hindquarters

Very strong with muscles hard and standing out noticeably under skin. Thighs broad and curved. Broad croup slightly sloped, with flat, broad arch. Pelvis long and broad. Upper and lower thigh long. Good hind angulation, when standing, the stifle is directly under the hip protruberance. Seen from side, leg from hock joint to foot not quite vertical. Seen from behind, legs straight, hock joints clean, with powerful rear pads.

Feet

Front feet small and catlike, with well arched toes, and hard pads; hind feet slightly longer.

Tail

Set on high, customarily docked and carried upward.

Gait/movement

Strong, powerful with noble bearing, reaching well forward, and with driving action of hindquarters. In profile, stride free and ground covering.

Coat

Short, glossy, smooth and tight to body.

Colour

Fawn or brindle. White markings acceptable not exceeding one third of ground colour.
Fawn Various shades from dark deer red to light fawn.
Brindle Black stripes on previously described fawn shades, running parallel to ribs all over body. Stripes contrast distinctly to ground colour, neither too close nor too thinly dispersed. Ground colour clear not intermingling with stripes.

Size

Height: Dogs 57-63 cms (22½-25 ins); Bitches: 53-59 cms (21-23 ins). Weight: Dogs approximately 30-32 kg (66-70 lbs); Bitches approximately 25-27 kg (55-60 lbs).

Faults

Any departure from the foregoing points should be considered a fault and the seriousness with which the fault should be regarded should be in exact proportion to its degree.

Note

Male animals should have two apparently normal testicles fully descended into the scrotum.

11

First Principles of Judging

'Well, I can fault him.' I heard these words at a show, spoken with such pride that I couldn't resist replying, though it was none of my business, 'Anybody who knows anything at all can fault a dog; the perfect one has yet to be born.' And again I reflected on these words of J. P. Wagner: 'Even a moron can easily learn to fault a dog, but it takes a lot of study and experience to appraise a dog's virtues.'

How right this is. The wrong way to judge a dog is to learn those faults I have listed, to seek them out, and allow them to blind one to all the fine qualities an animal may possess. There are a large number of fault judges, and I am always unhappy to read a criticism of a Boxer I know to be a good one conclude in harsh terms, referring only to faults everyone knows the dog to possess, particularly the owner. You know what I mean; something like 'bad feet', or 'light in eye', the obvious and most disagreeable thing about the exhibit. Don't judge like this. Learn to appraise what is good, learn to discern what is important, and appreciate the difficulties and problems of the breeders.

I am not saying ignore faults—that's impossible. When one becomes experienced they stick out like a sore thumb, but always judge the Boxer as a whole, appreciating the fundamentals. What are the fundamentals? A fair question and for the answer I again refer to Mr Wagner who has selected five: 1. type 2. balance, 3. soundness, 4. movement, 5. temperament.

Notice that he has not attempted to look at the dog in detail at this stage, nor has he listed a single fault. First type, or, in other words, 'Is it a good Boxer?' That must be the first question a judge asks himself, for if the answer is 'No, it's not my idea of a good Boxer,' then there's little left to be said.

Disregard those, by the way, who use that silly expression 'he's not *my* type,' for that's almost as stupid as that other one: 'I like them big,' or small, or this way or that. There's only one size for the Boxer, and that's the one laid down.

Before I knew Mr Wagner he judged one of my Boxers at the first championship show for the breed in this country after the war. After I had made one circuit of the ring he said, 'Thank you, madam, that's a very nice dog, but I'm afraid it's not a good Boxer.' How right he was.

Judge Boxers first for type, the all-over quality of the dog assessed against the first essentials: his character, general appearance and colour. The Boxer should be an alert dog, balanced, well constructed, and of a square, muscular figure, and noble bearing, able to stride out and freely cover the ground. That's the sort of animal you are looking for.

'For correct balance,' says Wagner, 'every part of an animal should be in proper proportion to every other part. To produce great beauty all things must balance and not be incongruous to the eye.'

Therefore there would seem to be no substitute for a good eye with which to assess beauty in a dog, or in a horse, or in a building, or anything else for that matter. One has this eye, or one hasn't, as far as I can judge, though undoubtedly much can be learned from the conversation of people who really know.

How rare these people are, and how well worth while it is to listen to them. Unhappily in this study of dogs every little person who has been at the game five minutes seems to take it on himself to express opinions—mostly wrong. Yet it is a study of many years and long experience. And so rewarding if entered upon thoughtfully and with a sufficiently humble mind.

As I have written before, there is no real substitute for knowledge, and yet we find that those who talk most are usually those who have yet to breed a really good dog. In no other walk of life do I find this. We all freely acknowledge that the best people to talk about Mount Everest are those who have climbed to the top. Yet in dogs it seems that those who have never done it have most to say.

However, I digress. After type and balance, soundness and the ability to move, Wagner says: 'No dog in a show-ring should be condemned for minor, or technical details that would not radically interfere with usefulness if over-all he is a better specimen than those showing against him. But whatever defects, particularly those of a hereditary character, are serious enough to affect usefulness should be severely penalized.'

Here then the judge must have knowledge of the history of the breed with which I have already dealt. I know of no better definition of soundness than these words: 'Soundness is the ability of the dog to do the work that it was supposed to do'.

Remember the Boxer is a guard dog, also able to cover long distances at a good speed and is a splendid jumper. Always keep that in mind. The dog's ability to move is the yardstick by which experienced judges can assess whether the animal is well constructed and sound.

You've probably heard the phrase, 'He can't move wrong,' and it's an apt one. A correctly made dog must move well if he is fit and in good condition. The Boxer's movement should be true in front and rear and he must step out with good, proud carriage. He can't do that if, for instance, he's upright in shoulder or steep in stifle.

Wagner's last fundamental is temperament—or spirit, if you like the word better—and he says of it: 'Temperament is governed by the nervous system, and no dog can wholly display his type and quality unless he has that spark that makes him alert and active. Temperament is the electric system which makes the machine work, and if it is feeble you have a pretty sluggish job.'

There is little to add to that except to say that good temperament is one of the things we must always insist on in our Boxers. A Boxer should not crawl in to win a prize, and neither should he show viciousness—which is just as bad. It *is* possible to produce an animal which is gay and alert, friendly, but never a coward.

All this, then: type, balance, soundness, movement and temperament come into the first appraisal of the dog, and the experienced eye can take this in at one quick glance. After these come other considerations.

Size in the breed in so far as height is concerned is clearly laid down, so as long as a dog comes within this Standard there is nothing to worry about. Weight is a bit more difficult. Though it is given as approximately 66 lb. for dogs and 62 for bitches I have never yet seen anyone weigh a Boxer, and so I see little point in bothering with exact figures. Again, the experienced eye must judge. I like to see good round bone and the dogs neither plump nor racy. If the height and bone are there, and the dog looks fit and muscular, that's all that is necessary on this score.

To those who tell me there can be no such thing as 'substance combined with elegance', and that they are contradictory terms, I can only say go and look at Waterloo Bridge or the Eiffel Tower. Surely they are both elegant structures, but they equally have substance. Over-elegance or too much substance are judgments which only the experienced can make, and I know of no quick or easy way of gaining this knowledge.

It is also apparent that there must be differences of opinion among judges on what is the desired degree of substance and of elegance, though a thorough study of placings made throughout the years at championship shows will reveal that there is far more agreement about dogs than one is led to believe.

But there it is; a Boxer must have 'substance *and* elegance'. I can think of no better way of expressing it. And here is a tip well worth remembering: the length of neck both in Boxers and in humans is a factor which contributes largely to elegance. A long, arched neck also gives noble bearing. No Boxer with a short, thick, throaty neck can be elegant.

A square, muscular figure is also a desired quality in our breed, and this appearance is given by the deep chest coming down to the elbows, and by the short back.

1 Good head. Correct balance between muzzle and skull. Lively expression, well carried ears

2 Gloomy head, with mask thrown too high. Overwrinkled and poor expression. Untidy ears

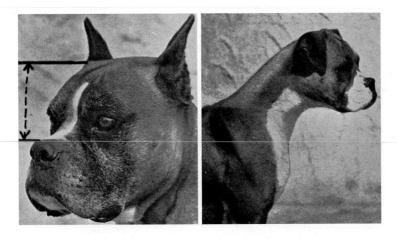

3 Clean head with excellent chin and correct, pronounced stop, indicated by dotted line

4 Exceptional neck, clean and arched

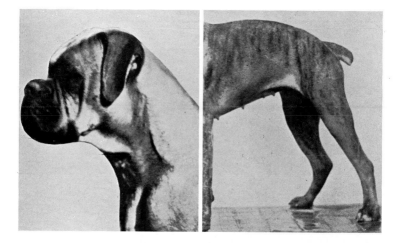

5 Throaty – a lot of loose skin in the neck

6 Roach back, poor hindquarters

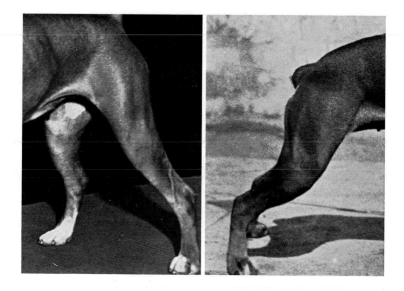

7 Powerful hindquarters with well turned stifle

8 Over-angulated, falling off in croup, low set tail

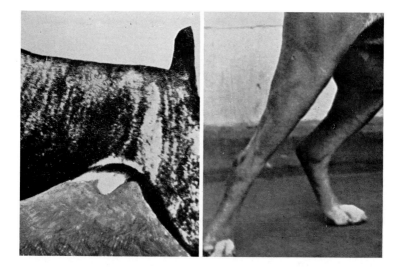

9 The correct, short, straight, level back, high set tail

10 Straight in stifle, cow hocked

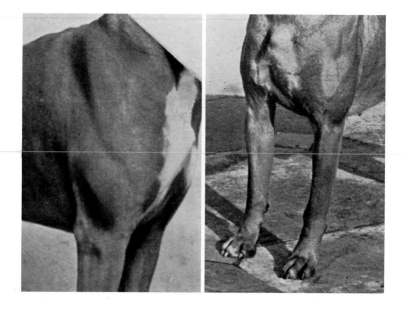

11 Upright shoulder, correct depth of brisket

12 Loaded in shoulder, front not absolutely true

13 Straight front, flat shoulders

14 Wide front, Bulldoggish

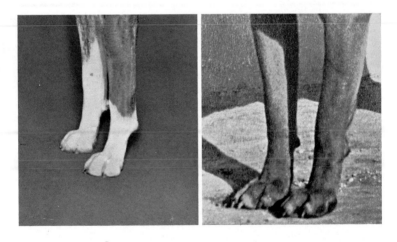

15 Beautiful tight feet, arched toes

16 Large flat feet, toe-nails uncared for

Though I fight shy of measurements other than height at the shoulder (which can also be deceptive) because they are practically impossible to make accurately, a rough guide which the eye can take in with experience is this: the length of the body from the front of the chest to the rear of the body should equal the height from the ground to the top of the shoulder. Also, the depth of the chest should be half the height of the dog at the withers.

But bear this in mind as a rough guide only and remember that a well-balanced dog can look deceptively small.

It's class and style you are also looking for, the dog which makes you look twice, the one who seems to take possession of the ring and loudly asks, 'Now who's going to take the *second* prize?' I have no way of explaining these things, but a dog to be a great one (and they are very few) must possess all those qualities. It's sex-appeal, the *x*-quality, call it what you will. You will recognize it when you see it, though it's difficult to express. Without it the dog is commonplace in the show-ring.

12

The Head and Behind the Head

The Head

'Special attention should be devoted to the head' reads the Standard, so let's have a look at it. There is no doubt that the Germans were right when they said 'the head imparts to the Boxer a unique individual stamp peculiar to the breed'. There is no other head remotely like it, and perhaps it is this fact which misleads many.

First look for a clean head, that is, one without deep wrinkles, except on the top of the skull when the dog is alert, and from the root of the nose running downwards on both sides of the muzzle. What you don't want is a Bulldoggy appearance which, of course, is something you are very likely to get because of the Boxer's ancestry.

Our effort is to get away from this outlook as far as we can and this not only applies to wrinkle, or folds in the skin, but also the chin, which should not be extravagantly turned up, and also to the furrow on the forehead which should not be forced in, especially between the eyes. There are those who mistake this furrow for the stop, which is something quite different.

A head, then, free from wrinkle except where mentioned, though the folds which run down from the root of the nose are very important, for they give the typical Boxer outlook and without them the head is plain.

The length of the muzzle should be one-third of the whole length of the head from the top of the skull to the tip of the nose. Faults crop up here regularly. Either the

114

muzzle is too short, again like the Bulldog, or it is too long, giving the appearance of the Great Dane. Correct length of the muzzle is important. It must be powerful in every way—wide and also deep, that is, through the muzzle from the top of the nose to the chin. When you grasp some muzzles they will squeeze up into nothing, showing that there is no bone there, but purely skin. This is another frequent failing.

The top of the muzzle is just as important as the inside of the mouth, to which so many immediately fly. When the head is placed parallel with the floor the tip of the nose should be slightly higher than the root. Not forced back and in exaggerated form (again beware the Bulldog) but just tip-tilted. Without this one gets the downfaced appearance, which spoils the head.

The width of the muzzle is partly given by the formation of the teeth and also by the well-padded lips which should not hang loosely and become what we call lippy. A lippy dog is usually one which drools all over the place and is a great nuisance to an owner especially when wearing decent clothes.

For years British Boxer people have worried about teeth because of a simple mistake in the Standard which calls for those in the top jaw to be set in a 'concave' line. The translators mean convex, but it's far simpler to say curved slightly outwards. This is quite a normal placement, like in the human top jaw.

Now the bottom line. If possible the teeth should be set in a straight line, though this is one of the most difficult things to achieve. Nature doesn't like dealing in straight lines, as a moment's study of your own figure will convince you. Curves are the more normal. But the straight line of bottom teeth in the Boxer does give the width in the lower jaw which is very desirable, and if the teeth are big and well spaced so much the better. You might just as well be prepared to accept the fact, though, that the straight line occurs infrequently.

Don't be too worried about it. Provided the jaw and the bite are serviceable and strong this is the important thing. Avoid dismissing a good dog because his teeth are not absolutely as per the blueprint. Unhappily this is just what the beginner does. Notice, however, that I am saying that the perfect formation is desirable, and that a badly formed jaw, such as the wry jaw, or one pinched in, or weak, are faults.

Before looking at the skull, just notice that the nose should be large and black but, again, don't penalize a dog too much if he isn't perfect. I once saw a champion bitch dismissed because one nostril was not quite wide enough which, of course, is quite ridiculous. Remember that we are making an examination in detail now, and that we have already agreed that the complete whole is of greater importance. This also applies to the whole of the head, which as the Standard says must be in harmonious proportion especially as between muzzle and skull.

Look for a lean skull, narrow between the ears; avoid thickness (which, by the way, increases with age). When people looking at a fully matured dog say 'he hasn't gone coarse' they are generally referring to the skull, which should not be wide and round like our dear old friend the Bulldog.

Moderate, well-set ears are our target, and it's so pretty to see the dog 'use its ears' when alert. By that I mean making them look 'alive'. (My goodness, how difficult words are!) We don't care for heavy, hound-like ears.

A lot of people seem to be worried about a pup's ears when they don't lie flat against the cheeks, but fly back. I never bother. Ears generally come right. There are the exceptions, but flying ears have been one of the smaller troubles. Look for ears moderate in size, set on high, and not dead or lifeless ears.

Flat cheeks, dark eyes and an alert expression. Where the expression comes from I'm not quite sure. Partly from the eyes, I suppose, which must be friendly and clear, without red rims or haw showing if possible. The dark mask also comes into this, for when the mask is thrown above the eyes the expression does become sombre and dull. It's best confined to the muzzle, fading before reaching the eyes. Oh, what trouble there has been about the dark mask!

Yet the answer is so simple, and the suggested slight revising of the Standard will put it right. In simple words, the dog's muzzle should be either white or black, and not the same colour as the rest of the dog. If there are white markings, then a black line round them is a good thing.

Don't get agitated about that present wording, which is extremely clumsy, and take it from me that white on the muzzle will not handicap your dog. If you don't believe me, look again at the head study of Lustig (between pages 32 and 33). Nobody has yet faulted Lustig's head. And before I leave this subject: notice I have not said *white* markings are essential. A good, solid, black mask confined to the muzzle is just as good.

So forget the dark mask controversy, which is purely a case of adding great confusion where just a little misunderstanding existed.

I must put in here that excessive undershotness is undesirable, and the showing of teeth and tongue, I regret to say, a crime. Top lip should rest on bottom in the perfect lip formation, but do not worry if the bottom protrudes a little, or the top slightly overhangs it. These are not desperate faults, though the showing of teeth and tongue are. The latter, of course, is the return to the Bulldog which was poison to the old German Boxer breeder.

And finally the 'stop'. Like the dark mask, the stop has been a bogey, and again for no good reason. Some of our breeders have confused the furrow with the stop and have wanted a deep cleft to appear between the eyes. I remember one man telling me he put his thumb between the eyes of his dog each day and pressed. In this way he thought he would get a good stop. I told him all he would get would be a sore thumb!

A deep cleft between the eyes is not required and this, in any event, is not the 'stop'. The 'stop' is the difference in measurement between an imaginary line drawn from the top of the skull and another continued along the top line of the muzzle.

Read again the words of the official Standard on the stop. It says: 'The forehead should form a *distinct stop* with the top line of the muzzle, which should not be forced back into the forehead like that of a Bulldog.' A distinct stop, yes, but not an excessive stop. We do not want a Bulldog head.

Often it has pained me to see a good dog put down for 'lack of stop' when anyone with knowledge of the breed would have realized that the animal's head had all that was required.

I cannot give my readers a measurement for the stop; that would be impossible, but too much can be as bad a thing as too little, for the tendency in each extreme is on the one hand a tendency to the Bulldog and on the other towards the Dane. And as I have frequently quoted, a Boxer must have his own individual head.

Behind the Head

So much for the most important of the individual parts. What about the others?

First the neck. As long as you can get it, for it's the neck which gives elegance; long, curved and graceful with no loose skin in the throat if possible, for this is ugly. Notice I say 'if possible', for I find that the bitches have better necks than dogs, and that it's extremely difficult to get a short back and a long neck. It's very unusual to find a powerful short-backed dog with a long, graceful neck. Sometimes it happens, and if it does you may easily have bred a hum-dinger. The best-necked dog I ever bred was light in bone which seemed to me to be Nature's way of saying you can't have everything.

But that's our aim: the neck, long, graceful and clean (that odd word which does not mean free from dirt but free from loose skin. Another word we use, by the way, is dry, which also means clean—sorry it's so confusing). And the back, short, straight, broad and very muscular. Efforts were made to alter this part of the Standard. I am glad they failed, for here there seems to be no confusion and the words, short, straight, broad and very muscular are ones we can all understand. Any other sort of back is not what is required.

A most difficult task in the early days was to breed out the roach back which was handed down to us. One of my bitch champions was slightly faulty in this respect, so I was careful to mate her to a male without the fault. The brisket should reach down to the elbows so that the dog does not appear leggy, with too much daylight under him. One wants a body which is compact, strong and completely natural in formation.

Look at the underline of the stomach. A gracefully curved line to the rear is what is required, not an abrupt sharp tuck-up which spoils balance.

Well-sprung ribs, not slab sided, and so to the back end which to me is just as important as the front. We require strong hindquarters with a well-turned stifle, which usually goes with a well-laid shoulder. The converse is also true. Upright shoulders usually go with straight stifles. Fat hams are needed, especially in bitches; unlike in the human race, to be broad in the beam is a compliment. And, above all, the back end of your dog must match the front. This is where the word 'balance' comes in again.

So often I see dogs with strong forequarters and mean, slim, straight hindquarters. This is a most undesirable fault, for the hindquarters give the dog his power to run and jump. Well-developed hindquarters, especially the second thigh, make good movement possible.

A croup that falls off too much is to me worse than a boil on the nose. It hits me in the eye so forcibly that it spoils the whole dog. At the same time I know the difficulty we have had in this country in getting away from that ugly falling away of the croup. A low-set tail goes with it, and this again is a most unhappy characteristic. We require a croup that is only slightly sloping and the tail set on as high as you can get it to give an alert appearance.

Look at the dog from behind. The hocks, well let down, should be parallel, for we know that cow-hocks mean weakness and bad movement. That leaves the pastern and the feet and about these there can be little doubt. The pasterns should not be absolutely upright, but if they are nearly so it adds to the appearance of the dog. Terrier people like the leg and the pastern to be in one line, but slightly slanting pasterns are correct in our breed. If you imagine that slant is bad for running take the trouble to look at the picture of the Derby winner and the extent of the slant of the pasterns will surprise you.

Still, we shall compromise on this and ask for a pastern *almost* perpendicular. The feet should be small and tight. I love to see a dog with beautiful cat feet, the toes arched and the nails even shorter than Nature ever intended. I'm aware that may sound ridiculous, but experienced exhibitors will know what I mean. As I have written elsewhere, don't condemn a good dog because his feet are not all you require, but to the exhibitor I would say work on the feet as much as you can.

Though you wouldn't dismiss a beauty queen because her back teeth were not perfect (you wouldn't notice it if she kept her mouth closed) you would instantly see if she was badly shod, and it would irk you. So look after those feet.

I have nothing to add about the tail except to say that those who fixed the length at two inches can never have docked one. In proportion to the body and gaily carried are the important points. Colour, weight and size: I have dealt with these elsewhere. A good colour—red, fawn or brindled—as against a weak or washed-out colour is obviously much to be desired, while white markings undoubtedly set off the whole dog like a white handkerchief in a breast pocket.

Again, don't be confused about the white. The Standard is clear; study it again and notice that white markings are very desirable. As for condition, I believe that good condition is essential for a show dog and this includes the coat which, kept short and shining, sets off the lovely animal we have been looking at.

13

Choosing a Pup

Unless you are rich and can afford to buy without regard to the cost, don't be in too much of a hurry. For those with a small amount of capital it is wise to limit the number of mistakes you are bound to make, and can ill afford, by starting right. For example, if it's your wish to start in a small way as a breeder, don't begin by buying a male.

That seems obvious, but to this day I am constantly being asked to supply males to beginners who want to start up 'in Boxers'. They seem surprised when I say: 'You are starting off on the wrong foot. You can use at stud the best dogs in the country for a reasonable fee. What you want is a well-bred young bitch. Then, with luck, you can breed a litter for yourselves.' I am, of course, referring to those who want to begin as breeders, and not to people who only want a pet—that is a different proposition. A dog in these circumstances can be a splendid companion, though personally I still prefer bitches.

We will assume, however, that the beginner is setting out to buy a good young bitch. How does he start?

First, I would suggest, by visiting shows and studying the form. Get around quietly, note who is doing the winning, and observe the condition and style of their dogs. But don't rush up to everybody and ask advice, because you will be dumbfounded by the varying ideas you will get. Also, buy the canine papers, study the advertisements and provide yourself with copies of the *Kennel Gazette*. Then get any books there are on the breed. Gradually you will acquire a lot of knowledge which will be invaluable. As you gradually find out the form you will discover there are people who have a reputation for successful breeding and straight dealing.

When looking at the advertisements, interest yourself more in facts rather than opinion. By facts I mean answers to simple questions like these: 'Has this owner bred any good dogs?' 'Can I get a bitch pup from a dam which has already had some good pups?' and 'Is the sire in the top flight?' These are points which matter to the novice—or should do. Later on, when more knowledge has been acquired, it will be possible to back your own judgment and cast a wider net.

Now let us assume you have decided on a breeder (always go to breeders) you are going to see. And I do mean *going to see*. In this country, at any rate, it's worth the time and trouble, that is, if you are keen on getting the best service. Make an appointment first (this is most important) and then go along and explain your problem. If you are lucky in your choice, the experienced breeder will be most helpful to you. They generally are. But don't make the mistake of not trusting him, or her. Don't take a friend with you who is supposed to know, and is obviously there as a sort of safeguard. The odds are that the friend won't know anything, and will only exasperate the expert. Go along and say, 'I know nothing, this is what I want, can you help me?'

Obviously you are taking a chance. But one must take chances in life, and if you have taken my advice up to now you are going to someone with a reputation. And experienced and established breeders of pedigree dogs are rightly jealous of their reputations. My bet is that you will get sound advice and, if it's available, a good pup. Though remember, even the most experienced make mistakes, though not as many as the inexperienced.

Let us suppose there are pups available at about two months old, and you have a choice. On the other hand it may well be that there is no choice, and possibly the breeder has nothing available at all. In this case you may be well advised to wait until something is available. Don't be impatient.

The question of price will arise. It varies very considerably, but don't expect the breeder to sell at a loss (this applies to pets as well as to show prospects) for all pups cost the same amount to rear. Secondly, for a good bitch pup such as you are after, there will be a number of prospective purchasers. It may well be that the breeder will consider some sort of terms if the price is more than you can afford. Notice I said 'it may be'. But be prepared to pay a good price for a good dog, for you will reap the benefit (with the usual amount of luck) in the end. I cannot give actual prices because circumstances vary so very considerably.

Let us have a look at the pup we have in mind. It is well bred, the mother is out of a line of winning stock, and father has proved himself as a sire by *already getting winners*. Here she is, then.

Notice the attractive colour and markings, and the good bone. See also that the pup is in good health, the eyes clear, and the skin glossy and loose on the body. Take the head. The skull is domed on the top, an excellent sign, for it means that it is unlikely to coarsen later on. The muzzle has great width, also depth, and the eyes are dark. The white markings on the head are even (excellent) and there is good black rim to the mask. (Already in this book we have noticed the permissible variations in the mask.) The feet have thick pads, the toes are well arched while the ears though a little large (they invariably appear like this in a pup) are not so heavy or low placed that they won't come right—we hope.

Now let's set the pup up. We want to see that the front is straight, though the pup's legs will quite naturally be a little knobbly. Pay heed to the back line; you want it straight and short, with the tail well set on. Note also the turn of the stifle. Already the brisket reaches to the elbow (in some that may come later), but the neck has not yet reached its full length by any means, for this is one of the last parts to develop. Here, then, is an extremely fine puppy. Look inside the mouth, though it won't tell you a great deal, for you will be more interested in the second teeth (when they come) than the first. But—and here is an important point—at this stage the pup should not be too undershot. In fact I prefer only the slightest amount, and am not worried if the bite is even. In our breed, for some reason, the under-jaw invariably grows more than the top.

So you can now pick a puppy? I wonder. Unfortunately the snags are many. I have known the most promising pups 'go wrong', and others not so good at the start turn out really well. This is part of the frustration and fascination of breeding dogs. And, believe me, the most experienced breeders can only say to you, 'In my opinion this is a very promising pup.' Anyone who goes further is without real knowledge. We can all make mistakes simply because the pup will change and go on changing till he's mature, or nearly so.

The only safe way to buy a certain winner (if there is such a thing) is to wait until the pup is grown up. But we can't all do that: (a) because the price will be enormously increased, and (b) because few breeders can afford to run on all their pups. A decision must be made, and one hopes it will turn out right. It is here, of course, that experience alone can help and even experience can let you down. I leave out, by the way, the method of the crystal ball— though sometimes I wish I had one.

A word about the height of the pup. As a rough guide the length of the front leg should equal the distance from the top of the shoulder to the bottom of the brisket. That is as good a guide as any, but our hope is that the height will go on increasing.

Now temperament. Good temperament, by that I mean an alert, bold, but friendly nature, is vital. Ones with bad temperament should be put down. Life is too short to bother with them. Anything hysterical, frightened, or vicious avoid like the plague. I have cured nervous dogs in my day, but I would never want to do so again, for the time and trouble are ill spent. Besides that, never, never, never start off a breeding programme with nervous dogs. Broadly speaking, nervous, ill-tempered parents have nervous, ill-tempered children, and both in humans and in animals they are intolerable. Fortunately, as far as animals are concerned, one is not bound to keep them. And if a breeder tells you the pup will grow out of its 'nerves' agree, but don't take the risk. I wouldn't keep a nervous or vicious dog if it was the best show specimen in the world. Such types can only do a disservice to the breed. And I write as one who has been through the mill.

14

Care of the Pup

So you've bought your bitch pup and you have brought her home. She's about eight to nine weeks old. What now? First, you had better know something about feeding. Give four or five meals a day, starting say at 7 or 8 a.m. with a bowl of warm milk and cereal, adding a little sugar to make it more acceptable. I'm a believer in making meals agreeable for dogs, for, like us, they have their fads and fancies. It's best to be tolerant, though never to the extent of being silly about it. Nor will I lay down exact amounts of food, for dogs, like us, vary considerably. Some eat a lot of food and thrive on it, others do well with far less. Add a raw egg to the morning milk or glucose if you can manage it, for pups seem to enjoy it and also benefit.

Generally, in the morning, I give the pups goat's milk plus cereal.

Your pup will need its next meal at midday, and I strongly recommend raw minced meat. As to the amount, use your judgment, for I've never brought myself to weigh the food. Give her enough to satisfy her need, and remove if all is not eaten. At tea-time, about four o'clock, repeat the meal as for breakfast, though varying the milk with broth, or soup, if it is convenient.

Another four hours (about 8 p.m.) your pup will again feel peckish, so another meal of meat, either raw or cooked, is required and then, lastly, try her with a nightcap of warm milk before you go to bed. As you see, it's quite a business, and for those who can't be bothered the answer is don't have a pup. At the same time don't kill yourself over it, and the pup won't hurt if you miss a meal occasionally because you are out, or something like that.

At the same time, regular meals are best. Imagine the pup is a baby. If you treat it as a child you won't go far wrong. Certainly give it cod-liver oil, and add bonemeal and other vitamins, now easily available.

Like a child, a small pup needs rest and quiet, and it does not, repeat *not*, need a lot of exercise. If, I say if, the sun shines, let her gambol for half an hour, but don't let her overtire herself. This is worse than no exercise at all.

Spring or summer pups are said to be best. Perhaps this is so, but my best litter was raised in a cold winter with snow on the ground much of the time. They never went out until they were four months old. (I had no special electric lamp then, but have now used it successfully.) Yet this winter litter was not only the best but the most healthy I've ever had. They had no illness of any kind. Perhaps I was lucky. On this, however, I insist: your pup must be kept warm, and away from draughts and cold winds. Scrap all you have heard to the contrary, and I promise you will benefit. A warm, contented, well-fed pup will grow stronger, faster and better than one 'toughened up' (as I sometimes hear it put) by the rigours of winter.

Add vegetables to those meals for the pup, for she will need a little roughage. Greens and carrots mixed with the meat are excellent. Quite early on I start giving Vetzymes in the prescribed dosage, while one of the meat meals can be varied with the cheaper forms of fish.

As the pup gets older the meals can be cut down, and the first to go is the tea-time milk, so that at six months (when the second teeth will have come through) you will be giving three meals a day. Notice I'm not counting that late nightcap, which I continue for some time yet if the pup wants it. To be frank, I do this for my own convenience, for the nightcap induces sleep and will keep the puppy quiet until much later in the morning. Maybe you will feel that way too.

When a meal is cut out increase the amount given at the other meals, for it does not mean that you are giving less food but more at less frequent intervals. Your growing pup needs all she can get. At six months she should be eating 1½ lb. of meat a day. Biscuit (preferably terrier meal) can be started at three months. Baked brown bread is a good substitute, and I sometimes give cooked maca-roni or cooked rice as a change. Nowadays many types of food are available which we didn't have in the past. They are easy to feed and are very good.

My dogs, especially if they are being shown, get three meals a day up to the age of about twelve months, and afterwards they have two—mid-morning and the main meal at about 5 to 6 p.m. But I make no hard and fast rule about this. Stud dogs and brood bitches, for example, need extra nourishment, and I always watch them closely to see if there is any sign of one getting thin. If so, he or she gets extra rations.

So take all I say as a guide only. Some dogs are greedy and must be cut down, otherwise they would get out of condition. One such was my champion bitch, Party Piece, who was a good show dog and also a wonderful brood. She raised one litter of ten by herself and kept them spotless and fat. But eat! Not only when feeding her pups, but all the time. Finishing up her own bowl quickly, it was her habit to dash around helping out all those who were slower and minus such a keen appetite. But I never complain about a 'good doer', nor should you, either, for they are heaven compared with a finicky eater. I had one dog who lost weight so fast on his way to a show that I was in danger of prosecution, especially if it meant being away a couple of days. He wouldn't touch food until he got home again. Not so Party Piece. As we said, the day Party was off her food there was real trouble. Her grandmother— Serenade—was just the same.

Here is a suggested diet for your pup from six months to twelve. Breakfast milk and cereal as before, but don't worry if she doesn't care for it. In this case try her with terrier meal soaked with gravy and mixed with chopped meat. Notice I am a great advocate of meat, but it can take many forms—horse meat, paunches, butcher's scraps, for example, remembering also fish as a substitute. Thank heavens these are all pretty easy to get nowadays, not like the war years and immediately after when, as you can imagine, one had to be thankful for pretty well anything.

For midday try a few biscuits, and then for the evening meal return again to the soaked terrier meal and cooked meat, with the added roughage. The optional nightcap is a matter for you and your pup. Some people keep the Vetzymes or a biscuit for last thing. Keep on giving the cod-liver oil or similar product. Good, raw mince is excellent.

Here is an easy way to prepare a main meal. Cook up your meat, or whatever is on the menu for the day. When ready, place in a large bowl the required amount of terrier meal, then pour over the gravy from the meat and leave to soak. While this is cooling, chop up the meat and then mix together. Add the roughage and the extra vitamins and give to the pup the meal when it is still warm, but not while hot. Today, of course, there are good canned varieties available.

As the pup grows, watch her condition carefully, and vary the amount of food accordingly. If she is thin, it's a good idea to add about a tablespoonful of grated suet to her main dish.

So much for the principal meals, except to add that the fully mature dog can be reduced to one big meal a day, though that odd biscuit at night and the vitamins won't come amiss at any time. If the dog gets too fat reduce the biscuit. Don't cut down the meat (1½-2 lb. for a fully grown dog) and the roughage except as a last resort. Raw meat of good quality is always splendid food.

Some people I know have introduced a day of fasting with their routine, but I have never done this. I believe in offering water to a dog in the same way as I give food. In other words, it is not constantly available but is offered fresh and frequently. Nor am I a great believer in giving dogs bones, except puppies when a large one (not a bone which splinters easily) helps to loosen the temporary teeth. Subsequently the constant gnawing of a bone merely serves to wear down the enamel-covered crowns of the teeth. One way in which bones are useful is this: boil them in a pressure cooker until they are reduced to dust and then they form a valuable calcium intake. An occasional meal of liver is useful, and so is tripe which is particularly good for pups. As a general rule a grown dog's food should be served dry rather than sloppy.

Back again now to the day you took your bitch pup home. In all probability she has not been house trained, and if she is to be a house dog the job has got to be started right away. Otherwise you are going to rue the day you bought the dear little thing. Actually, with Boxers it is not such a difficult task, provided common sense is used. In all probability the pup is already used to attending to her duties on newspaper, for I always place paper on the floor of the kennel in which young pups take their first steps into the world.

In their youth Boxer pups quickly get the idea that paper is the right place on which to perform. If the weather is suitable you will soon start taking the pup out at regular intervals and praising her when she attends to her business. You will be amazed how quickly she will catch on. Night-time is a bit of a problem, and it is fatal to let a pup wander about the house. Something will happen as sure as Fate. I have found that behaviour improves if at night the pup is tethered to a radiator, or some substantial object. A dog travelling-box also makes a good bedroom for a pup. Put it inside and close the door when retiring. Let me repeat over again, she must sleep out of a draught and in the warm. Therefore the kitchen is, perhaps, the best room in the house for her.

I am a believer in inoculation, and if the pup has not had her 'shots' before you got her see your vet about it. These are normally given at about six weeks. Make certain, by the way, that your vet understands dogs, and if you have one specializing in small animals so much to your benefit. Even vets vary, and a good one is the salt of the earth. One of mine used to feel it to be a point of personal honour that all my Boxers were fit. When there was illness he worried as much as I. Such a vet is a godsend. I shall not encroach on the veterinary field by advising which of the many methods of inoculation is best—that is the vet's job. But this I will say: carry out his instructions to the letter.

As yours is a show pup, don't let her scrabble about all

over the house. I once knew a beautiful pup spoiled because the owner let him run up and down stairs at a tender age. As you might expect, he damaged his front. Never allow the pup to pull and pant when she is walking on a lead. How I hate dogs that do this! *Make* her walk properly, and if she refuses, take a little switch with you and remind her that to pull and scrabble sideways is an offence.

Notice I didn't say beat your pup. Only a fool and a bully would do that. But correct her with a tap and show her that you are going to have *your* way. A nicely behaved pup is a blessing, and a badly behaved one an abomination. It is up to you to see she is properly behaved. Always praise good behaviour, and encourage with a tit-bit exemplary conduct.

It is a good thing if your pup knows her basket, or box, where you have decided she shall sleep. See that it is off the floor and out of a draught. She will soon learn simple words like 'basket' or 'bed'. Though I do not go in for obedience work myself, I know that Boxers are most intelligent and master the simple things I have suggested in next to no time. All knowledge they gain is by constantly doing the same thing, so regular habits are invaluable.

Of course, your pup will want to chew things, especially when the second teeth are coming, and so it's wise to give her something to chew rather than let her find something for herself. Serenade used to eat lampshades quite regularly. When I gave her a rubber bone, or a ball (never a small one), she stopped.

For training on the lead I have always used a light chain choke collar. The pressure reminds the pup that it doesn't pay to pull, though I hate to see anyone jerking strenuously on a choke collar. In my experience that is seldom needed with a Boxer.

Naturally your pup will be prone to minor ailments, and I always advise newcomers to call the vet if they are in doubt about the pup's health. Be safe rather than sorry, and act too soon rather than too late. Don't be a know-all and run risks, for your bitch has a great future if you are wise.

For the first time, also, take early advice about worming (this is most important) and then follow the instructions faithfully. When the puppy has simple diarrhoea it can be checked nowadays by a tablet from the vet, but remember, it may not be simple diarrhoea, but a symptom of something worse. Still, you must use your own judgment. The best simple laxative for a puppy is milk of magnesia, and the best safeguard from disease your constant care and attention.

A puppy is naturally boisterous. If it isn't, there is something wrong with it. If your pup doesn't leap out of her basket in the morning to meet you, suspect the worst. Look to see if the eyes are clear and bright. If they are full and there is mucus running from the nose, take her temperature at once. Normal for a pup is 101°F (38.3°C). Even if she is normal this is not an absolute guarantee that all is well, for such is the trickiness of the various forms of distemper that a temperature can be normal and the pup very ill. If the mucus and the lethargy persist call the vet. Even if it's a false alarm, don't worry. Everything you do to ensure the health of your pup, especially in the early months, is worth while. And you'd better shrug off the vet's bills as just one of those things. With luck you won't get many.

You may have to deal with a simple wound, or cut, yourself, for dogs get them as often as children. Use your wits about this, remembering that to cleanse and apply a simple remedy are the first essentials. Hysteria and convulsions are not often experienced in our breed, thanks be, but you might have to deal with this condition during the teething period.

This is what you should do: hold the dog to prevent injury; remove to a quiet place, covering with a coat or blanket if necessary, keep it in the dark, administer a sedative and call the vet.

Keep your pup clean by grooming every day so that the skin is retained in a good condition and there are no dead hairs left in the coat. Use not too harsh a brush. Clean out the ears regularly with cotton wool, warm water and benzyl benzoate (BP) and, later on, if the tips of the ears become heavy, massage them with the fingers and olive oil. Toe-nails should be your special care, especially if the pup is to be shown. How short should the nails be kept? The answer is as short as you can possibly get them. I've heard the excuse given, 'I couldn't cut her nails because she wouldn't let me.' That is ridiculous. Few dogs like having their nails cut; they must be made to endure it. And on this I warn you, unless you keep this job up and start early, the quicks will grow long and you are asking for trouble. Use a pair of proper canine nail clippers, and also file the nails back in addition. Constant work will repay you.

I'm often asked if road work improves a dog's feet. One thing is certain: it doesn't do any harm (in the right doses) and possibly some good. But no amount of road work will produce good feet if they are soft, thin and flat to begin with. If the pup has good feet and they are properly cared for, you should be all right. Don't bath the pup too often for it removes the natural oil from the skin, but occasional bathing for a special occasion, like a show, does no harm. When you do it use a good shampoo, and see that the lather is completely removed. Then dry the pup carefully and don't let her out of your sight until you present her in the show-ring.

15

Your First Show

We shall assume once again that your bitch pup has turned out well, and you have decided to show her. Like everything else in the dog game, don't be in too much of a hurry. It's simple to say that, for showing becomes a disease. I've known experienced breeders rush a dog into the ring long before it was ready. Do this, and you will suffer. It is permissible to show a pup as soon as it reaches the age of six months, but unless there is a special puppy class you will have to compete against dogs up to twelve months old. The special puppy class is limited to dogs of six months and over and nine months and under. Don't make the mistake of giving away too much in age. Enter a special puppy class when your bitch is eight months and the full puppy class when she is about nine or ten. If you don't do this your pup will have to be very good to beat the maturer entrants. Be wise, restrain that desire to rush ahead. It's not good for your morale, or your pup's future, to bring it out too soon and get in the habit of being beaten.

I should have mentioned earlier, perhaps, that you can check any details regarding the registration of your pup with the Kennel Club, 1 Clarges St, London W1Y 8AB, for only registered pups are allowed to be entered in properly regulated and approved shows, and these are the only ones you are interested in. Shows are advertised regularly in the canine press, and a note to the secretary of the society concerned will bring you an entry form and a schedule by return. I do not propose to explain these, for the rules and conditions are clearly set out. Go for a small show first, for you must get experience, and the competition at open and championship shows in our breed is extremely keen. That will come later. So for the moment the sanction and limited shows are the ones you are after. It will be worth your while to purchase a copy of the Kennel Club Rules and Regulations which will give all the information required.

But before you go into the show-ring there is a lot of work to be done. Your pup must be trained for it. In addition, you have to learn how to handle, and get the best out of her. Go to a show and watch the experienced handlers, professional and amateur, presenting the dogs in the ring. Spend a day watching closely. There are a thousand and one wrinkles to be picked up which can only come with experience. Teach your bitch to pose, looking her best, and to trot smartly at your side as you move up and down the ring. Ringcraft classes are often available.

It requires a lot of practice, and if you neglect it your chances will be spoiled. It's no use being nervous, so that's something to get over to begin with. If you are nervous the dog will know about it, and she'll not like it. That is why I said start with a small show, for at these you will get over your nervousness when you discover there isn't anything to be nervous about. Don't give a brass farthing for anybody; that is the right frame of mind to be in. Give the impression that you, at any rate, think your dog to be the best in the ring. Wear sensible clothes, too. That's simple enough, but it's a lesson a lot of women haven't learned. A dog show isn't a cocktail party. At the same time you must be neat, and to look attractive is not a disadvantage. Wear low-heeled shoes so that you can walk briskly and purposefully and don't wear a picture hat (it will get in the way). This may seem gratuitous advice, but I've known this sort of thing done. Nor do you want a low-cut dress, or a very short skirt. Wear something with pockets because there will be lots of bits and pieces to put in them, and speaking of shoes again, never wear a new pair at a show, for a blister on the foot is all kinds of hell.

You mustn't be shy, nor must the dog be shy. Get her used to people and crowds by taking her about with you. Also let her meet people individually, for the judge will want to place his hands on her, and also look into her mouth. Teach her to act boldly in these circumstances, but never to snap. She must also get used to the proximity of other dogs and not mind noise like hand-clapping or the sudden boom of a loud speaker.

The pup must learn to trot with head up, moving smoothly on a show lead, which is a thinner type than that used normally; one that will roll up easily in the hand and will not obscure the pup's neck. Usually you will have to move round in a circle, going anticlockwise, but it may be the other way, so learn to lead your dog with either the right hand or the left. She will also have to move straight up and down and pose for several minutes at a time. You are permitted to take in the ring a tit-bit which will claim the dog's attention. Perhaps a ball will help, or anything else she is used to. The object is to keep her alert. How simple it is to write that! But keeping a pup alert on a hot day, or in a stuffy hall, is something which tries the skill of even the most experienced exhibitors. But you *must* be able to do it. Nothing is worse than a dull, lethargic Boxer in the show-ring. Its chances are absolutely ruined.

Many Boxer handlers in this country are very poor, and if you acquire handling skill you will have a distinct advantage. For years it was the habit when posing to stretch dogs out so that the rear legs were pulled back to the limit. This was making the task difficult for no reason at all. The right way, as ever, is the simple way.

Your dog must stand still, perfectly balanced, with its weight taken on all four feet. Then it's up to you to keep it alert, on its toes, wearing a keen expression. That's the difficult part, but it can be achieved. Some dogs are born showmen, and are interested in everything that is going on. If you have one like that, thank your lucky stars. And here's a good tip: don't fuss your dog. If it's standing nicely let it continue to do so. How often has over-handling spoilt a dog's chances. Get it right and then be content. And if you are aware of your dog's faults ignore them, for by constantly putting them right you will only draw attention to them. You will be surprised at what a judge overlooks. Move smartly at the judge's bidding, and watch points all the time. Don't allow yourself to be jockeyed out of position by other exhibitors (there are some not above trying it) and always anticipate what the judge requires. For example, if he wants to view the rear of the dog don't stand in his light; move to the front. Don't chatter to the handler next to you, and don't let your attention wander, deserving the caustic comment I once heard made by a judge: 'The fact that you ladies have dogs in the ring is purely coincidental'. Don't get pushed into a corner; and don't, above all things, adopt what I call 'the crouch' when moving your dog. Stand up and stride out.

There are two ways of handling. First, the loose-lead style, that is with the dog standing up unassisted, head held high, alert and noble. This is the best way, but I must admit it's difficult. If your dog can do it, never alter this method. It's the best in the world: the natural way and the most impressive.

Next is the 'topping and tailing' style, favoured by the Americans and often seen nowadays in the British rings, though some judges won't allow it. For this method to be effective the dog must be beautifully balanced, lead right up under the chin, revealing the neck. Keep the back straight and level, the tail held up to show that it is well set on, and the hindquarters correctly positioned so that the turn of the stifle is clearly illustrated.

This method, well done, is effective and smart, but badly done is hopeless. Let me repeat, the dog must be in perfect balance, with the weight evenly distributed on all four feet. All this takes practice and yet more practice. But you must get it right to do your dog justice.

Now preparation for the show-ring. A manicure and a bath are absolutely required. Your bitch must be spotlessly clean. There is also some stripping to be done, though not nearly as much as in some other breeds.

As this is a smooth-coated dog your object is to make it appear smooth all over. First read Regulations for the Preparation of Dogs for Exhibition, so that you do not inadvertently infringe these rules. Stripping is permitted, so first snip off the whiskers on the foreface and then, with a stripping comb, remove the slightly ragged and longer hair down the sides of the neck. Also see that the insides of the ears are smooth and clean, and that there are no long hairs under the brisket and loin, around the base of the tail and down the inner stifle. On the day, then, satisfy yourself that your dog goes into the ring as if it has just stepped out of a bandbox.

And now one or two simple things a beginner always forgets. Dogs usually go to shows in cars. Take practice journeys, for as sure as I write this the light of your life will be sick on the first occasion she travels in a car, and will finish the journey looking miserable.

Take her with you when travelling so that she accepts it all as a part of life. Before she goes into the ring see that she attends to her business. Best to do this at home for it's a bad thing to mess up the show ground. Do not throw down litter. Show days are fast days. Save the main meal until you arrive home tired and, I hope, with a prize card in your pocket.

16

Breeding

The Sire

I hope that after all that you've made your bitch a champion. If not, you may well have learned a lot that will help you to do so later. Now we will turn our attention to breeding. When your bitch pup is anything from eight to twelve months old she will come into season. There is no rule about this. Some pups first come into season at eight to nine months, and others go much longer, perhaps a year. Thereafter it may be every six months, or up to twelve before she is on heat again. As a general rule in Boxers, I do not advise mating at the first season, for if she is only eight months old the bitch will be far from mature.

Your bitch, let us say, is to be missed first time, so make quite certain that she does not come in contact with a male dog. Also make sure you do not invite every dog in the neighbourhood to your back door by allowing the bitch to micturate indiscriminately. It is possible to buy a preparation which will discourage the males. Use this freely, and also exercise the bitch securely on a lead. It will be necessary to observe this precaution for about 21 days. Don't use the preparation if you are going to mate her. There is another preparation which controls the season. Ask your veterinary surgeon.

If you have decided to breed from her at the second season start thinking about the preparations a long way ahead. You will need a sire, and the right one will be a matter of careful thought. I do not propose to write a chapter on the scientific approach to breeding. That has already been done, and far better than I could write it. I prefer, rather, to pass on some general hints which have brought me a certain amount of success, and to leave the genes and the chromosomes to others. Let us then deal in simple terms.

To arrive at the best possible sire for your bitch read and understand the background of the breed and study the facts contained in the records (see Appendices). From these you will observe that by their reproductive achievements some blood-lines have exerted more influence on the breed than others. As you cannot afford to speculate as you have one bitch only, I would advise you to follow a line which is known to have had success. Any sire is as good as his children. No more, or no less. For that is the acid test. He may be brilliant himself as a show dog, but the question you must ask is, 'What have his children achieved?' Not for you the experimental mating. That can well be left to those with the time and money who can afford to make mistakes. Though there are other considerations for the experienced, the safest way for newcomers is to rely on a stud dog who has consistently sired winners.

If you have taken my advice all through, I hope your foundation bitch will be a well-bred female, without obvious faults, even though she may not be brilliant. For her mate I would advise a dog known to have a good record as a sire and one, if possible, in the same family group. There is another important consideration. As a general principle avoid mating animals which have any similar major faults.

Study the pedigrees. Notice how the successful sires have been line-bred— that is the mating of dogs that have near relatives in common. In some lines there has also been successful in-breeding—that is the mating of close relatives, like father to daughter, mother to son, and brother to sister.

This latter method will fix a type quicker than any other, but only the very experienced should try it, for a sure knowledge of the breed for many generations is essential. In-breeding fixes faults as well as virtues. It has this advantage. The faults are quickly brought to the surface where they can be seen and appropriate steps taken in subsequent matings to deal with them. Out-crossing is more likely to hide faults for the time being, only to allow them to reappear when least wanted.

I would put it this way. All breeding is a gamble. It is so easy to make a terrible mistake, forcing one to start all over again. Yet, on the other hand, the gamble may come off and be brilliantly successful. Good-looking parents often have good-looking children. But my advice to you, at this stage, is to play as safe as you can. Accept it as a general principle that a closely bred dog is more likely to reproduce his own type.

In this country the records show that only a limited number have been dominant sires. Undoubtedly Int. Ch. Seefeld Picasso was in a class of his own in his day. Of British champion bitches only very few have produced two or more champions.

These *facts* must provide food for thought, for they clearly reveal that success has come from certain clearly defined blood-lines. You must decide on these for yourself.

Of course I know that these figures do not reveal every side of the subject, but the yardstick of success in breeding can only be judged by wins in the show-ring. There may be better dogs elsewhere, but it is not possible to recognize them. Poor sometimes though it may be, competition must be our guide.

My own success and that of other leading Boxer breeders has undoubtedly been brought about by concentration on specific blood-lines. At first I line-bred to fix type, and then out-bred when forced to do so. The decision to out-breed must be made by every breeder of several years' standing at some stage, for one must come to a point when it is apparent that no improvement is taking place. It is then that a vital step must be taken. Even so, it is wise to keep within well-defined family limits. It is only possible for me to illustrate my point by referring to my own breeding programme. Naturally others have done the same sort of thing successfully in other directions.

To get my first champion I bred grandmother to grandson—two animals without major faults. They were a Lustig daughter to a Lustig great-grandson. Next, I mated half-brother to half-sister and this produced two champions. One of them was a dog who by any reckoning was a dominant sire. He produced 7 of the 43 champions bred in the whole of the British Isles during the period he was at stud.

Finally came my experiment in out-breeding. I mated a daughter of this champion descendant of Lustig to a descendant of Dorian who, you will remember, was Lustig's first cousin. The result was two champions, and another dog with one certificate. The same plan has also brought success to others.

So, then, by experience I have arrived at these simple conclusions: (1) Buy a good bitch pup from a successful line; (2) mate her to a successful sire from the same family if this is possible. In simple words, exploit success. Do *not* be afraid to go outside your own kennel, even if you dislike the owners. It's the dog's blood you want.

Avoid shy or vicious dogs in any breeding plan, and do not countenance the theory that big bitches make the best mothers. They don't. Neither is a long back desirable in a female. Have regard to colour, for attractive puppies are easier to sell and better to keep. My best reds have been obtained when one parent has been a brindle. It is risking a lot from the colour standpoint to mate two washed-out fawns together.

Expect white puppies to show up because of the white ancestors in the breed, and don't blame the stud dog when it occurs, for *both* parents are to blame—if that's the word to use. Neither is it possible to forecast how many white pups there will be in a litter. I have known a bitch have several whites in her first litter and then, mated exactly the same way again, have none in her second. Some mistakenly blame the male if the litter is small in number. This, also, is a complete fallacy, for a stud of proven capabilities could father hundreds of pups at one mating if the female could produce that number of eggs for him to fertilize. She can't. So dismiss advertisements which claim that a stud dog is 'siring big litters'. The bitch alone decides the number of pups. That is why it is essential that she should have been properly fed and be in perfect condition.

The Mating

So, then, Mr and Mrs Beginner, with these and probably some more thoughts in mind, get out the pedigrees, the records, and your notes on the faults and virtues of the proposed dam and possible sires, and make your decision on which male to use at stud. Having made up your mind, stick to the plan and don't be put off by others who may not necessarily be looking at the problem from your point of view. It should not matter to you whether the stud dog is in the same town, or county, for the job is worth doing well. A journey of a few hundred miles shouldn't make any difference to your choice. It is elementary not to use the dog next door unless he is the best one for the job. I once travelled across the world for a stud dog and never regretted it. Owners of bitches sometimes seem to forget that for a modest fee they can get the services of a stud dog produced as the result of years of work and study and not a little expense.

The first day your bitch comes into season get in touch with the owner of the sire you propose to use, discuss the situation and book the dog. If it is a popular sire it may be wise to make a preliminary arrangement with the owner some time ahead. You will then receive preference. Take your bitch to be mated. In the old days we had to crate bitches and send them by rail, but it was always a worry. Nowadays it is rarely necessary.

What is the right day for your bitch to be brought, or sent, for mating? There is no hard and fast rule. I have related that Alma von der Frankenwarte was successfully mated only very late in her season. That was most unusual. It is far better to take the bitch too early rather than too late. The only way is to watch her closely. While she is still discharging colour it is too early. Wait until the colour changes to a paler shade. The bitch will also do her best to tell you when she is ready. When the moment arrives she will make advances to any male dog, and will lift her tail as an invitation. This is a sure sign. Don't delay any longer.

When you arrive with your bitch for the event it is far better that you should leave the actual job of mating to the dog and the owner (for they are fully experienced in these matters), giving assistance only when asked to do so. You may be required to hold the bitch's head, and generally look after her. On the other hand, the owner of the stud dog may prefer you to keep out of the way and only return to the dogs when they are tied. Don't be alarmed if the owner of the stud tapes the female's mouth, for this is a simple precaution sometimes required, and does not hurt her.

Quiet is necessary, for some stud dogs are easily distracted. Don't talk, don't move about, and don't have any other dogs near. The two animals may remain tied for anything up to half an hour. After it is over, both owners will be wise to swab their animals down with something like diluted TCP, but only touching the *outside* of the bitch's parts. This is a simple precaution against any infection, skin or otherwise, after the two dogs have been in such close contact.

There are certain customs of the trade you should be told about. (1) The stud fee is payable in advance. (2) The owner of the stud dog *may agree* to take the pick of the litter in lieu of the stud fee. (This arrangement is by mutual agreement, and is frequently varied.) (3) If the bitch misses (does not have pups) it is usual for the owner of the stud dog to give a free service next time she is on heat, provided he still has the dog, and provided you still have the bitch. He is not required to do this, and is doing you a kindness, because you have only paid for one service from a proven dog. Still, most owners of stud dogs think it a bit hard if there is no result.

But the owner of the bitch does not receive this consideration by right, nor can it be expected that the free service will be given to another bitch or by another dog, though I sometimes agree to this if it is convenient, and it is a deserving case. The same applies if the bitch has only one puppy, say, or only all-white puppies. In the event of this happening there is no claim on the owner of the stud dog, for the dog is no more to blame than the bitch. But, again, in these circumstances some owners of stud dogs will be helpful. Others take a tougher line, and are quite within their rights. But we must make it clear that the owner of the bitch is *entitled* to only one service for the fee, and everything done above this is by good will. Don't ask for two services, for if the dog is in demand it is a burden to the owner. But accept if offered. If your bitch has to stay with the owner of the stud dog, if by chance she is not ready when she arrives, it is usual for a boarding charge to be made after the first day, but that again depends on the circumstances of the owner concerned.

A stud dog should not be over-used, but twice a week is not out of the way when he is at the peak of his powers; but he should be in top-class condition and receiving all the meat he requires, plus eggs and milk. If there is a period when he is not getting bitches in whelp it is a simple matter for a test of his virility to be made by a vet, but nine times out of ten it will be found that the bitch was to blame.

The bitch must also be in good condition and, *above all, not too fat.* And you can't expect her to have a good litter if she hasn't been fed on the best food—which is meat. Don't overdo the biscuit; avoid bread and other starchy foods. It is also wise to worm her before she goes for the mating, and not afterwards. Use also the proved additives to diet like bone meal. There are many others.

Whelping

If everything has gone well, about 63 days from the day of the mating your bitch should have pups. During the period of pregnancy care for her well. Feeding is most important. She needs to look in good condition, with a bloom on her coat. Here is the sort of diet I use. Breakfast: cereal with egg, honey, milk and sugar. Main meal: as much meat as she wants, with fish as an alternative. Very little biscuit, but say one big cupful soaked in gravy and mixed with the meat. Add to the food one dessertspoonful of cod-liver oil, a moderate serving of green vegetables and a teaspoonful of calcium glucanate. I also use bonemeal and Stress.

To prevent acid milk, a teaspoonful of bicarbonate of soda may be added to the morning feed. This can be kept up until the pups are a week old.

Other than extra food, I do nothing more than usual. Do not mess around trying to feel how many pups the bitch is going to have. Leave her alone, exercise regularly, and don't fuss. After about six weeks you will notice (that is, if she is in whelp) that she will be looking after herself a little more carefully. She won't romp about, and if by chance you have other dogs she will give up playing with them and remain at your side. In other words, the expectant mother is taking things quietly.

In good time prepare her whelping-box, and place it in a quiet, warm place. Believe it or not, these are the most important words in this book. *Quiet and warmth are essential during whelping and the early stages of nursing.* I keep telling people that, and yet I am frequently being called in to assist when things have gone wrong and find the bitch and her pups in a busy kitchen, or a draughty shed, or next to a lot of noisy dogs. Do pay heed to this advice again: QUIET and WARMTH.

A good whelping-box is an essential. It can easily be made for you by a local carpenter. Have it constructed with a hinged top and the front open, save for a strip along the bottom fitted with hinges and clips. Later on, when the pups are beginning to walk, this piece can be let down to form a ramp which they can use to get in and out of the box. Inside the box, all round, fix a rail about six inches from the floor level. This is a wise precaution and prevents pups being squashed. Inside and high up fix with clips a tubular electric heater which can be kept on night and day in the early stages. The size of the box depends on the size of the bitch. She should be able to stretch out lengthways very comfortably in each direction. Also in the puppy room have some other form of heating—such as a safe electric fire, or radiator. An easily obtainable infra-red lamp is good for heating. When the great day arrives you want the room kept at a constant temperature of about 70°F (21.1°C).

Introduce the bitch to her new quarters early on and let her get used to them. If you are perceptive, she will indicate to you when the pups are about to arrive—it may be a day or so early. She will suddenly go off her food, and will be reluctant to come out of the box to attend to her business. See that the temperature of the room is right, and that all is quiet. In front of the box hang a piece of material cutting down the light, and ensuring there is not the slightest risk of draught. Remove also any bedding you may have had in the box, and put down strips of newspaper. Turn on the red lamp, suspended about four feet above the bed.

I always stay up with my bitches while they are whelping, but I do not fuss. If there is any difficulty I always call in a vet, for if it is decided that a caesarian operation is necessary the decision must be taken early and not after the bitch is so exhausted.

In the healthy, normal whelping the bitch requires no assistance from you. Each puppy is delivered in an individual sac which the bitch removes. She also severs the navel cord and licks the puppy until dry. If, however, she finds difficulty, and our breed sometimes does, this is something you can do for her. Do not cut the cord too near the puppy. It is also wise to let the bitch lick and cuddle her new born until she starts to deliver the second pup. Then, when her attention is diverted, remove it so that she can't accidentally knock it.

If by any chance a pup is still wet and cold, rub it with a rough towel, and keep it very warm. It may be that if this is a weak one you may have to give it artificial respiration by pulling the forelegs outwards and forward and then backwards against the chest with steady regular movements. Swing it, head downwards, a few times. As soon as the pup gasps, wipe out the mouth and nose with lint soaked in warm water. Then place the pup in a basket, which should be kept near, with a towel in the bottom

The Whelping Box

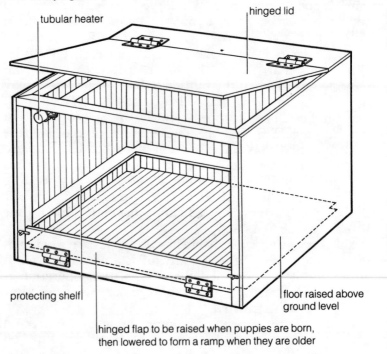

tubular heater

hinged lid

protecting shelf

floor raised above
ground level

hinged flap to be raised when puppies are born,
then lowered to form a ramp when they are older

an infra-red lamp is available that will give the correct heat

covering a hot-water bottle. Make all your movements
quietly and unobtrusively. At a convenient moment
change the newspaper bedding as it will have become wet
and soiled, and when all is over (and not before) substitute
a dry, warm blanket.

Whelpings vary and the period of time between each
pup may be anything from a few minutes to an hour or
more. But if the mother seems to be in excessive pain, or
discharging badly, or too few pups arrive in proportion to
her size, or none arrives after some period of labour,
'phone your vet. He may advise an injection of pituitrin,
or an operation. It is so important not to leave the decision
too long.

Make certain that none of the pups has a cleft palate (this sometimes occurs) and if they have, nothing can save them. They must be destroyed. It is also wise to put down any whites provided there are enough pups left to deal with the milk. It is essential that both mother and children should be content. If they are not, something is wrong. Listen to them. If they sound like bees in a hive all is well, but squeaking and fidgeting can warn you that this is not the case. Have the bitch's milk tested for acidity if there are any doubts. It is, of course, a safeguard to have a foster in reserve, but I think you must gamble first time that all will go well.

For the purpose of our story we will assume a normal whelping. Wipe clean with a warm damp flannel the mother's breasts and hindquarters, drying off with a clean towel, and then place the pups on the nipples, where they will suck vigorously. Before you go to bed to take a well-earned rest, the bitch will be glad of a drink of warm milk, egg and glucose, which I also offer during whelping.

Next morning pop in early and see that the temperature of the room is still correct. Everything should be quiet save for contented little noises within the whelping-box. Draw aside the curtain and invite the bitch to take a walk. She won't want to, but gently you must insist. Take her outside to spend her money, and while she is away get someone to change the blanket and have everything neat and ready for her return. A good mother won't be away for more than half a minute, so you must be quick. At this stage don't handle the pups too much, and don't worry the bitch by taking them away to examine them. Though I write this, I have never been able to resist a quick look, to decide which are boys and which are girls, and which are nicely marked.

A word about the mother's diet now she has her pups. She will require plenty of liquid to drink (I advise milk, honey, glucose and egg beaten up with it, though fresh water is all right if she wants it) and again as much meat as she will eat twice, even three times, a day.

About the tenth day the eyelids of the puppies begin to part, and don't be alarmed because the eyes are a cloudy blue, for that is normal at this stage.

Don't let us be gloomy, but if by some misfortune you lose your bitch during whelping try hard to get a foster and while awaiting her arrival keep the pups alive by hand feeding. It is possible, but hard work. This also applies if the bitch's milk is not satisfactory, for to let them feed from her in these circumstances can only mean death to them.

Without a bitch's help, keeping the pups clean and warm is the problem, but I've known it achieved—in fact I've done it myself, though I do not pretend that it's anything but a trying job. Keep the pups warm by placing them in something like a basket with a hot-water bottle or electric pad in the bottom. The temperature of the room must remain at 70°F (21.1°C). Keep the top of the basket covered. Feed the pups every three hours with a medicine dropper, using the best tinned sweetened milk. I find this very satisfactory. To get some rest myself I kept the pups beside my bed, and attended to them every three hours for seven days.

After the first week, feeds can be given every four hours from a bottle. By the time they are three weeks old the pups are able to lap.

Soon after birth will arise the question of docking, and in the next chapter I shall give detailed notes on this simple, but important, operation.

17

Docking

Boxer pups should be docked when not younger than four days old and normally before they are seven days. It is not possible to state exactly which day, as it will depend on the strength of the pups. If robust, the fourth day is perfectly all right, but if not so strong give a little longer.

If the pups are prematurely born count the first day as from the correct date of birth. This means that the fourth day would be the 67th day after mating (63 plus 4).

This is important as the blood of a premature puppy does not coagulate easily. (I have known a whole litter bleed to death.)

Two people are required for docking, and I should certainly call a vet. One holds the puppy. Tie a small bandage tightly at the root of the tail, after pulling back as much skin as possible towards the quarters. (The object is to reserve enough skin to pull over the tip of the tail after docking.) The second person, using an ordinary pair of docking scissors, should smartly cut the tail, doing so on the slant, that is, with the cut sloping from the top of the tail to the bottom. This rough diagram will illustrate:

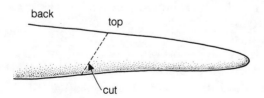

I prefer blunt scissors rather than sharp. Some breeders use an elastic band; it is effective, but I prefer the old-fashioned way and do not heed those who denounce docking. It is not cruel and we have never lost a pup. There should be no loss of blood although sometimes a drop is lost, and there may be a slight squeak from the pup. Some vets will not do the job, others will.

The length is important. The Standard of the Breed says the tail of a boxer should be two inches long. This is absurd, for the measurement obviously refers to a mature dog. How is it possible to dock a tail at four days knowing what length the tail will be 12 months later? Besides that, each dock must suit the individual pup. Other reference books say cut the tail at the second joint (from the root). This also is ridiculous, for at four days one cannot distinguish the joints. Both these instructions must have been given by people who have never docked a puppy. Here is a simple practical hint. Bend the puppy's tail down between its back legs. Note where the tail just covers the pup's anus. With the docking scissors knick out a little hair at this spot so that when the tail is released one can see where to cut.

For the practised eye, it is possible to note also where the pup's tail tapers. The place to cut is just the root side of the spot where the tapering begins.

Above all, don't get a tail too short—it can spoil a good dog (as I know to my cost). Better have it too long. One can always redock later, using an anaesthetic, though this, of course, is not desirable, but nevertheless possible. A too-short dock can never be rectified.

After docking, immediately apply a little tincture of perchloride of iron, or of Friar's balsam. There should be little or no bleeding. Healing powders are excellent. So are permanganate crystals.

If expertly done, taking off the tail is no more than cutting toe-nails. Some will make a slight fuss about this.

It should not be necessary to say that it is wise to send the bitch out for a walk, or keep her in another part of the house, while docking is going on. But it is surprising how thoughtless people can be. Obviously the small cry of the pup (not always made: some don't seem to feel anything at all) will upset her if she is present.

Do the docking in a good light, preferably on a table covered with an old piece of clean towelling. (The iron dressing will stain it.) Have the dressing close at hand, and don't in any circumstances let the pups get cold. This is important, especially in winter, as cold will aggravate any shock. Always, in all circumstances, keep them warm.

Now, if the job is neatly and well done, you should have no trouble at all. After 30 minutes or so the bitch will be feeding her youngsters and neither she nor they will realize that the pups' long tails have gone.

I always remove dew-claws at the same time as docking. In this operation make certain that all the dew-claw has been removed. I have known many instances where a part is left. This will grow, and require another operation. Apply the same dressing as for the tails.

18

Completing the Circle

We now enter the final stage. First a word about your bitch. Massage her breasts, and apply hot fomentations if there is danger of them becoming lumpy and hard, and also examine the nipples for sores which should be bathed. You should have been keeping the pups' toe-nails short from the first week, for they can make the dam mighty sore.

Weaning is commenced at about three weeks, and most probably I have already been giving a little extra food from a bottle, using the best sweetened tinned milk. Now I give the pups their first taste of raw minced meat, and it's a good idea to nail a piece of meat to a bread board and put it in the puppies' box. The pups will come and sniff and then begin to suck, more out of curiosity at first. In this way they will get a lot of nourishment without any danger of swallowing large lumps.

If the weather is cold keep the temperature of the room well up to 70°F (21.1°C), and don't listen to those who say you are mollycoddling the youngsters. Now they are busy climbing in and out of their box up and down the ramp I described, and the bitch doesn't want to be with them all the time. A good mother, though, will not be far away and will jump in to let her pups have a snack every now and then. Soon, also, she will be vomiting her food to the pups if you allow her, but I try to prevent this.

From four weeks onwards I give six meals a day, alternating sweetened tinned milk and minced meat. In addition the pups get a little calcium phosphate and cod-liver oil each day. At eight weeks the meals are reduced to five, but the quantities are increased. I also introduce a

little baked brown bread and gravy, and cooked vegetables.

Worming must be attended to at five weeks and seven
weeks, and again at ten weeks if necessary. Also look after
your bitch, for with care she can be brought back to the
show-ring, maybe all the better for having had a litter.
Massage her breasts morning and night with camphorated
oil, and do not allow her to visit the pups after this has
begun. Already she should have returned to normal diet,
but keep her well fed on meat to aid recovery, and use one
of the tried preparations on her coat, which will most
probably (though not necessarily) have become pretty
thin. As a general principle, I would not mate her at her
next season, unless she goes 12 months without coming
into season, and not then if she isn't right back to full
health and strength.

There can, of course, be variations on this theme,
depending on the vigour of the bitch, though I am against
wearing the mother out with repeated litters and without
rests in between.

This, then, has completed the circle, but finally a word
about keeping Boxers on a large scale. This is only possible
in the country, for a number of young dogs of five months
and upwards can be pretty boisterous creatures, and they
need properly constructed runs in which to let off steam.

In this climate concrete runs surrounded by six-feet
high chain-link netting are, in my experience, the most
suitable, while an exercising paddock in addition is a
blessing. Stoutly constructed kennels need light, water and
heat laid on, with a kitchen, isolation kennel, show
preparation room, etc., as part of the equipment. With it
must go an adequate staff.

As this type of set-up can only be enjoyed by the few
there is no need for me to go into the detail. Fortunately,
for the many, it is quite possible to keep one or two Boxers
in a house, or even a flat, and it is for these owners—the
great majority—that this book has been written. And I
hope some benefit has been gained by reading it.

There is no doubt at all in my mind that dogs are at

their best when given individual attention. The character of the Boxer thrives when he, or she, is the pet of the household. Make the Boxer your friend and you will never regret it.

19

The Modern Scene

In 1954 the Wardrobes Kennel of Mr and Mrs H. Wilson Wiley came into prominence. Three years earlier they had made into a champion a daughter of Ringleader (Wardrobes Alma of Greenovia) and after this success they purchased another Ringleader daughter (Wardrobes Gay Taffeta) and mated her to their own dog, the Viking son, Wardrobes Starlight of Belfoyne. This was a happy combination, for Taffeta produced two champions for her owners—Wardrobes Hunting Pink, a consistent winner, and Wardrobes Sari. A litter sister to these two bitches, Wardrobes Silver Spurs, was the dam of Mr and Mrs Wiley's top champion, the striking red bitch Ch. Wardrobes Miss Mink, who was the fourth Boxer to go Best in Show All Breeds at a championship show. This was at the L.K.A. in 1955. Later on she added to her fine record with more Best-in-Show wins, and eventually became Britain's leading show Boxer. This record was to be beaten in the seventies by another Wardrobes bitch—Ch. Wardrobes Clair de Lune who won 31 Challenge Certificates.

Mink's total of 27 certificates up till the end of 1969 was a remarkable record for that time in Britain. Her dam produced five champions altogether (Mink, Sable, Swinging Kilt, Red Sash and Madam Georgette) and the sire in each instance was Mrs Hullock's Ch. Winkinglight Justice. A great performance. In turn, Mink, mated to Kilt, was the mother of Ch. Wardrobes Wild Mink. These and other successes were to put Mr and Mrs Wiley at the head of British breeders. Their champion Wild Mink proved most successful, having sired 11 English champions up to the end of 1969, including the great winning bitch Ch.

Wardrobes Side Saddle of Arnogar who with 24 almost reached her grand dam's record of 27 Challenge Certificates.

The passing of time is bound to bring changes. As the years went by some of our original Boxer breeders died and kennels went out of existence. Others in changed circumstances were unable to carry on. But, as in other walks of life, more enthusiasts take their places.

They have been able to build on the work already put in, and looking at the Boxer scene at the end of 1983 there is no doubt that the overall quality of the breed has gone right on improving. Today it stands pretty high. That does not mean that the dogs are better than our great ones of the past. But in the show-rings today there are many *more* good ones. Their owners have the stalwarts of the past to thank.

Looking at my latest list of champions, I see that the top dogs have come from kennels where the owners have not only used outstanding stock, but have drawn on their great knowledge of the breed, and their skill in presenting and handling their animals. These are the secrets of success.

Mr and Mrs Wiley continued their success story but have now cut down. I give special praise to Mrs Felicia Price of the Felcign prefix. On her own she took on the best and brought off some splendid victories. Unhappily she has died and a colourful character has gone.

Another splendid performance has been that of Mrs Withers, owner of the Witherford Boxers. Not only has she owned and bred many winners in Britain, but she sent back to Germany, the home of the breed, a brindle and white marked puppy that went to the top in that country and in other parts of Europe.

The dog, Witherford Hot Chestnut, with all possible honours heaped on him, has also proved an exceptional sire. I regard this as a great achievement. It proves that British breeders, given a little time and opportunity, can take on the best in the world.

Mention must also be made of the following who kept the flag flying in the sixties: Mrs Knight (Swanfield), Mrs Thornley (Cherryburton), Mrs Ingram (Bockendon), Dr

McKellar (Makreen), Mrs Hambleton (Marbelton), Mrs Pat Heath (Seefeld), Mrs Greathead (Rytonways) and Miss Grover (Ackendene). Unhappily Mrs Thornley and Dr McKellar have passed on.

So on to the seventies and eighties with more champions made up. We've come a long way from those early days I've written about, and new names have come into the picture, which is just as it should be. In 1970 Mrs Withers and Mrs Hambleton (of the ones mentioned earlier) each produced a title winner, and a bitch I particularly noted was Miss Susan Harvey's Ch. Faerdorn Truly Scrumptious, whom I selected as Best in Show in the club's championship event out of more than 300 Boxers.

Of the '71 crop Mrs Hambleton's Ch. Marbelton Desperate Dan was a great winner, and he kept going into '72 and '73, with Crufts as his particular happy hunting ground. In 1975 he won his twenty-ninth C.C.

The name Int. Ch. Seefeld Artmaster (owned by Mrs Heath and Mrs Crompton, bred by Mrs Banks) catches the eye, for he was not only a successful dog himself, but was the son of that great sire of the breed, Int. Ch. Seefeld Picasso.

Picasso's record as a sire was the best for any Boxer in Britain at that time. He not only sired many champions in the UK, but many others abroad. Altogether his progeny have won well over 100 certificates between them. It is a triumph for Pat Heath, a most knowledgeable and likeable person.

Appendix A comprises a full list of champions up to the end of 1987. In 1972 and 1973 I notice that Mrs Thornley was bringing out good ones, as were Mrs Jean Heath, Mrs Izett and Mrs Garrett, Mrs Tripe and Mrs Rahder, while a most popular winner and champion was Mrs Andrews' Lestar Lucky Lady. I must not leave out the West Country breeders, Miss Grover and Mrs Malcolm, who went to the top.

Among the highlights of 1974 and 1975 were the continued successes of Mrs Withers with her Ch. French Spice of Witherford, and Mrs Hambleton and Mr and Mrs Donnachie with the brindle bitch Ch. Marbelton Tyzack's

Super Trouper.

A new star was Ch. Starmark Sweet Talkin' Guy, a red and white marked male owned and bred by Jean Heath. He took 17 tickets in 1975 and became the leading Boxer for that year. Mrs Heath suffered severe illness, but happily returned to the ring to add to her successes. Alas, she has now gone.

Mrs Angela Kennett, from the North, achieved an unusual victory by making up two red and white males in the same period. I don't recall this being done before. The dogs were Ch. Thunderbolt of Trywell and Ch. Tremendous of Trywell. My husband, Stafford Somerfield, and Miss Susan Harvey made up a daughter of Ch. Faerdorn Truly Scrumptious, previously mentioned. She rejoiced in the name of Ch. Faerdorn Truly Gorgeous.

Mrs Joy Malcolm, a consistent breeder over many years with her Skelders, added to her laurels with Ch. Tartan Tigress; Ch. Rytonways Triple Crown did well for his owner-breeder, Mrs Greathead, winning his title; while Mrs Dudlyke kept the Welsh colours flying with her Ch. Silverstein Sundance Kid.

Mrs Pat Heath, rarely out of the winners, came back with two more champions, Ch. Seefeld Coral Dawn and Ch. Seefeld Dark N'Delicious and two other champions carried her prefix — Ch. Seefeld Miss Pimms (owner Mr and Mrs Russell) and Ch. Seefeld Goldsmith (owner Stafford Somerfield). Goldsmith was bred by Mrs Rita Gathercole, who well deserves a mention as the breeder of four champions.

Ch. Houdini of Sombong, owned by Mrs R. Evans, was a worthy champion, and Ch. Secret Love of Stainburndorf won a title for Mrs Penn and Mr and Mrs Greenway. Those who have read about the early days will note this prefix for it was owned by the late Mr Allon Dawson, one of the breed's pioneers. He handed it on to Mrs Penn. Northern Ireland comes into the winners' list with a very nice fawn bitch, Ch. Tirkane Avaunt, owned and bred by Miss Ann Ingram, daughter of an old friend, Mrs Ingram, who was among the earliest breeders of Boxers in Northern Ireland.

Ch. Marbelton Desperate Dan, certificate record holder in males, proved his value as a sire with Mr Barker's Ch. Hazefield Ladybird of Haiglea and the home-bred Ch. Marbelton Rainfly. Mrs Withers' Ch. Witherford Cool Mango was another to score at stud, producing Mr and Mrs Fellows' Ch. Lovesong of Witherford. Cool Mango had four champions to his credit at the end of 1975.

That leaves one further champion for this two-year period, a very lively red and white marked bitch by Picasso named Ch. Tarpen Sea Moon, a first for enthusiastic Northern breeders—Mr and Mrs Alton.

The champion dog of 1976 was Miss June Grover's Ch. Ackendene Willy Wagtail, a very smart brindle I made second in the Working Group at Crufts. He later won the Group at Birmingham.

Others with a 1976 title are: Mrs Kennett and Mrs Duncan's Ch. Alldane Golden Wonder of Trywell; Mrs F. M. Davies' Ch. Matholm Cool Desire of Snarestone; Mrs Lindsay's Ch. Lindayne Francesca; Mrs Joy Malcolm's Ch. Scallywag of Skelder; Mrs Boyle's Ch. Camsail Lovebird; Mr and Mrs Ward-Davies' Ch. Kinbra Uncle Sam of Winuwuk; Mr Chris Cray's Ch. Goldseal of Klansted.

Fourteen new champions were added in 1977 and bitches dominated the show scene, nine being made up compared with five dogs of which Mrs Fairbrother's Ch. Gremlin Summer Storm took most of the limelight.

Joy Malcolm kept among the leaders with her Ch. Skelder Burnt Almond, a brindle bitch by Ch. Starmark Sweet Talkin' Guy, whose owner Jean Heath sadly died. Guy in the hands of his new owner, Mrs Sillitoe, continued to win certificates and to sire winners. His last triumph was at Crufts in 1979, where he went Best of Breed, and my Ch. Gold Bangle of Panfield took the bitch ticket.

Right in the forefront of top sires was Pat Heath's incomparable Ch. Seefeld Picasso. Three times he appears as the father of new champions in 1977, and to add to that, his sons, Ch. Seefeld Artmaster and Ch. Seefeld Goldsmith, sired one each in that year. What a remarkable dog he was. His death later on was a great sadness, but he'd had a splendid life and he left a wonderful heritage.

Dr Cattanach's Ch. Steynmere Summer Gold, by Gold-smith and a double Picasso grandson, was a most interest-ing dog who went to the United States where American breeders were glad to have his bloodlines. Ch. Thayman Cinna deserves mention for she was nearly six when she got her third ticket for her devoted owner, Mrs Norman. Cinna was an Artmaster daughter.

Some may question the continued reference to Picasso, but the facts cannot be ignored. I must also mention Ch. Simoor Status Quo, owned by Mrs Jackie Carter, and another Picasso champion son.

So to 1978 when the number of new title holders dropped to eleven, six of them bitches, and five males which indicates there are no easy champions in Britain. Not a lot of change among leading breeders and owners— Pat Heath as ever, Dr Cattanach and Mrs Malcolm claiming success. Miss Anne Podmore, with stout heart, continued with Ch. Dallgery Golden Bracken and at the age of seven, or thereabouts, he made her dream come true by joining the title holders.

An import, Norwegian Ch. Cavajes Herakles, had been brought in to strengthen Mrs Heath's stud team and he twice figured as the sire of new champions. So did Artmaster and the old man himself, Picasso, couldn't be kept out. It seems a pity that males get the star billing over the females, but a bitch cannot have the same opportunity to produce champions.

Mrs Kennett kept the Trywells going, and Daphne North bred her first champion, Ch. Carinya Petticoat, by Ch. Gremlin Summer Storm who achieved yet more honours in '79 and '80.

Miss Susan Harvey, an outstanding breeder (she made up champions in earlier years like Scrumptious and Gorgeous) was the first breeder, jointly with myself, to start the ball rolling in 1979 with the Goldsmith daughter, Gold Bangle. At the time of writing the old lady is still with us.

Goldsmith also sired Jovaltone Penny from Heaven for Mrs Gray and brought the first champion success to this breeder. Ackendene Royal Streaker was in there with Mrs

Queen the owner. He was bred by Miss Grover, especially
known for her outstanding brindle champion Ackendene
Willy Wagtail. Pirol von Belcane sired Steynmere Golden
Link. Mrs Withers, not seen so often in the ring now,
brought in Pirol from Germany.

Her Witherford Cherry Cobbler sired Mrs Boyle's Ch.
Camsail Mudlark. Mr and Mrs Hambleton, consistently
successful show-goers and breeders, came through with
Ch. Marbelton Peep Show by Hasty Harry. Harry did well.
He also sired Ch. Marbelton Tyzacks Misty Blue, bred by
Mr and Mrs Donnachie and owned by the Hambletons.

More American blood had come here earlier in the
shape of Kreyon's Back In Town of Winuwuk who, among
other champions, sired Mrs Combe's Ch. Kimbra Bicen-
tennial. The Kreyon dog was imported by Mr and Mrs
Ward-Davies, keen and clever Cotswold breeders, who
were to have outstanding success. This brindle Yankee was
to throw some excellent stuff over the years, including Ch.
Kimbra Uncle Sam of Winuwuk.

Summer Storm, still proving himself a significant sire
and showman, achieved the double with a dog and a bitch,
Mrs Williams' Ch. Willrait Nota Bene and the brindle
female Ch. Dusky Damsel of Chellowside. Mrs Kennett,
never far away, and Mr and Mrs Duncan, were back at the
top of the line with Ch. Alldane Golden Joy of Trywell by
her Ch. Thunderbolt of Trywell. And special mention for
a great tryer from the West Country, Mrs Davey, who bred
Ch. Kitwe Sylvia.

One for whom more success was to come later was
Landor Prince Charming of Janmer, an outstanding red
and white male, owned by Mrs James and Mrs Adams,
who not only took his championship but later was Best in
Show at the Working Breeds. Most unhappily he died
young. A Scottish success was Ch. Braxburn Eros, bred
and owned by Mr and Mrs MacLaren, who have taken
keen interest for many years and who have raided
successfully from across the Border.

So 1979 saw titles claimed by fourteen Boxers, with
bitches again taking the honours, eight of them against six
dogs. This is interesting, as dogs have a longer and more

consistent show life generally, though there are exceptions.

20

Into the Eighties

1980 was soon marked by the outstanding success of Mrs Jackie Carter. She made up a dog and a bitch from the same litter, a performance rarely achieved. These two exciting 1980 youngsters were Ch. Simoor Status Symbol (the dog) and Ch. Simoor State of Grace. The sire was Mrs Carter's own dog, Ch. Simoor Status Quo, and the dam Winuwuk Kissing Cousin of Simoor. Notice the breeding: Simoor Status Quo is by Picasso, now passed on full of honours, and the Winuwuk bitch a daughter of Ch. Kimbra Uncle Sam of Winuwuk by Kreyon's Back In Town of Winuwuk.

Ch. Winuwuk Good Golly, by the American imported sire, Winuwuk Milray's Red Baron of Valvay, piled up certificates for Mr and Mrs Ward-Davies, and others to take the coveted titles were Ch. Collis Winter Gold (Mrs Greathead), Ch. Devonaire Belle Star (Mrs V. Carnill), Ch. Mauraine Sweet Jolie Girl (Mrs Webb) and Ch. Snarestone Skyrocket of Skelder (Mrs Malcolm).

Two of those were by Ch. Sweet Talkin' Guy, who triumphed again even from the grave. Mrs Malcolm again proved a consistent breeder and exhibitor and was top kennel in 1979 and 1980.

Another kennel in the headlines now was Tyegarth, owned by Miss Sheila Cartwright, who made up the group winner, Ch. Tyegarth Famous Grouse. Grouse's litter brother, Tyegarth Glenmorangie of Jenroy, became a champion for Mrs Townshend. They are by Ch. Gremlin Summer Storm out of Tyegarth Old Fashioned.

In 1980 Boxer breeders were alarmed by the emergence of an hereditary condition affecting the nervous system known as Progressive Axonopathy. The disease was a distinct threat and had to be taken very seriously. The clubs did not shrink from taking action, and a panel was formed to produce a scheme of control. To their great credit, owners of dogs found to be carriers withdrew them from stud.

Dr Bruce Cattanach was the leader in the arduous work of research and strong support was given by the British Boxer Club under its chairman, John Luckhurst, a veterinary surgeon. Thanks to their diligent efforts and those of the panel, the dreaded disease was largely conquered. There are hopes it will be eradicated altogether.

Marian Fairbrother was once again prominent in 1980, and her Ch. Gremlin Summer Storm became the C.C. record holder in the breed with 33 certificates. Altogether, Marian's Gremlin Boxers at that time had notched up a total of 109 C.C.s. Marian was to become president of the parent club, a deserved honour.

The exhibit she overtook was Mrs Constance Wiley's Ch. Wardrobes Clair de Lune, an attractive bitch who took 31 C.C.s and was then retired. Mrs Wiley retired as an exhibitor but, fortunately for the breed, remained as a judge.

In the year 1980 the top winning Boxer was Mr and Mrs Ward-Davies' Ch. Winuwuk Good Golly with 11 C.C.s. She is an outstanding brindle and white marked bitch who put these popular breeders right out in front. Altogether there were 13 new champions, seven dogs and six bitches. Golly was by Winuwuk Milray's Red Baron of Valvay who came to Britain from the United States to have great influence. It is interesting to note the success gained by mating Baron to daughters of Back In Town.

As well as the Simoor duo already mentioned we must notice again the performance of Ch. Tyegarth Famous Grouse, the prepotent brindle and showman owned by Miss Cartwright.

Another dog coming along was to place an indelible stamp on the breed. Ch. Steynmere Night Rider, a dark brindle and white owned by Dr Cattanach, set up an outstanding performance as a sire. We take a little credit here as his sire was That's Right of Panfield (a son of my Gold Bangle) whom we exported to Australia where he had marked success. Five times he was just kept out of the top winning spot at home.

Mrs Wiley, patron of the British Boxer Club, was able to report an outstanding year for the club. A landmark was the setting up of a show centre on Towcester racecourse. The B.B.C. was the first breed club in Britain to have a permanent home of its own. Many took a hand in this achievement, particularly Mrs Knight, the secretary.

The breed was in a very healthy condition. Registrations remained high at over 4,000, making it the tenth most popular breed. It has been higher, but to have settled down around this figure reveals continued popularity.

1981 was an unusual year. Only three males became champions, being outnumbered two to one by bitches. Outstanding was Mrs Best's Ch. Wrencliffe Let's Try Again, another by Red Baron; Mrs Fairbrother's Ch. Gremlin Summer Storm was in second place with Grouse third. Golly was still up close, and Mrs Malcolm came along with Skelder Burnt Offering, a brindle bitch by Storm, to claim her title.

It is significant that altogether 38 animals figure in the list of certificate winners for '81, indicating that a high standard existed. Storm, by the way, beat his son Grouse by one C.C. Try Again and Storm took seven each and Grouse six.

On to 1982 dominated by two splendid brindle males, which between them scooped up 26 of the 38 certificates available for dogs. They were Ch. Norwatch Brock Buster, owned by Mrs Watchorn, and Ch. Faerdorn Pheasant Plucker belonging to Miss Susan Harvey and Mr R. P. Hughes.

Both were top class and among the very best shown in Britain. They possessed great style and temperament, and commanded the ring. Top spot went to Brock Buster as he captured two more reserve certificates. It was my pleasure to give Pheasant Plucker Best of Breed at the famous Crufts show.

The sire of each has already been mentioned here, demonstrating how top dogs often (not always) produce good sons and daughters. Buster's sire was Night Rider and sire of Plucker was Famous Grouse. So Panfield came up, after all those years, as owners of the grandsire of one of the top modern dogs. Elizabeth Somerfield, who started this book, would have been gratified.

In the 1982 lists we must mention Golly again, being one of three to take four C.C.s. The others were Ch. Wrencliffe Let's Try Again by Baron, and Ch. Biloran Miss Nancy by Ch. Biloran Mr Similarity. So there was also deserved success for Mr and Mrs W. A. Law of the Biloran affix. Buster's litter brother, Norwatch Glory Boy of Rayfos (owned by Mr and Mrs Greenway) also got his title. Two champions in one litter! Thus Night Rider came into the records again. Their dam is Norwatch Mustang Wine.

For the second year running in 1983, Ch. Norwatch Brock Buster was top dog with an excellent total of 14 tickets and eight reserves. Buster was twice winner of the Working group. Plucker was reserve Best in Show at the Working Breeds and out of the blue came Antron Prize Guy owned by Mrs S. Tonkin. Though having to wait some time for his title, he had the greatest success for the breed I can remember in the big ring. He took Best in Show All Breeds at a championship show, a reserve Best in Show, a Working group, two C.C.s and later a third.

He was cleverly handled by Miss Tonkin, a youngster who had everyone talking. A newcomer, she deserves many congratulations on her outstanding success.

Much to everyone's regret Marian Fairbrother, a leading breeder and exhibitor frequently mentioned in this book, died while still actively engaged in the sport. She, like a previous president of the British Boxer Club (Elizabeth Somerfield), was one of the friends who clubbed together with Mary Davis many years ago to buy one of the early imports. They will be long remembered.

Marian never gave up and even when no longer able to show in her old style, she still appeared in the ring and won. Her friend, Daphne North, took Storm over.

Best bitch of 1983 was interesting. Ch. Kanix Scarlett, owned by Mrs Wilberg, came from Norway to take the top female spot with 5 tickets. Mr and Mrs Wilberg, Boxer enthusiasts, have now come to live in Britain.

Another bitch, winner of 5 C.C.s, was Ch. Moljon Dream Again of Marbelton, but Scarlett pipped her on reserves. Dream Again was by Mr and Mrs Hambleton's import from Germany, Dandy v Starenschloss. Dandy is just one of the Hambleton imports who has proved successful at stud. So the Marbelton affix was there again, and they were to have another outstanding year in '84.

The breed Standard was under review yet again in 1984. I hope any changes will be very seriously considered. I see no reason to change anything save, perhaps, for one or two minor revisions. Working with the old Standard we have produced many splendid animals which must indicate that there is very little wrong with it. The breed today has reached a degree of excellence of which the best of the old timers would certainly approve.

Summing up the four years 1980 to 1983 inclusive, it will be seen that two brindle sires had a tremendous influence and are largely responsible for the dominance of brindles in British Boxers today. Mrs Fairbrother's Ch. Gremlin Summer Storm and Miss Cartwright's Ch. Tyegarth Famous Grouse are father and son. Storm sired four champions in the period, and Grouse five. I cannot recall a father and son doing better. Grouse was in fact the top sire in 1982 and 1983.

Looking through the records for the last four years other sires with two or more champion progeny were: Winuwuk Milray's Red Baron of Valvay, Ch. Starmark Sweet Talkin' Guy, Ch. Simoor Status Quo and Ch. Steynmere Night Rider. The stars in the ring at this time were: the Ward-Davies' bitch Ch. Winuwuk Good Golly, Ch. Wrencliffe Let's Try Again (also by Baron), and Summer Storm. Near, or at the top, was Faerdorn Pheasant Plucker, the brilliant brindle dog with a difficult name, owned by Miss Harvey. He was among the best I've seen in the United Kingdom.

But one cannot keep Summer Storm out of the records.

In 1980 he took his tally of certificates to 33, setting up a new record for the breed taking the top place from Ch. Marbelton Desperate Dan (1975) and Ch. Wardrobes Clair de Lune (1973).

The following year was marked by the fierce competition between Pheasant Plucker and Brock Buster. Both were exceptional, and both claimed 13 certificates in 1982. It was thrilling to see them competing against each other, sometimes one and then the other getting the top spot. They are still fighting it out, and I would not like to say how the battle will finish. Sufficient to say both are beautiful Boxers that all followers of the breed would be proud to own. Golly and Let's Try Again were the female stars, and a great credit to their sire, Baron.

In 1983 the pattern was very much the same with Brock Buster getting top place with 14 certificates (27 C.C.s altogether) but the battle was not yet over. They were both in there at the start of 1984. Skelder must be praised for consistent winning and Mr and Mrs Wilberg were in the honours again with the red bitch, Ch. Kanix Scarlett.

It is impossible in the space available to mention everyone who deserves recognition, but I've tried to pick out the highlights. Once again I give it as my opinion that the breed continues to make progress. Breeders have brought in outstanding males from Germany, Holland and the United States to combine with the best of the British stock. The art is to get the right mix, and I think this has been done.

21

More Progress

The previous chapter is called 'Into the Eighties'. Now it is possible to see what has happened as we speed on into the nineties. The Boxer has made more progress. Once again, UK breeders have demonstrated that they have the skill to produce good dogs and now the British Boxers are comparable to those in any other country. Some would claim they are better, but I would be content to say equal. The United States also have many splendid ones.

The discerning reader will note that when the breed first came to England Boxers did not get very far in competition with other breeds, particularly for group and Best in Show winners. That has changed. Now they are often given the top spot or are near to it. They will remain there. This improvement has been due to the mix of wise buying in Germany, Holland and the USA, plus the skill to use the new blood. The result is outstanding.

Some of our older breeders have had to give up because of advancing years but they have handed on their skills to enthusiastic young people who are making new records. Good luck to them. This book will show them that their advance has been based on the valuable contributions made in the past.

In 1984 there were again 38 sets of C.C.s on offer and these were awarded by 44 different judges to 33 different Boxers (13 dogs, 20 bitches). Once again two dogs dominated the show scene: Ch. Rayfos Cock Robin was top C.C. winning Boxer with 11 C.C.s and he was closely followed by Ch. Marbelton Dressed to Kill who won 9 C.C.s. Dressed to Kill, by reason of his group win at the Autumn S.K.C. and group and reserve Best in Show at

L.K.A., was top Boxer in the *Dog World* competition. Ch. Faerdorn Pheasant Plucker added to his score by winning the supreme award at the spring S.K.C. show.

Leading bitch was Ch. Moljon Dream Again of Marbelton who won 5 C.C.s but the Scottish Ch. Socotras Royal Game and Ch. Belowen State Treasure came close behind with 4 C.C.s.

Top kennel was Marbelton (Mr and Mrs Hambleton) who accumulated 15 C.C.s (5 of them in partnership with Moljon). Ch. Wanderobo Hurley Burley of Marbelton returned to the ring after whelping a litter and won the C.C. at Midland Counties, and that's always good to see. The Marbeltons, during the year, topped the century in Challenge Certificates, a feat which demonstrates their success over the years.

A year later Ch. Marbelton Dressed to Kill created breed history by becoming the first male to win two Best in Show awards at all-breed Championship shows. He did this at Birmingham and at Southern Counties. One has to go back to Ch. Wardrobes Miss Mink to beat that – she did it four times! Dressed to Kill was awarded 14 C.C.s bringing his current total to 23, and he ended the year as top working dog. His nearest rival was the previous year's big winner, Ch. Rayfos Cock Robin.

At the end of the year a new star appeared at Seefeld, Rupik Bellringer of Seefeld, who after winning his first ticket went on to reserve Best in Show at Midland Counties. Ch. Trywell Twelfth Night won 7 C.C.s but she was overtaken by the young Ch. Norwatch Slightly Sozzled who won 7 C.C.s and 4 reserve C.C.s. It was a very close thing! Top sire was Ch. Tyegarth Famous Grouse with 18 C.C.s awarded to his offspring. He was closely followed by Ch. Norwatch Glory Boy of Rayfos whose progeny won 15 C.C.s. Top kennel was again Marbelton. Top puppy was Skelder Pot Luck who gave great promise for the future. Also impressive was the achievement made in the whelping box of Norwatch Mustang Wine whose children became very successful.

There were extra C.C.s this year bringing the total to 39 sets, and 11 new champions were made up.

A bitch dominated 1986. This was the outstanding Ch. Trywell Twelfth Night who, by winning 13 C.C.s, claimed one third of the bitch certificates and brought her current total to 20. Twelfth Night beat the record for the most C.C.s awarded to a bitch in one season. This had previously been held by Ch. Wardrobes Miss Mink and Ch. Winuwuk Good Golly who both had 11. Runner-up to Twelfth Night was Ch. Skelder Pot Luck, who gained 7 C.C.s. She had come through from top puppy a year earlier.

The top winning male was Ch. Rayfos Cock Robin, who by gaining a further 6 C.C.s (with Best of Breed each time) took his total to 26, thus taking over from Inkling, Picasso and Guy in the C.C. lists for the top red male. Robin won Best in Show at the BBC Golden Jubilee show. He was closely followed by the striking brindle, Ch. Katar Dancing Shadows.

Another highlight of the year was the achievement of Ch. Garnet Gelert of Steynmere who took both the group and Best in Show All Breeds at Bournemouth.

The year 1987 brought Walkon into prominence. Walker and Yvonne Miller piled up 11 C.C.s, 8 reserve C.C.s and 6 Bests of Breed with three different Boxers. They had the top winning kennel. The runners-up were Marbelton, with 8 C.C.s, 8 reserve C.C.s and 4 Bests of Breed.

Forty different Boxers were awarded Challenge Certificates and 13 new champions were made up. Unlike many of the other years in the decade, no particular Boxer dominated the show scene and indeed, up until the Cotswold Boxer Club's show in December, nine different champions were contenders for the accolade of top Boxer '87. This reveals the progress made in the breed with so many of them deserving top honours. However, on the basis of C.C.s and reserve C.C.s, the top Boxer was Ch. Marbelton Burley Chassis who gained 5 C.C.s, 5 reserve C.C.s and one Best of Breed. Joint top males were the cousins, Ch. Tyegarth Blue Kiwi and Ch. Jenroy Pop My Cork to Walkon, who were each awarded 5 C.C.s and 4 reserve C.C.s with 4 Bests of Breed. The other close contenders were Ch. Slightly Sloshed of Sunhawk and Walkon and Ch. Roxess Daze of Wine and Roses. Most successful breeders were Helen and Eddie Banks with 11 C.C.s, 9 reserve C.C.s and 6 Bests of Breed.

Top sire was, once again, Ch. Tyegarth Famous Grouse whose pups amassed the grand total of 17 C.C.s, 16 reserve C.C.s and 10 Bests of Breed. These awards were shared by nine different Boxers, two of which became champions during the year. Ch. Norwatch Brock Buster sired three champions. Of the 13 'new' champions, the Tyegarth brothers, Grouse and Glenmorangie, were either sire or grandsire of no less than eight.

Boxers that won a Working Group were Ch. Jenroy Pop My Cork to Walkon at Birmingham City; and six days later at Richmond, after winning his second C.C., Steynmere Forceful William.

Returning to the ring after a long absence, one of the most experienced breeders, Pat Withers, piloted Ch. Witherford Gay Jasmin through to her title, the first for a decade. Jenny Townsend produced her third-generation champion in Lot Less Bother. She also bred Ch. Jenroy Pop My Cork to Walkon. The Winuwuks and the Seefelds both made up champions. Ch. Slightly Sloshed of Sunhawk and Walkon became a champion for the Millers and the fifth to be produced by Helen and Eddie Banks's Norwatch Mustang Wine. Another highlight was the victory of Sheffordian Ruby Tuesday of Norwatch who, after nine reserve C.C.s, gained her title. The following week her young son, Norwatch Sunhawk Raffles, won his, keeping these two fine kennels to the fore.

To sum up. Looking back over recent years I am convinced that not only have British Boxers improved in style and show presence but today they are prepared and handled so much better. There were exceptions in the past, of course, and there were also outstanding dogs in the early days, but not nearly so many. Some stood out, but the classes were not uniform. Today the line-up is excellent and there are now very good dogs who can't even get into the first three places.

The key is to mate good dogs to good bitches, paying

regard to line-breeding. Observe in the pages of this book how the established breeders, by careful selection, come through to the top time and again. But this does not mean that surprises do not occur occasionally. They do, and newcomers should always remember that the best sires are available to them. There is no substitute for experience and study. Look at the top dogs again. Their bible is the Standard.

I shall not attempt to change in any way the views and principles of Dibbie Somerfield. After many years they still hold firm. But in my opinion no good has been done by the Kennel Club's mucking about with the Standard. A few minor changes were needed, but observe how the breed has improved by sticking to the views of the old-timers. They knew what they were doing. By following on, even greater success will be achieved.

APPENDIX A

BRITISH BOXER CHAMPIONS 1939–1987

Note: *Owner* gives the name of owner at the time of becoming a champion.

B/W = Brindle and White   R/W = Red and White   F/W = Fawn and White   B = Brindle   F = Fawn

Name	Sex	Colour	Birth	Sire	Dam	Breeder	Owner
1939							
Horsa of Leith Hill	D	B	3.7.36	Sieger Hansl von Biederstein	Gretl von der Boxerstadt	Mrs Sprigge	Mrs Caro
1947							
Panfield Serenade •	B	B/W	14.4.45	Juniper of Bramblings	Alma von der Frankenwarte	Mrs Somerfield	Breeder
Thornick Beta of Oidar	B	B	3.9.44	Stainburndorf Minesweeper	Stainburndorf Prudence	Mrs Pickford	Mr & Mrs Dyson
Cuckmere Krinetta	B	F	8.5.45.	Cuckmere Krin	Bluemountains Lottery	Mrs Martland	Mrs Siggers
1948							
Holger von Germania	D	F/W	15.10.45	Rex von Hohenneuffen	Dutch Ch. Favoriet vom Haus Germania	Mr Zimmerman	Miss Bing
Panfield Tango	D	F	16.4.46	Panfield Flak	Alma von der Frankenwarte	Mrs Somerfield	Breeder
Bucko of Gerdas Hofstee	D	B/W	19.8.47	Dutch Ch. Faust vom Haus Germania	Britta van Gerdas Hoeve	Mr Vandenberg	Mr Jakeman
Florri of Breakstones	B	F/W	6.3.47	Champus von der Fischerhutte	Maragay of Maspound	Mesdames Dunkels and Gamble	Breeders
Monarchist of Maspound	D	B	12.2.45	Mutineer of Maspound	Marienlyst of Maspound	Mrs Guthrie	Breeder

Name	Sex	Colour	Birth	Sire	Dam	Breeder	Owner
Asphodel of Knowle Crest	B	F	21.5.47	Stainburndorf Jaguar	Ch. Thornick Beta of Oidar	Mr & Mrs Dyson	Breeders
Cuckmere Bomza Fiesta	B	B/W	4.10.47	Ch. Cuckmere Andrew	Bomza Revelmere Lulu	Mrs Stephens	Mrs Siggers
Holmehill Faust of Gerdas Hofstee	D	B	19.8.47	Dutch Ch. Faust vom Haus Germania	Britta van Gerdas Hoeve	Mr Vandenberg	Mr & Mrs Gemmell
Annelie von Eddy's Gluck	B	B/W	20.8.46	Tom von der Sievershohe	Flamme von Vierlingen	Mrs Laurniot	Mrs Bishton
1949							
Golf von Kunzerndorf	D	F	17.2.46	Rex von Hohenneuffen	Draga von Kunzendorf	Lotte Wolf	Mrs Fearfield
Alrakim Orburn Akaboo	B	F/W	3.5.47	Ch. Holger von Germania	Marageth of Maspound	Miss Rands	Mrs Guthrie
Orburn Kekeri	B	F/W	3.5.47	Ch. Holger von Germania	Marageth of Maspound	Miss Rands	Mrs Hullock
Gernotson of Jonwin	D	B/W	3.11.47	Gremlin Gernot von der Herreneichen	Revelmere Cristel	Mr Bowman	Mrs Sykes
Panfield Ringleader	D	F	19.3.48	Ch. Panfield Tango	Ch. Panfield Serenade	Mrs Somerfield	Breeder
Bobbysox of Greentubs	B	B/W	1.6.48	Ch. Cuckmere Andrew	Alrakim Maureen	Mr Cooke	Mr & Mrs Blackham
Lustig of Gerdas Hofstee	D	R/W	19.8.47	Dutch Ch. Faust vom Haus Germania	Britta van Gerdas Hoeve	Mr Vandenberg	Mrs Payton-Smith
Gremlin Sungari	B	F/W	6.5.48	Ch. Panfield Tango	Gremlin Bossi von Rhona	Mrs Fairbrother	Mrs Pugh

Name	Sex	Colour	Birth	Sire	Dam	Breeder	Owner
Cuckmere Andrew	D	B/W	6.7.46	Am. Ch. Quality of Barmere	Ozark Jerris of Blossemlea	Miss Grant	Mrs Siggers
1950							
Linbox Leo	D	F/W	21.3.48	Gremlin Gernot von der Herreneichen	Linbox Boxdorf Mira	Mr & Mrs Linds	Breeders
Panfield Rhythm	B	F/W	19.3.48	Ch. Panfield Tango	Ch. Panfield Serenade	Mrs Somerfield	Breeder
Panfield Flash	D	F/W	26.4.49	Ch. Panfield Tango	Panfield Comedy	Mrs de Salis	Mrs Somerfield
Winkinglight Viking	D	F/W	24.9.48	Breakstones Helios vom Haus Germania	Ch. Orburn Kekeri	Mrs Hullock	Mrs Anson
Max of Boxholme	D	B/W	14.2.48	Golf von Germania	Nevada of Monkswood	Mrs Pugh	Mrs Fotherby
Panfield Bliss	B	B/W	17.4.48	Collo von Dom	Britta van Gerdas Hoeve	Mr Vandenberg	Mrs Somerfield
Hella of Belfoyne	B	B/W	3.5.49	Ch. Holger von Germania	Fiffi Patch of Belfoyne	Mr Rathbone	Breeder
Winkinglight Venturer	D	F/W	24.9.48	Breakstones Helios vom Haus Germania	Ch. Orburn Kekeri	Mrs Hullock	Miss Anderson
1951							
Florizel of Breakstones	D	F/W	9.7.49	Dutch Ch. Faust vom Haus Germania	Christine of Breakstones	Mesdames Dunkels and Gamble	Breeders
Burstall Delight	B	B	11.9.49	Ch. Panfield Ringleader	Burstall Gremlin Torni	Major D. F. Bostock	Breeder
Fenella of Breakstones	B	B/W	9.7.49	Dutch Ch. Faust vom Haus Germania	Christine of Breakstones	Mesdames Dunkels and Gamble	Breeders
Gremlin Inxpot	D	F/W	25.10.49	Axel von Bad Oeyn	Gremlin Moonbeam	Mrs Fairbrother	Breeder

Name	Sex	Colour	Birth	Sire	Dam	Breeder	Owner
Burstall Gelasma	B	B/W	4.6.50	Immertreu Kavelier	Cedar of Bramblings	Miss Duckett	Major D. F. Bostock
Panfield Zick	D	F/W	21.8.50	Axel von Bad Oeyn	Panfield Flame	Major Leach	Mrs Somerfield
Flacius of Knowle Crest	D	F/W	2.8.49	Finemere's Flip of Berolina	Ch. Asphodel of Knowle Crest	Mr & Mrs Dyson	Breeders
Panfield Tap Dancer	B	F/W	25.2.47	Gremlin Gernot von der Herreneichen	Panfield Edelweiss	Mrs Plumstead	Mrs Fleming
Greatsea Masterpiece	D	B/W	20.6.49	Finemere's Flip of Berolina	Charterlea Vesper	Dr & Mrs Preston	Mrs Welden
Wardrobes Alma of Greenovia	B	F/W	29.5.50	Ch. Panfield Ringleader	Awldogg Veronica of Greenovia	Mr & Mrs Green	Mrs C. W. Wiley
Panfield Zest	D	F/W	2.3.50	Ch. Panfield Ringleader	Panfield Starborne Caper	Mrs Somerfield	Mrs Kidd
Ajax of Gunnholme	D	F/W	26.11.50	Hans van der Zaankant	Fedora of Knowle Crest	Mr & Mrs Greig	Breeders
1952							
Klesby Sparklet	D	F/W	24.4.50	Ch. Holger von Germania	Skolar of Klesby	Mrs Hucklesby	Breeder & Mrs Price
Panfield Awldogg Attar	D	B/W	5.11.50	Ch. Panfield Ringleader	Awldogg Zena	Mr & Mrs Lissenden	Mrs Somerfield
Panfield Party Piece of Greentubs	B	B/W	26.12.50	Ch. Panfield Ringleader	Lisa of Greentubs	Mr Cooke	Mrs Somerfield
Geronimo Carissima	B	F/W	28.5.51	Am. Ch. Awldogg Southdown's Rector	Geronimo Chloe	Mrs Thompson & Mr Hatherly	Mrs Thompson

Name	Sex	Colour	Birth	Sire	Dam	Breeder	Owner
Burstall King	D	F/W	11.9.50	Axel von Bad Oeyn	Burstall Duskie	Major D. F. Bostock	Breeder
1953 Felcign Cover Girl	B	F/W	24.9.51	Ch. Winkinglight Viking	Zita of Ceboy	Mr Boyce	Mrs Price
Knowle Crest Isis	B	F/W	14.8.51	Am. Ch. Applause of Emefar	Genista of Knowle Crest	Mr Davies	Mr & Mrs P. Dyson
Zattopeck Maxceboy	D	F/W	24.9.50	Ch. Winkinglight Viking	Zita of Ceboy	Mr Boyce	Breeder
Spaldene Spruce	B	F/W	5.10.50	Ch. Panfield Ringleader	Charterlea Marina	Mrs Harvey	Major D. F. Bostock
Felden Feebee	B	F/W	16.10.51	Gremlin Klever of Felden	Panfield Sheba	Mrs Mould	Breeder
Anndale Sheafdon Hooch-Mi	B	F/W	3.8.51	Ch. Florizel of Breakstones	Sheafdon Paprika	Miss Haggie	Major D. F. Bostock
Gremlin Indelible	D	B/W	8.6.51	Ch. Gremlin Inxpot	Gremlin Chutni	Mrs Fairbrother	Mr Craggs
Awldogg Jacobus	D	F/W	11.9.51	Am. Ch. Awldogg Southdown's Rector	Awldogg Zena	Mr & Mrs Lissenden	Major D. F. Bostock
Blacknowe Beau Ideal	D	B/W	26.4.52	Ch. Florizel of Breakstones	Blacknowe Ballerina	Miss Miller Thomas	Breeder
Anndale Aleader	D	F/W	11.5.50	Ch. Panfield Ringleader	Anndale Gay Lady of Greentubs	Mr McKee	Breeder
Stainburndorf Vanderlion	D	F/W	13.5.52	Stainburndorf Frohlich von Dom	Stainburndorf Babette	Mr Thornton	Mr Ridley

Name	Sex	Colour	Birth	Sire	Dam	Breeder	Owner
Geronimo Duich of Coigach	D	F/W	7.3.50	Cerne Combat	Geronimo Gretel	Mrs Dellar	Mr & Mrs Hunter
1954 Gremlin Inkling	D	F/W	14.1.53	Ch. Gremlin Inxpot	Mandy Lou of Wrymark	Mr Wright	Mrs Fairbrother
Panfield Beau Jinks	D	B/W	7.1.53	Mazelaine's Texas Ranger	Ch. Panfield Party Piece of Greentubs	Maj. & Mrs Somerfield	Breeders
Klesby Cherry Brandy	B	F/W	27.2.52	Klesby Starlight	Orburn Griselda	Mrs Handford	Mrs Hucklesby
Glad Eyes of Chetawayo	B	F/W	18.10.52	Bontrapu Blitz	Gremlin Design	Captain Hughes	Breeder
Winkinglight Justice	D	B/W	13.3.53	Winkinglight Jandan Jupiter	Winkinglight Vesper	Mrs Hullock	Breeder
Wardrobes Hunting Pink	B	F/W	17.4.53	Wardrobes Starlight of Belfoyne	Wardrobes Gay Taffeta	Mrs C. W. Wiley	Breeder
Braxburn Flush Royal	D	F/W	1.5.53	Gremlin Winkinglight Vigilant	Geronimo Candy'n Cake	Miss Warden	Breeder
Wardrobes Sari	B	B/W	14.4.53	Wardrobes Starlight of Belfoyne	Wardrobes Gay Taffeta	Mrs C. W. Wiley	Breeder
Sheafdon Toplocks Welladay	B	F/W	17.1.51	Axel von Bad Oeyn	Toplocks Panfield Stella	Mrs I. V. Wilson	Miss J. Haggle
Panfield Texas Tycoon	D	B/W	30.10.53	Mazelaine's Texas Ranger	Ch. Panfield Party Piece of Greentubs	Maj. & Mrs Somerfield	Breeders

Name	Sex	Colour	Birth	Sire	Dam	Breeder	Owner
1955							
Burstall Zipaway	B	F/W	8.1.53	USA Ch. Mazelaine's Gallantry	Beaulaine's Bonadea	Major D. F. Bostock	Breeder
Vicki of Felpham	B	F/W	7.10.51	Ch. Winkinglight Viking	Bodil of Schulensee	Capt. Mathews	Mrs Hullock & Mr Wynn
Burstall Fireaway	D	F/W	8.1.53	USA Ch. Mazelaine's Gallantry	Beaulaine's Bonadea	Major D. F. Bostock	Breeder
Mayerling Sugar Bush	B	F/W	21.4.53	Borestone Klesby Sublime	Yacomb Folly	Mrs Hemery	Breeder
Stainburndorf Dandylion	D	F/W	26.3.53	Stainburndorf Frochlich von Dom	Stainburndorf Babette	Mr Thorton	Mr Ridley
Sheafdon Spellmaker	D	F/W	22.11.53	Mazelaine's Texas Ranger	Ch. Toplocks Welladay of Sheafdon	Miss Haggie	Miss Haggie
Trispia Rachel	B	F/W	3.11.53	Trispia Nabob	Brenalvie Ballet Dancer	Mrs Jarvis	Mrs Bicknell
Wardrobes Miss Mink	B	F/W	30.10.54	Ch. Winkinglight Justice	Wardrobes Silver Spurs	Mrs C. W. Wiley	Breeder
1956							
Tinkazan Merriveen Speculation	B	F/W	16.10.54	Felmoor Raineylaine's Raffles	Merriveen Moussec	Mrs P. Dellar	Mrs J. Scheja
Wardrobes Rustle of Silk	B	F/W	12.7.55	Ch. Winkinglight Justice	Ch. Wardrobes Hunting Pink	Mrs C. W. Wiley	Breeder
Burstall Jazzaway	D	F/W	10.10.54	Ch. Burstall Fireaway	Ch. Burstall Delight	Major D. F. Bostock	Breeder
Wardrobes Miss Sable	B	B/W	30.10.54	Ch. Winkinglight Justice	Wardrobes Silver Spurs	Mrs C. W. Wiley	Mrs M. Norrington
Kelfry Merry Monarch	D	F/W	24.10.55	Rob Roy of Tomira	Breakstones Merry Widow	Mr & Mrs P. Kelly	Major D. F. Bostock

Name	Sex	Colour	Birth	Sire	Dam	Breeder	Owner
1957							
Wardrobes Swinging Kilt	D	B/W	29.1.56	Ch. Winkinglight Justice	Wardrobes Silver Spurs	Mrs C. W. Wiley	Breeder
Merriveen Fascination	B	F/W	16.10.54	Felmoor Raineylaine's Raffles	Merriveen Moussec	Mrs P. Dellar	Breeder
Mitsouko of Maspound	D	F/W	1.2.56	Ch. Winkinglight Viking	Marney of Maspound	Mrs K. Guthrie	Breeder
Sonna New Moon of Heighington	B	F/W	8.2.54	Ch. Winkinglight Viking	Sonna Trinket	Mrs Anson	Mr & Mrs E. East
Burstall Little Caesar	D	B/W	24.9.55	Rob Roy of Tomira	Panfield Texas Diana	Mr Ernest Dawson	Major D. F. Bostock
Wardrobes Madam Georgette	B	B/W	29.1.56	Ch. Winkinglight Justice	Wardrobes Silver Spurs	Mrs C. W. Wiley	Breeder
Wardrobes Red Sash	D	F/W	29.1.56	Ch. Winkinglight Justice	Wardrobes Silver Spurs	Mrs C. W. Wiley	Breeder
1958							
Panfield Sneatonhall Ensign	D	F/W	23.10.55	Mazelaine's Texas Ranger	Eve of Gunnholme	Mrs Egerton	Major & Mrs Somerfield
Burstall Icecapade	B	F/W	1.10.55	Rob Roy of Tomira	Ch. Anndale Sheafdon Hooch-mi	Major D. F. Bostock	Breeder
Meteor of Knowle Crest	D	F/W	12.4.54	Fireball of Emefar	Ch. Knowle Crest Isis	Mr & Mrs P. Dyson	Breeders
Felcign Fiona	B	F/W	10.8.56	Felcign Faro	Ch. Felcign Cover Girl	Mrs F. Price	Breeder

183

Name	Sex	Colour	Birth	Sire	Dam	Breeder	Owner
Stainburndorf Bontrapu Xoanon	D	F/W	15.7.56	Ch. Stainburndorf Vanderlion	Bontrapu Nicola	Mrs Lowe	Mr Dawson & Mrs Ridley
Witherford Crystal Clear	D	B/W	11.6.56	Winkinglight Jandan Jupiter	Witherford Cotton Candy	Mr Jakeman & Mrs Withers	Mrs Withers
Wynskip Crofter	D	B/W	2.4.57	Wynskip Winkinglight Janitor	Wynskip Tara	Mr R. Wynn	Breeder
Wardrobes Wild Mink	D	F/W	11.7.57	Ch. Wardrobes Swinging Kilt	Ch. Wardrobes Miss Mink	Mrs C. W. Wiley	Breeder
Felcign Fabulous	B	B/W	10.4.57	Felcign Faro	Felcign Glitter	Mrs F. Price	Breeder
Lejeune Sporting Edition	D	B/W	5.12.54	Mazelaine's Texas Ranger	Ardenoak Special Edition	Mrs A. L. Neale	Breeder
Braxburn Waza Waza	D	B/W	30.1.57	Ch. Braxburn Flush Royal	Rossut It's Magic	Mrs J. Maclaren	Breeder
Wardrobes Joybells of Beitunia	B	F/W	2.4.57	Ch. Wardrobes Red Sash	Kenmirjoy Jingle Bells of Beitunia	Mr Lye	Mrs C. W. Wiley
1959							
Tingdene Felcign Fargo	D	B/W	10.4.57	Felcign Faro	Felcign Glitter	Mrs Price	Mr & Mrs Millard
Witherford Sweet Talk	B	B/W	29.10.57	Winkinglight Jandan Jupiter	Witherford Cotton Candy	Mr Jakeman & Mrs Withers	Mrs Withers
Mickleham Firebird	B	F/W	4.11.54	Stainburndorf Mickleham Solo	Fredibet Firedancer	Misses Hutchinson	Breeders
Panfield Esquire	D	B/W	24.4.57	Ch. Panfield Sneatonhall Ensign	Ch. Panfield Party Piece of Greentubs	Major & Mrs Somerfield	Breeders

Name	Sex	Colour	Birth	Sire	Dam	Breeder	Owner
Wardrobes Madam Marcasite	B	B/W	28.1.58	Ch. Wardrobes Swinging Kilt	Beauty of Shrublands	Mr H. Miles	Mrs C. W. Wiley
Burstall Barnstormer	D	F/W	31.10.57	Rob Roy of Tomira	Ardenoak Minuet	Messrs E. Hodges and E. Dawson	Major D. F. Bostock
Summerdale Shamus	D	F/W	4.6.58	Rainey Lane's Sirocco	Summerdale Selmus Debutante	Mr M. Summers	Mr M. Summers and Mrs Fairbrother
Wardrobes Red Fan	B	F/W	27.3.58	Ch. Wardrobes Red Sash	Wardrobes Bella Bikini	Mrs C. W. Wiley	Breeder
Merriveen Medallion	D	B/W	20.3.58	Mazelaine's Texas Ranger	Ch. Merriveen Fascination	Mrs Dellar	Mrs Dellar & Miss Haggie
Wardrobes Joriemour Witch Doctor	D	F/W	3.3.58	Ch. Wardrobes Wild Mink	Joriemour Carla	Mrs Clark	Mrs C. W. Wiley
Summerdale Snazzy	B	F/W	4.6.58	Rainey Lane's Sirocco	Summerdale Selmus Debutante	Mr M. Summers	Mr M. Summers & Mrs Fairbrother
Wild Star of Greentubs	B	F/W	22.7.58	Ch. Wardrobes Wild Mink	Bomza Starmoney	Mr & Mrs W. R. Cooke	Breeders
1960							
Wardrobes Sapphire Mink	B	B/W	11.7.57	Ch. Wardrobes Swinging Kilt	Ch. Wardrobes Miss Mink	Mrs C. W. Wiley	Breeder
Felcign Francesca	B	F/W	17.6.58	Felcign Faro	Ch. Felcign Cover Girl	Mrs F. Price	Breeder
Witherford Dawn Sky	D	B/W	25.12.58	Ch. Witherford Crystal Clear	Witherford Sunwarm	Mrs P. Withers	Breeder

Name	Sex	Colour	Date	Sire	Dam	Owner	Breeder
Burstall Highblo Valda	B	F/W	15.2.57	Rob Roy of Tomira	Benbox Dainty Dinah	Mr Kelleher	Major D. F. Bostock
Summerdale Normlin Freelancer	D	B/W	23.2.59	Rainey Lane's Sirrocco	Miss Camille of Normlin	Mrs Archer & Mrs Fairbrother	Mr M. Summers & Mrs Fairbrother
Joriemour Ballerina	B	B/W	25.12.53	Flash of Wrymark	Leeta's Legacy	Mrs Clark	Breeder
Wardrobes Side Saddle of Arnogar	B	F/W	31.7.59	Ch. Wardrobes Wild Mink	Odette of Arnogar	Mrs Garroway & Mr Arnot	Mrs C. W. Wiley
Burstall Kinvike Clarion Call	D	F/W	17.9.59	Ch. Burstall Barnstormer	Karendorf Replica	Mrs Gathercole & Flt-Lt Bell	Major D. F. Bostock
Felcign Hot Cargo	D	B/W	10.3.59	Ch. Merriveen Medallion	Ch. Felcign Fabulous	Mrs Price	Breeder
Wardrobes Silhouette of Arnogar	B	F/W	31.7.59	Ch. Wardrobes Wild Mink	Odette of Arnogar	Mrs Garraway & Mr Arnot	Mrs C. W. Wiley
Radden Renown	D	B/W	4.9.57	Ch. Wardrobes Red Sash	Ch. Wardrobes Miss Sable	Mrs Norrington	Breeder
Dorcliff Decision	B	F/W	14.4.59	Ch. Wardrobes Wild Mink	Dorcliff Quaker Girl	Mrs D. Greenwood	Breeder
1961							
Makreen Dreamboat	B	B/W	17.6.59	Ch. Tingdene Felcign Fargo	Makreen Highland Fling	Dr J. J. McKellar	Breeder
Gremlin Normlin Legend	D	B/W	23.2.60	Rainey Lane's Sirrocco	Miss Camille of Normlin	Mrs Archer	Mr M. Summers & Mrs Fairbrother
Panfield Lucky Star	D	B/W	31.10.58	Ch. Panfield Texas Tycoon	Belvedere Fantasia	Mrs Bradshaw	Mr Hodge

Name	Sex	Colour	Birth	Sire	Dam	Breeder	Owner
Beauty Spot	B	B/W	28.10.58	Ch. Burstall Little Caesar	Lynton Lass	Mrs J. Meakes	Breeder
Trelfont Tenacity	D	B/W	15.11.58	Ch. Tingdene Felcign Fargo	Flashlight of Helexion	Mrs J. A. Wallsom	Breeder
Braxburn It's Dinah Might	D	B/W	12.7.56	Ch. Braxburn Flush Royal	Rossut It's Magic	Mrs J. Maclaren	Mr K. Burns
1962 Starmark Strawberry Fair	B	R/W	17.1.59	Ch. Wardrobes Wild Mink	Radden Rapture	Mrs Heath	Breeder
Wardrobes Autumn Haze of Amerglow	D	R/W	17.10.60	Ch. Wardrobes Wild Mink	Merriveen Destiny	Mrs Paterson	Mrs C. W. Wiley
Cloudesley Golden Guinea	B	R/W	20.4.59	Ch. Wardrobes Wild Mink	Cloudesley Copper Bright	Mrs Smith	Breeder
Tip Topper of Klewco	D	B/W	28.4.60	Ch. Witherford Dawn Sky	Ch. Pink Gin of Klewco	Mrs Bishton	Breeder
Chesara Contraband	B	B/W	27.1.61	Ch. Felcign Hot Cargo	Chesara Merriveen Cassandra	Mrs Elsden	Breeder
Pink Gin of Klewco	B	R/W	4.10.58	Hengistholm Mixmaster	Chattermag of Klewco	Mrs Bishton	Breeder
Witherford Pistachio Mint	B	B/W	28.11.60	Ch. Witherford Dawn Sky	Witherford Candlelight	Mrs Withers	Breeder
Summerdale Logic	D	R/W	17.7.61	Rainey Lane's Sirrocco	Ch. Wardrobes Miss Sable	Mrs Norrington	Mr Summers & Mrs Fairbrother

Name	Sex	Colour	Date	Sire	Dam	Owner	Breeder
Winkinglight Juryman	D	R/W	23.7.61	Ch. Winkinglight Justice	Mistinguette of Maspound	Mrs Hullock	Breeder
Panfield Free 'n' Easy	B	R/W	27.10.60	Ch. Summerdale Normlin Freelancer	Merriveen Festoon	Mrs Somerfield	Mr Mizen
1963							
Jetera Jaunty Jane	B	B/W	26.4.59	Rossut Black Magic	Jetera Dinah Marksis	Mrs Owen	Breeder
Radden Pro Rata	D	R/W	17.7.61	Rainey Lane's Sirrocco	Ch. Wardrobes Miss Sable	Mrs Norrington	Breeder
Cherryburton Autumn Rose	B	R/W	28.12.61	Ch. Wardrobes Autumn Haze of Amerglow	Cherryburton Delight	Mr A. Makinson	Mrs Thornley
Bockendon Bewitching	B	R/W	4.4.62	Bockendon Beechnut	Widneyland Bittesehr	Mrs Ingram	Mrs Seale
Cuckmere Jo	D	R/W	28.3.62	Ch. Wardrobes Wild Mink	Cuckmere Prima Donna	Mr Barlow	Breeder
Wardrobes Wilsiclea Autumn Serenade	B	R/W	28.12.61	Ch. Wardrobes Autumn Haze of Amerglow	Cherryburton Delight	Mr A. Makinson	Mrs C. W. Wiley
Witherford Cool Cat	B	B/W	15.7.61	Ch. Witherford Crystal Clear	Witherford Sun Warm	Mrs Withers	Breeder
Gremlin Normlin Notanda	B	B/W	7.3.60	Rainey Lane's Sirrocco	Normlin Nonita	Mrs Archer	Mrs Knight
Wardrobes Flashing Stream	D	R/W	27.10.62	Ch. Wardrobes Autumn Haze of Amerglow	Ch. Wardrobes Silhouette of Arnogar	Mrs C. W. Wiley	Breeder
Summerdale Shatter	B	R/W	4.5.62	Rainey Lane's Sirrocco	Normlin Maxona's Leprachorn	Mr Summers & Mrs Fairbrother	Breeders
Regor Fireball	D	R/W	30.8.61	Rainey Lane's Milltown	Summerdale Sharee	Mr & Mrs Handley	Breeders

Name	Sex	Colour	Birth	Sire	Dam	Breeder	Owner
Greentops Drummajor	D	B/W	19.2.60	Mazelaine's Hit Parade	Greentops Quality	Mr R. Hill	Breeder
1964							
Makreen Saturday Told	B	R/W	22.12.62	Ch. Tingdene Felcign Fargo	Ch. Markeen Dreamboat	Dr McKellar	Breeder
Summerdale Defender	D	R/W	16.5.62	Rainey Lane's Sirrocco	Rainey Lane's Delectable	Mr Summers and Mrs Fairbrother	Breeders
Marbelton Top Mark	D	B/W	16.11.61	Ch. Witherford Dawn Sky	Waylands Top Trick	Mrs Hambleton	Breeder
Wardrobes Emerald of Arnogar	B	R/W	22.6.61	Ch. Wardrobes Wild Mink	Odette of Arnogar	Mrs Garraway & Mr Arnot	Mrs Wiley & Mrs Heath
Wardrobes Thunderbird	D	R/W	17.10.60	Ch. Wardrobes Wild Mink	Merriveen Destiny	Mrs Paterson	Mrs Wiley & Mrs Dixon
Wardrobes Cherry-burton Wild Honey	B	R/W	29.12.62	Ch. Wardrobes Autumn Haze of Amerglow	Cherryburton Stainburndorf Sunshine	Mrs Thornley	Breeder
Seefeld Holbein	D	R/W	17.12.62	Seefeld Radden Rembrandt	Mixonne Mitzie Moonbeam	Mrs Harris	Mrs P. Heath
Pensing Anita	B	B/W	9.2.62	Regor Merry Thought	Normlin Paragonetta	Mrs Singleton	Breeder
Wardrobes Rytonways Autumn Gold	D	B/W	20.10.62	Ch. Wardrobes Autumn Haze of Amerglow	Rytonways Fashion	Mrs Greathead	Mrs Wiley & Mrs Greathead
Radden Skean Dhu	D	R/W	27.2.63	Ch. Radden Pro Rata	Radden Rose Petal	D. & G. Davitt	Mrs Norrington
Makreen Tam O'Shanter	B	B/W	30.9.63	Felcign Hot Diggotty	Makreen Jago	Mrs Kimblin	Mrs Cushman
Bockendon Cresta Run	B	B/W	18.11.59	Ch. Tingdene Felcign Fargo	Retrial of Bockendon	Mrs Ingram	Breeder

Name	Sex	Colour	Birth	Sire	Dam	Breeder	Owner
1965							
Hazefield Bossanova	B	R/W	5.6.63	Yacomb Tempest	Glenside Bolero	Mrs Izett	Breeder
Rytonways Autumn Fashion	B	B/W	20.10.62	Ch. Wardrobes Autumn Haze of Amerglow	Rytonways Fashion	Mrs Greathead	Mrs Woodward
Gunlaw of Klewco	D	B/W	6.11.62	Ch. Tip Topper of Klewco	Chattaway of Klewco	Mrs Bishton	Mr Duncan
Burstall Miss Lacy	B	R/W	1.8.62	Ch. Burstall Barnstormer	Soft Pads	Mrs Lockwood	Mr & Mrs Mair
Wardrobes Morning Canter	D	R/W	19.7.63	Ch. Wardrobes Autumn Haze of Amerglow	Ch. Wardrobes Side Saddle of Arnogar	Mrs C. W. Wiley	Breeder
Bricklesea Cleopatra	B	R/W	3.5.61	Ch. Burstall Little Caesar	Dominoe Lady	Mr W. G. Glake	Mrs Alderton
Swanfield So Smart	D	R/W	22.7.63	Panfield Nassau Adonis	Merriveen Festoon	Mrs Wolfe	Mrs Knight
Phalnagrave Phoenix	D	B/W	25.8.63	Cherryburton Outrider	Cherryburton Touch of Gold	Messrs Ryan & Taylor	Mr & Mrs R. Lee
1966							
Kinvike Kamelia	B	R/W	7.5.62	Ch. Burstall Kinvike Clarion Call	Minstead Golden Charmer	Mrs Gathercole	Mrs Gathercole & Mrs P. Haslam
Felcign Barbery	B	B/W	5.8.64	Felcign Hot Diggotty	Felcign Candy Capers	Mrs Price	Breeder
Véljers Glowworm of Beaverslodge	D	R/W	12.11.62	Wardrobes Delharts Mack The Knife	Dormouse of Beaverslodge	Mrs Clemons	Mrs Burgess

Name	Sex	Colour	Birth	Sire	Dam	Breeder	Owner
Bamarhills Golden Quest	B	R/W	17.3.64	Rainey Lane's Sirrocco	Bamarhills Happy Talk	Mrs Collins	Mrs Hillson
Starmark Mike	D	R/W	21.6.64	Ch. Cuckmere Jo	Cherryburton Vanity	Mrs Marshall	Mrs Heath
Ackendene Royal Fern	D	R/W	5.7.63	Rainey Lane's Sirrocco	Ackendene Fair Comment	Miss J. Grover	Breeder
Marbelton Mosaic	B	B/W	25.10.64	Ch. Marbelton Top Mark	Marbelton Red Ribbon	Mrs Rowe	Mrs Hambleton
Delapoer War Paint	D	B/W	17.4.63	Wardrobes Delharts Mack The Knife	Delapoer Silver Dolphin	Mrs Llewellyn Davies	Breeder
Liedeberge Musetta	B	B/W	28.5.64	Ch. Salola Jazz's Willy Um	Liedeberge Charmaine	Mr P. C. F. Perrett	Breeder
Salola Jazz's Willy Um	D	B/W	7.8.62	Mickleham Xcelsior	Salola Red Topaz	Miss Hutchinson & Miss Boor	Breeders
Summerdale Walk Tall	D	R/W	8.11.64	Summerdale Knockout	Ch. Summerdale Shatter	Mr Summers & Mrs Fairbrother	Mrs Law
Wardrobes Hunters-moon	D	R/W	10.4.64	Ch. Wardrobes Autumn Haze of Amerglow	Ch. Wardrobes Side Saddle of Arnogar	Mrs C. W. Wiley	Breeder
1967 Cheza Hatari	B	R/W	14.2.62	Ch. Wardrobes Thunderbird	Royalhill Carioco	Miss D. Nichols	Mrs Gwatkin
Calidad Oh Be Cheerful	D	B/W	4.2.64	Diamond Bay	Scapa Ella	Mrs Garratt	Breeder

Kingstyle Spitfire	D	R/W	6.12.62	Ch. Wardrobes Autumn Haze of Amerglow	Lindenville Romance	Mrs Wayling	Mr & Mrs Wayling
Seefeld Musk Rose	B	R/W	17.12.62	Wardrobes Delharts Mack The Knife	Seefeld Radden Rosina	Mrs P. Heath	Breeder
Ackendene Royal St John	D	R/W	11.5.65	Ch. Ackendene Royal Fern	Ackendene Spinning Coin	Mrs Van Herk	Miss J. Grover
Silverstein Sundance	D	R/W	15.5.63	Silverstein Sierra	Silverstein Hybeam Mucky	Mrs Dudlyke	Breeder
Felcign Flamenco	B	R/W	14.7.65	Ch. Tingdene Felcign Fargo	Felcign Fabiola	Mrs Price	Breeder
Witherford Stingray	D	B/W	18.4.65	Witherford Firegold	Polidice Cornishay Summer	Mrs Withers	Breeder
Swanfield Southern Sweetie	B	R/W	2.6.65	Ch. Swanfield So Smart	Swanfield Ardane Star Turn	Mrs Knight	Breeder
Wardrobes Cherryburton Bumblebee	D	R/W	20.10.65	Cherryburton Diplomat	Ch. Wardrobes Cherryburton Wild Honey	Mrs Thornley	Mrs C. W. Wiley
Sovrin Stainburndorf Salamander	B	R/W	29.10.64	Stainburndorf Saga	Summerdale High Fashion	Mrs P. Penn	Breeder
Cloudsley Seefeld Samantha	B	B/W	21.2.65	Seefeld Radden Rembrandt	Seefeld Mona Lisa	Mrs Marley	Mrs M. Smith
Marbelton Double-O-Seven	D	B/W	30.5.66	Ch. Marbelton Top Mark	Marbelton Red Lace	Mrs Hambleton	Breeder
Summerdale Stormkist	B	R/W	6.3.62	Rainey Lane's Sirrocco	Panfield Blonde Princess	Mr & Mrs Ward-Davies	Mrs Hillson

Name	Sex	Colour	Birth	Sire	Dam	Breeder	Owner
Valabeau Gold Sari	B	R/W	14.3.65	Ch. Wardrobes Rytonways Autumn Gold	Normlin Springtime	Mr & Mrs W. C. Malcolm	Breeder
1968							
Mickleham Bossy Boots	B	R/W	21.6.66	Felcign Hot Diggotty	Mickleham Maggie May	Miss Hutchinson & Miss N. Boor	Breeders
Hajema Easter Sonnet	B	R/W	10.4.66	Gremlin Trecedar's Catch Me Red	Hajema Honeybun	Mr & Mrs Austing	Breeders
Delapoer Pale Face	D	B/W	29.1.66	Ch. Delapoer War Paint	Terrandor Spectacular	Mrs Williams	Mrs Llewelyn Davis
Rayfos Rainmaker	D	B/W	17.6.65	Sheafdon Medallist	Astree Summerdale Merry Tune	Mr P. Greenway	Breeder
Felcign Prince Hal	D	R/W	25.6.66	Felcign Hot Diggotty	Felcign Fabiola	Mrs F. Price	Breeder
Carfanlain Opus Too	D	R/W	18.8.65	Carfanlain Ibix of Beaverslodge	Bryderi Bashful Queen	Mr Thomas	Breeder
Lindayne Mountain Mist	B	R/W	30.6.65	Wardrobes Delhart's Mac The Knife	Lindayne First Foot	Mrs Lindsay	Breeder
Delapoer Pied Piper	D	B/W	29.1.66	Ch. Delapoer War Paint	Terrandor Spectacular	Mrs Williams	Mr & Mrs Mair
Wardrobes Clair de Lune	B	R/W	5.6.67	Ch. Wardrobes Huntersmoon	Bartondourne Dainty Lady	Miss J. C. Day	Mrs C. W. Wiley
Yooneek Dedication	D	R/W	16.5.64	Ch. Wardrobes Autumn Haze of Amerglow	Yooneek Good Fortune	Mrs V. Tripe	Breeder

Panfield Nassau Adonis	D	R/W	22.4.62	Rainey Lane's Sirrocco	Nassau Cheriton Black Magic	Mr Odling	Mrs P. Knight
Marbelton Pewter Pot	B	B/W	16.10.66	Ch. Marbelton Top Mark	Marbelton Raindrop	Mrs Hambleton	Mrs Gallagher
Felcign Saffron Velvet of Skelder	B	R/W	5.1.67	Felcign the Mandarin	Viva Velvet of Skelder	Mrs Malcolm	Breeder
Glenaulds Gossip	B	R/W	15.4.66	Summerdale Knockout	Stainburndorf Gremlin Cinna	Mr & Mrs Mair	Breeders
1969							
Thelroy Highwayman	D	R/W	23.7.66	Ch. Radden Pro Rata	Marbelton Paper Moon	Mr J. D. Moss	Breeder
Seefeld Picasso	D	R/W	12.11.66	Ch. Seefeld Holbein C. D. (Ex.)	Ch. Seefeld Musk Rose	Mrs Heath	Breeder
Devonaire Tudor Rose	B	B/W	10.5.67	Ch. Starmark Mike	Marbelton Markova	Mrs Carnhill	Breeder
Felcign Makreen Medlar	B	R/W	21.11.66	Felcign the Mandarin	Makreen Truly Fair	Dr McKellar	Mrs F. Price
Wardrobes Wilsiclea Fantasy	B	R/W	17.3.66	Ch. Wardrobes Huntersmoon	Ch. Wardrobes Wilsiclea Autumn Serenade	Mr Makinson	Mrs C. W. Wiley
Bockendon Firelight Glow	B	B/W	12.10.67	Witherford Firegold	Bockendon Born Free	Mrs P. Ingram	Breeder
Farfield Mayfly of Skelder	B	B/W	30.3.67	Velvet Touch of Skelder	Farfield Ting a Ling	Mr Whitfield	Mrs J. Malcolm
Turk of the Leam	D	R/W	14.1.66	Jock of Strathcullen	Miss New Year Wonder	Mr Forster	Mr J. Mallam
1970							
Ridgeway Bandido	D	R/W	17.6.67	Ch. Delapoer Pale Face	Ridgewood Kerensa	R. Partridge	Mrs Brimfield

Name	Sex	Colour	Birth	Sire	Dam	Breeder	Owner
Witherford Cool Mango	D	B/W	29.4.68	Ch. Witherford Stingray	Ch. Witherford Cool Cat	Mrs P. Withers	Breeder
Melvich's Melissa	B	B/W	12.4.69	Ch. Witherford Cool Mango	Melvich's Miss Marchena	Mrs M. Bell	Breeder
Hazefield Barrister	D	R/W	14.3.67	Seefeld Radden Rembrandt	Ch. Hazefield Bossonova	Mrs Izett	Breeder
Newlaithe Ariadne	B	R/W	10.12.68	Ch. Hazefield Barrister	Newlaithe Maisue Teddy Girl	Mrs Beardsell	Breeder
Faerdorn Truly Scrumptious	B	R/W	26.11.68	Ch. Summerdale Normlin Freelancer	Faerdorn Gay Enchantment	Miss S. Harvey	Breeder
Hazefield Beatnik	B	R/W	7.12.68	Ch. Seefeld Holbein C. D. (Ex.)	Ch. Hazefield Bossonova	Mrs Izett	Breeder
Marbelton Music Box	B	B/W	7.1.68	Ch. Marbelton Double-O-Seven	Marbelton Red Ribbons	Mrs Rowe	Mrs Hambleton
Farfield Pedro	D	B/W	2.7.68	Ch. Wardrobes Huntersmoon	Radden Ailsa Amaryllis	Mr Whitfield	Major J. R. Nicholls
1971 Janeen Continental Gold	D	R/W	20.2.68	Ch. Wardrobes Ryton-ways Autumn Gold	Whytebarton Solitaire	Mrs Pryor	Mrs Woodward
Seefeld Artmaster	D	R/W	3.8.69	Int. Ch. Seefeld Picasso	Marven Marcasite	Mrs P. Banks	Mrs P. Heath & Mrs S. Crompton
Starmark Sweet Someday	B	R/W	3.12.68	Starmark Chuck-a-Luck	Starmark Michaela	Mrs J. Heath	Breeder

Name	Sex	Colour	Birth	Sire	Dam	Breeder	Owner
Barnstone Bon Voyage	D	R/W	6.10.68	Barnstone Busby	Barnstone Blue Bonnet	Mrs J. M. Robinson	Breeder
Marbelton Desperate Dan	D	B/W	4.3.70	Ch. Marbelton Top Mark	Charnvyl Personality Girl	Mrs Hambleton	Breeder
Brenrays Venetian Lace	B	B/W	30.1.68	Wardrobes Mack Chandy	Mickleham The Pipers Tune	Mr & Mrs Snape	Breeders
Wardrobes Moon-flower	B	R/W	4.4.69	Ch. Wardrobes Hunters Moon	Touchline of Skelder	Mrs Chapman	Mrs C. W. Wiley
Cherryburton Tiger Pete	D	B/W	15.5.69	Cherryburton Peto Myrlin	Cherryburton Velvet Ribbon	Mrs Saville	Mrs Thornley
Ackenden Precious Bane	B	R/W	14.10.68	Felcign Hot Diggotty	Ackenden Poldice Pippaway	Mr Moss	Miss Grover
Operastar Magic Flute	B	B/W	25.6.66	Witherford Firegold	Operastar Dascha vom Wittekindgrund	Mrs Murray	Breeder
1972							
Calidad Redcoat	D	R/W	6.5.70	Int. Ch. Seefeld Picasso	Calidad Sandfire Fantasia	Mrs Garratt	Breeder
Coperscope Wynbok Sophia	B	R/W	27.2.70	Int. Ch. Seefeld Picasso	Wynbok Wilhelmina	Mrs Marley	Mrs M. I. Walkden
Yooneek Presentation	D	R/W	27.4.69	Ch. Yooneek Dedication	Yooneek Keepsake	Mrs V. Tripe	Breeder
Seacrest Drummage of Mindenwood	D	B/W	24.8.68	Ch. Marbelton Top Mark	Seacrest Stormcall	Mr A. Stephenson	Mr A. Butters
Calidad Bright Boots	B	B/W	28.5.71	Int. Ch. Seefeld Picasso	Calidad Sandfire Fantasia	Mrs Garratt	Breeder

Name	Sex	Colour	Birth	Sire	Dam	Breeder	Owner
Thye Bulan	B	R/W	22.8.69	Ch. Wardrobes Hunters Moon	Thye Ming	Mrs Y. Baxter	Breeder & Mrs Wiley
Starmark Pretty Flamingo	B	R/W	5.7.70	Ch. Cuckmere Jo	Starmark Michaela	Mrs J. Heath	Breeder
Sunshine of Riddagshausen	B	R/W	29.10.70	Wardrobes Moonshine of Riddagshausen	Josephine of Riddagshausen	Mrs R. M. Hughes	Breeder
1973							
Steynmere Ritzie Miss	B	B/W	14.10.71	Int. Ch. Seefeld Picasso	Black Rose of Cherokee Oaks	Dr B. M. Cattanach	Breeder
Rahdavons Remember Me	D	R/W	6.8.70	Radden Upper Crust	Rahdavons Racherine	Mrs W. Rahder	Breeder
Lestar Lucky Lady	B	R/W	30.8.69	Int. Ch. Seefeld Picasso	Lestar Gay Dancer of Honister	Mrs D. Andrews	Breeder
Clayva Argonaut	D	B/W	15.10.70	Ch. Phalnagrav Phoenix	Clayva Carbonel	Mr & Mrs R. Varley	Breeders
Felcign Royal Ruse	D	R/W	16.2.69	Ch. Felcign Prince Hal	Felcign Bracken	Mrs Price	Mr S. Riley
Kinvike Kollector's Item	B	R/W	21.4.72	Int. Ch. Seefeld Picasso	Cherryburton Fine Art	Mrs Gathercole	Breeder
Bockendon Buchanan	D	R/W	6.4.72	Int. Ch. Seefeld Artmaster	Bockendon Nuts'n May	Mrs Ingram	Breeder
1974							
French Spice of Witherford	D	B/W	26.6.72	Ch. Witherford Cool Mango	Lynpine Polly Pare Kins	Mr & Mrs Walker	Mrs P. Withers

Name	Sex	Colour	Birth	Sire	Dam	Breeder	Owner
Marbelton Tyzacks Super Trouper	B	B/W	25.6.72	Ch. Marbelton Desperate Dan	Tyzacks Spanish Moon	Mr & Mrs Donnachie	Mrs Hambleton Mr & Mrs Donnachie
Thunderbolt of Trywell	D	R/W	28.11.71	Int. Ch. Seefeld Picasso	Trywell Tamerisk	Mr & Mrs Goss	Mrs A. Kennett
Faerdorm Truly Gorgeous	B	R/W	9.8.72	Int. Ch. Seefeld Picasso	Ch. Faerdorm Truly Scrumptious	Miss Harvey	Mr Somerfield Miss Harvey
Tartan Tigress of Skelder	B	B/W	11.9.71	Ch. Cherryburton Tiger Pete	Cherryburton Saffron Tarten of Skelder	Mrs Thornley	Mrs Malcolm
Tremendous of Trywell	D	R/W	9.4.72	Rytonways Tamouray Dark Intrigue	Trywell Country Girl	Mrs E. Maxwell	Mrs A. Kennett
Rytonways Triple Crown	D	B/W	15.11.71	Rytonways Tamouray Dark Intrigue	Rytonways Clantilew Sea Mist	Mrs Greathead	Breeder
Silverstein Sundance Kid	D	R/W	21.9.71	Ch. Silverstein Sundance	Brickbats Bardot	Mrs Dudlyke	Breeder
Seefeld Coral Dawn	B	R/W	9.5.72	Int. Ch. Seefeld Picasso	Ashgate Fancy Pack	Mrs Cullen	Mrs P. Heath
Houdini of Sombong	D	R/W	25.8.72	Sombong Chili Sauce	Marbelton New Penny	Mrs Rollings	Mrs R. Evans
Secret Love of Stainburndorf	B	R/W	12.9.72	Ch. Felcign Royal Ruse	Lady Tina Truffle	Mrs Anderson	Mr & Mrs Greenway
Seefeld Miss Pimms	B	R/W	14.4.72	Int. Ch. Seefeld Picasso	Simoor Keyen Miss Brandy	Mrs J. Carter	Mr & Mrs Russell
1975							
Tirkane Avaunt	B	R/W	6.6.73	Braxburn Atilla	Tirkane Afterall	Miss A. Ingram	Breeder
Hazefield Ladybird of Haighlea	B	R/W	18.11.71	Ch. Marbelton Desperate Dan	Hazefield Breakaway	Mr E. A. Carson	Mr Barker

Name	Sex	Colour	Birth	Sire	Dam	Breeder	Owner
Starmark Sweet Talkin' Guy	D	R/W	27.8.73	Wardrobes Tamouray Jonker	Ch. Starmark Sweet Someday	Mrs J. Heath	Breeder
Lovesong of Witherford	B	B/W	4.10.72	Ch. Witherford Cool Mango	Lynpine Black Pudding	Mr C. Walker	Mr & Mrs Fellows
Seefeld Goldsmith	D	R/W	1.8.73	Int. Ch. Seefeld Picasso	Cherryburton Fine Art	Mrs Gathercole	Mr Somerfield
Marbelton Rainfly	B	R/W	17.4.74	Ch. Marbelton Desperate Dan	Silver Slipper of Marbelton	Mrs Hambleton	Breeder
Seefeld Dark N' Delicious	B	B/W	1.2.72	Int. Ch. Seefeld Picasso	Seefeld Miss Degas	Mrs P. Heath	Breeder
Tarpen Sea Moon	B	R/W	4.9.73	Int. Ch. Seefeld Picasso	Tarpen Barbarella	Mrs Alton	Breeder
1976							
Matholme Cool Desire of Snarestone	B	B/W	20.7.72	Ch. Witherford Cool Mango	Matholme Odette Von Gertrudenhof	Mr & Mrs Mathews	Mrs F. M. Davies
Alldane Golden Wonder of Trywell	D	R/W	18.8.74	Ch. Thunderbolt of Trywell	Alldane Golden Blossom	Mr & Mrs Duncan	Mrs Kennett and Mr & Mrs Duncan
Lindayne Francesca	B	R/W	5.6.73	Int. Ch. Seefeld Artmaster	Lindayne Heat Wave	Mrs G. Lindsay	Breeder
Ackendene Willy Wagtail	D	B/W	13.12.74	Ch. French Spice of Witherford	Ackendene Flirty Bird	Miss J. Grover	Breeder
Scallyway of Skelder	B	B/W	25.12.72	Donovan of Skelder	Snarestone Newscast of Skelder	Mrs F. M. Davies	Mrs J. Malcolm

Name	Sex	Colour	Date	Sire	Dam	Owner	Breeder
Camsail Lovebird	B	B/W	21.4.75	Ch. Witherford Cool Mango	Camsail Calypso	Mrs E. R. Boyle	Breeder
Kinbra Uncle Sam of Winuwuk	D	B/W	6.4.75	Kreyons Back in Town of Winuwuk	Kinbra Alice Blue Gown	Mr E. R. Coombes	Mr & Mrs Ward Davies
Goldseal of Klansted	D	R/W	11.3.74	Seefeld Hallmark	Rjondane Magic Starlight	Mr W. Glanvill	Mr C. Cray
1977							
Gremlin Summer Storm	D	B/W	10.1.75	Gremlin Famous Footsteps	Gremlin Mere Magic	Mrs M Fairbrother	Breeder
Wrencliffe Careful Choice of Inglethorn	B	R/W	2.9.73	Marisburn Student Prince	Wrencliffe Silver Raindrop	Mrs M. Best	Miss H. Short
Skelder Burnt Almond	B	B/W	17.12.75	Ch. Starmark Sweet Talkin' Guy	Burning Bright of Skelder	Mrs J. Malcolm	Breeder
Hilario of Stainburndorf	D	R/W	21.3.75	Stainburndorf Fabian	Rayfos Renee	Mrs Robinson	Mrs Penn and Mr Greenway
Liedeberge Annalise	B	B/W	1.6.75	Kreyons Back in Town of Winuwuk	Liedeberge Chiamano Mimi	Mr P. Perrett	Mrs J. Cox
Steynmere Summer Gold	D	R/W	6.8.75	Ch. Seefeld Goldsmith	Ch. Steynmere Ritzi Miss	Dr B. Cattanach	Breeder
Bockendon Cotton Jenny	B	R/W	1.9.75	Ch. Starmark Sweet Talkin' Guy	Bockendon Bright Water	Mrs P. Ingram	Breeder
Thayman Cinna	B	R/W	23.10.71	Int. Ch. Seefeld Artmaster	Thayman Madam Chloe of Calverly	Mrs Anne Norman	Breeder
Seefeld Tinkerbelle	B	R/W	24.6.74	Int. Ch. Seefeld Picasso	Cherry Burton Tiger Belle	Mrs Bowman	Mrs P. Heath

Name	Sex	Colour	Birth	Sire	Dam	Breeder	Owner
Melvich's Miss Mudge	B	B/W	31.1.72	Trelgandorf Sea Wolf	Melvich's Marina	Mrs M. Bell	Breeder
Simoor Status Quo	D	R/W	12.2.75	Int. Ch. Seefeld Picasso	Simoor Queen's Counsel	Mrs J. Carter	Breeder
Lengwyn Lyric	B	R/W	1.7.73	Int. Ch. Seefeld Picasso	Rismort Radiant Star of Lengwyn	Mrs L. G. Greed	Breeder
In a Spin of Witherford	B	B/W	3.10.73	Ch. Witherford Cool Mango	Amber Boogalou	Mrs Barnet	Mrs P. Withers
Newlaithe Quibbler	D	B/W	5.3.75	Rytonways Tamouray Dark Intrigue	Hazefield Best Seller of Newlaithe	Mrs C. Beardsell	Breeder
1978							
Kalendar's Gold Mink of Steynmere	B	B/W	21.11.75	Ch. Steynmere Golden Link	Kalendar's Tartan Gold	Mrs S. Osborne	Dr B. Cattanach
Seefeld Mustard Seed	B	B/W	23.7.75	Nor. Ch. Cavajes Herakles of Seefeld	Seefeld Rose Marie	Mr Elsey and Mrs Heath	Mrs Heath
Dallgery Golden Bracken	D	B/W	25.9.71	Radden Upper Crust	Dallgery Picturesque	Miss A. Podmore	Breeder
Mescalero Cool Breeze	B	R/W	17.3.75	Ch. Witherford Cool Mango	Flibertigibet of Mescalero	Mrs M. Smith	Mrs P. Withers and Mrs D. Hawkins
Whytebarton Three Wishes	B	R/W	30.10.74	Int. Ch. Seefeld Artmaster	Whytebarton Fair Dawn	Mrs B. White	Breeder
Seefeld Sunbeam	D	B/W	18.8.75	Int. Ch. Seefeld Picasso	Caefennie Abby	Mr and Mrs Barnett	Mrs P. Heath

Name	Sex	Colour	Date	Sire	Dam	Owner	Breeder
Seefeld Shadowfax	D	R/W	4.1.77	Nor. Ch. Cavajes Herakles of Seefeld	Seefeld Beau Folly	Mrs P. Heath	Breeder
Skelder Scorching	D	B/W	23.3.77	Ch. Starmark Sweet Talkin' Guy	Burning Bright of Skelder	Mrs J. Malcolm	Breeder
Carinya Peticoat	B	B/W	6.9.76	Ch. Gremlin Summer Storm	Charogne of Carinya	Mrs D. North	Breeder
Alldane Golden Topper of Trywell	D	R/W	25.8.76	Ch. Thunderbolt of Trywell	Alldane Golden Blossom	Mr and Mrs Duncan	Mrs A. Kennett and Mrs S. Blackley
Steynmere Moonflame	B	B/W	17.8.77	Int. Ch. Seefeld Artmaster	Steynmere Summer Symphony	Dr B. Cattanach	Breeder
1979							
Gold Bangle of Panfield	B	R/W	30.10.74	Ch. Seefeld Goldsmith	Ch. Faerdorn Truly Gorgeous	Miss S. Harvey and Major S. Somerfield	Major S. Somerfield
Ackendene Royal Streaker of Zondora	D	B/W	26.6.75	Ch. Ackendene Royal St John	Ackendene Royal Gloss	Miss J. Grover	Mrs P. Queen
Steynmere Golden Link	D	R/W	3.6.74	Pirol Von Belcane	Ch. Steynmere Ritzi Miss	Dr B. Cattanach	Breeder
Jovaltone Penny from Heaven	B	R/W	8.4.76	Ch. Seefeld Goldsmith	Kinvike Krown Jewel of Jovaltone	Mrs V. Gray	Breeder
Marbelton Peep Show	B	B/W	13.3.76	Marbelton Hasty Harry	Too True of Marbelton	Mrs M. Hambleton	Breeder
Marbelton Tyzacks Misty Blue	B	B/W	2.4.77	Marbelton Hasty Harry	Tyzacks Hi Trouper	Mr and Mrs Donnachie	Mrs M. Hambleton
Kinbra Bicentennial	D	B/W	1.7.76	Kreyon's Back In Town of Winuwuk	Kinbra Alice Blue Gown	Mr E. R. Coombes	Breeder

Name	Sex	Colour	Birth	Sire	Dam	Breeder	Owner
Dusky Damsel of Chellowside	B	B/W	30.7.77	Ch. Gremlin Summer Storm	Keelbec Mandolin of Adinas	Mrs Patchett	Mrs J. Blackburn
Braxburn Eros	D	R/W	1.1.77	Wanderobo Afire	Braxburn Skalla	Mr and Mrs J. MacLaren	Breeder
Wilrait Nota Bene	D	B/W	23.7.76	Ch. Gremlin Summer Storm	Wilrait Impromptu Chorus	Mrs R. Williams	Breeder
Camsail Mudlark	B	B/W	11.3.78	Witherford Cherry Cobbler	Ch. Camsail Lovebird	Mrs L. Boyle	Breeder
Landor Prince Charming of Janmer	D	R/W	14.11.77	Landor Red Duke	Felcign Pink Orchid	Mrs L. James	Mrs James and Mrs Adams
Alldane Golden Joy of Trywell	B	R/W	7.2.78	Ch. Thunderbolt of Trywell	Alldane Golden Blossom	Mr and Mrs Duncan	Mrs Kennett and Mr and Mrs Duncan
Kitwe Sylvia	B	B/W	29.8.77	Kitwe Blue Mink	Kitwe Victoria	Mrs L. Davey	Breeder
1980							
Winuwuk Good Golly	B	B/W	23.6.78	Winuwuk Milray's Red Baron of Valvay	Goodness Gracious of Winuwuk	Mr and Mrs Ward-Davies	Breeder
Collis Winter Gold	D	B/W	26.12.77	Rytonways Tamouray Dark Intrigue	Sukreen High-life	Mrs C. Handford	Mrs L. Greathead
Devonaire Bella Star	B	B/W	6.6.76	Ch. Starmark Sweet Talkin' Guy	Devonaire Tudor Rhythm	Mrs V. Carnill	Breeder
Mauraine Sweet Jolie Girl	B	B/W	20.11.75	Ch. Starmark Sweet Talkin' Guy	Cherry Blossom of Starmark	Mr and Mrs Webb	Breeders
Simoor Status Symbol	D	R/W	28.3.79	Ch. Simoor Status Quo	Winuwuk Kissing Cousin of Simoor	Mrs J. Carter	Breeder

Name	Sex	Colour	Birth	Sire	Dam	Breeder	Owner
Snarestone Skyrocket of Skelder	B	B/W	22.12.78	Ch. Skelder Scorching	Snarestone Ivory Fashion	Mrs F. Davies	Mrs J. Malcolm
Simoor State of Grace	B	B/W	28.3.79	Ch. Simoor Status Quo	Winuwuk Kissing Cousin of Simoor	Mrs J. Carter	Breeder
Ymar Right Royal Raver	B	B/W	24.2.78	Urban Van Het Dennendaal	Ymar Her Royal Highness	Mr and Mrs M. Foan	Breeders
Tyegarth Famous Grouse	D	B/W	14.2.78	Ch. Gremlin Summer Storm	Tyegarth Old Fashioned	Miss S. Cartwright	Breeder
Aramis of Charnvyl	D	R/W	14.8.77	Marisburn Student Prince	Georgie Girl of Charnvyl	Mr Rogers	Mrs P. Clarke
Biloran Mr Similarity	D	R/W	29.3.78	Dicarl Todhunter Too of Biloran	Biloran Lady Tippins	Mr and Mrs W. Law	Breeders
Glorious Twelfth of Redfyre	B	B/W	7.5.79	Ch. Tyegarth Famous Grouse	Redfyre Dolly Bird	Mr Howard	Mrs N. Byerley
Tyegarth Glenmorangie of Jenroy	D	B/W	24.11.78	Ch. Gremlin Summer Storm	Tyegarth Old Fashioned	Miss S. Cartwright	Mrs J. Townshend
1981							
Braxburn Cornelius	D	B/W	3.5.79	Braxburn Thor	Braxburn Catalina	Mr and Mrs MacLaren	Breeders
Steynmere Night Rider	D	B/W	18.5.79	Aus. Ch. That's Right of Panfield	Ch. Kalendars Gold Mink of Steynmere	Dr B. Cattanach	Breeder
Wrencliffe Let's Try Again	B	B/W	20.3.80	Winuwuk Milray's Red Baron of Valvay	Wrencliffe Sweet Pepper	Mr M. Best	Breeder
Tyzacks Posh Paws	B	B/W	11.5.79	Tyzacks Bootlegger	Tyzacks Nippy Nellie	Mr and Mrs Donnachie	Breeders
Marbelton Don't Dilly Dally	B	B/W	5.8.78	Aus. Ch. Marbelton Vander Valk	Marbelton Bit of a Madam	Mr M. Hambleton	Breeder

204

Name	Sex	Colour	Birth	Sire	Dam	Breeder	Owner
Skelder Burnt Offering	B	B/W	29.4.79	Ch. Gremlin Summer Storm	Skelder Burnt Amber	Mr J. Malcolm	Breeder
Roylark Kiss Me Kate	B	B/W	8.9.79	Charnvyl Buccaneer	Charnvyl Backchat of Roylark	Mr and Mrs Watson	Breeders
Winuwuk Salak Lucky Strike	B	B/W	26.1.78	Kreyons Back in Town of Winuwuk	Sulak Pirate Treasure	Mr and Mrs Merrett	Breeders
Tyegarth Wee Dram	B	B/W	18.8.79	Ch. Tyegarth Famous Grouse	Tyegarth Auld Lang Syne	Miss S. Cartwright	Breeder
1982							
Faerdorn Pheasant Plucker	D	B/W	7.11.80	Ch. Tyegarth Famous Grouse	Faerdorn Ginger'n'Spice	Miss S. Harvey	Breeder
Norwatch Brock Buster	D	B/W	9.9.80	Ch. Steynmere Night Rider	Norwatch Mustang Wine	Mrs H. Watchorn	Breeder
Mindenwood Jake the Fake	D	B/W	12.4.78	Ch. Newlaithe Quibbler	Burnguard Burlesque	Mr B. Butters	Breeder
Biloran Miss Nancy	B	B/W	10.6.80	Ch. Biloran Mr Similarity	Biloran Mrs Thingummy	Mr and Mrs W. Law	Breeders
Think Big of Trywell	D	R/W	21.7.79	Alldane Golden Triumph of Trywell	Jackman's Pride	Mr Beedell	Mrs S. Blackley
Seefeld Smarty Pants	B	B/W	1.7.79	Ch. Seefeld Shadowfax	Seefeld Fancy Pants	Mrs Heath and Mrs Gunn	Mrs Heath
Norwatch Glory Boy of Rayfos	D	R/W	9.9.80	Ch. Steynmere Night Rider	Norwatch Mustang Wine	Mrs H. Watchorn	Mr and Mrs P. Greenway

Name	Sex	Colour	Birth	Sire	Dam	Breeder	Owner
Yankee Ballard of Jimbren	B	R/W	16.8.80	Winuwuk Milray's Red Baron of Valvay	Jimbren Sweet Mimosa	Mrs P. Poole	Mr & Mrs Groves
Marbelton Making Whoopee	B	B/W	21.7.79	Marbelton Bread Winner	Marbelton Mrs Buswell	Mr & Mrs Hambleton	Breeders
1983							
Tyegarth Double Whiskey of Tyzack	B	B/W	3.11.80	Ch. Tyegarth Famous Grouse	Tyegarth Toshan	Miss S. Cartwright	Mr & Mrs Donnachie
Kanix Scarlett	B	R/W	4.5.81	Nor. Ch. Tonan Supersonic Sonmar	Nor. Ch. Kanix Kamelia	Mr & Mrs Wilberg	Breeders
Socotra's Royal Gam	B	B/W	2.7.82	Ch. Tyegarth Famous Grouse	Kinbra Proper Madam	Mr & Mrs Strachan	Breeders
Wanderobo Hurley Burley of Marbelton	B	B/W	3.7.81	Dandy von Starenschloss	Wanderobo Star	Mr and Mrs Buswell	Mr and Mrs Hambleton
Bonedome Bucks Fizz	D	B/W	2.7.80	Karstorps Zilver Zolomon	Bonedome Bramble	Mr T. Furnival	Mrs P. Ingram
Skelder Sky High	D	B/W	18.4.80	Ch. Snarestone Skyrocket of Skelder	Stainburndorf April Love of Skelder	Mrs J. Malcolm	Mrs Malcolm and Mr Fairhurst
Summer Shadow of Gremlin	D	B/W	17.5.81	Ch. Gremlin Summer Storm	Peepejays Kings Rhapsody	Mrs A. Whiting	Mrs M. Fairbrother
Belowen State Treasure	B	R/W	8.1.81	Ch. Simoor Status Symbol	My Treasure of Belowen	Miss Campbell	Breeder
Moljon Dream Again of Marbelton	B	B/W	22.4.82	Dandy von Starenschloss	Moljon Sporting Favour	Mrs M. Davies	Mrs Hambleton and Mrs Davies

Name	Sex	Colour	Birth	Sire	Dam	Breeder	Owner
1984							
Rayfos Cock Robin	D	F/W	16.10.82	Ch. Norwatch Glory Boy of Rayfos	Rayfos 'Arf A Tick	Mr & Mrs P. Greenway	Breeders
Roylark Call Me Madam	B	F/W	21.11.81	Charnvyl Optimist	Charnvyl Silhouette	Mr A. Watson	Mr & Mrs Hulme
Antron Prize Guy	D	B/W	7.11.80	Ch. Ackendene Willy Wagtail	Antron Arabian Knight	Mrs S. Tonkin	Breeder
Marbelton Dressed To Kill	D	B/W	1.11.82	Quinto Manolitov D. Klappeheide of Marbelton	Marbelton Sugar Cube	Mrs M. Hambleton	Breeder
Britroys Game For A Laugh	B	B/W	20.1.81	Ch. Faerdorn Pheasant Plucker	Britroys Element of Surprise	Mrs J. Livy	Breeder
Sheffordian John-Joe	D	B/W	24.4.81	Ch. Tyegarth Famous Grouse	Sheffordian Sadie	Mrs J. Carter	Breeder
Hiltwood Levishie	B	F/W	13.2.80	Lindayne That's Jazz	Withendorf Coquette	Mrs J. Blade	Breeder
Ch. Tirkane Auditor	B	B/W	20.1.82	Ir. Ch. Tirkane Toastmaster	Braxburn Vendetta	Miss A. Ingram	Breeder
Seefeld Coral Gem	B	F/W	11.5.82	Jamaican Ch. Seefeld Hawkbit Copper Beech	Seefeld Coral Flame	Mrs P. Heath	Breeder
Tyegarth Brainduster	B	B/W	28.8.82	Ch. Tyegarth Famous Grouse	Biloran Little Claret	Miss S. Cartwright	Breeder
Kiki Dee of Alexval	B	B/W	23.5.78	Valabeau Viktor	Brunswick Midget Jem	Mrs J. Allison	Mrs D. Mastaglio

Name	Sex	Colour	Birth	Sire	Dam	Breeder	Owner
1985 Norwatch O'Toole of Rayfos	D	B/W	29.5.81	Ch. Steynmere Night Rider	Norwatch Mustang Wine	Mrs H. Watchorn	Messrs & Mesdames Greenway and Webster
Tinkers Trade of Harmaur	B	B/W	14.11.82	Ch. Tyegarth Famous Grouse	Janetiken Laurette	Mrs Potts & Mrs Wragg	Mrs Wragg
Tyegarth Gin'N'Cin	B	B/W	21.4.83	Ch. Tyegarth Famous Grouse	Biloran Little Claret	Miss S. Cartwright	Breeder
Bucksteps Bit 'O Bother at Jenroy	B	B/W	4.7.82	Ch. Tyegarth Glenmorangie	Bucksteps Bits 'n' Pieces of Jenroy	Mrs J. Whittaker	Mrs J. Townsend
Ice Maiden of Rayfos	B	F/W	21.6.82	Ch. Norwatch Glory Boy of Rayfos	Faerdorn Spiced Ginger	Mr J. Norman	Mr & Mrs Greenway
Trywell Twelfth Night	B	B/W	3.8.82	Ch. Steynmere Night Rider	Brigadoon Tigermouth of Trywell	Mrs A. Kennett	Breeder
Snarestone Pinnochio of Tyzack	D	B/W	12.6.83	Ch. Steynmere Night Rider	Snarestone Bisy Lizzie	Mrs F. M. Davies	Mr & Mrs M. Donnachie
Norwatch Slightly Sozzled	B	B/W	26.5.84	Ch. Tyegarth Famous Grouse	Norwatch Mustang Wine	Mrs H. Watchorn	Breeder/ Mr Banks
Willrait Titianesque	B	F/W	2.3.84	Ch. Kinbra Uncle Sam of Winuwuk	Sweet Scarlet of Willrait	Mrs R. Williams	Breeder
Marbelton Drunken Duncan	D	B/W	8.4.84	Ch. Marbelton Dressed to Kill	Ch. Wanderobo Hurley Burley of Marbelton	Mrs M. Hambleton	Breeder
Tyegarth Blue Kiwi	D	B/W	24.4.84	Ch. Tyegarth Famous Grouse	Biloran Little Claret	Miss S. Cartwright	Mr V. Zammit

Name	Sex	Colour	Birth	Sire	Dam	Breeder	Owner
1986							
Faerdorn Flash Bang Wallop	D	R/W	24.1.84	Ch. Faerdorn Pheasant Plucker	Faerdorn All Things Nice	Miss S. Harvey & Mr R. Hughes	Mrs C. Evans
Ryecroft Jazz Singer	D	B/W	20.4.83	Ch. Faerdorn Pheasant Plucker	Scrumpy of Tyegarth at Ryecroft	Mr F. Unsworth	Breeder
Katar Dancing Shadows	D	B/W	26.8.83	Ch. Summer Shadow of Gremlin	Sunhawk Night Dancer	Mr & Mrs L. Stait	Breeders
Susancar Lucy Lastic	B	B/W	1.10.84	Dolf the Buhe Farm of Marbelton	Shy Talk of Susancar	Misses S. & S. Carter	Breeders
Alexval Vienna	B	R/W	31.5.83	Ch. Biloran Mr Similarity	Alexval Vivacious	Mrs D. Mastaglio	Breeder
Skelder Pot Luck	B	R/W	1.12.84	Skelder Pot Black	Skelder Slapstick	Mrs J. Malcolm	Breeder
Camsail Firefox	D	R/W	29.7.82	Ch. Braxburn Cornelius	Camsail Tiger Moth	Mrs L. Boyle	Breeder
Garnet Gelert of Steynmere	D	R/W	17.10.84	Ch. Steynmere Night Rider	Garnet Gemma	Mrs P. Walker	Dr Cattanach
Tonantron Glory Girl	B	B/W	14.7.83	Ch. Norwatch Glory Boy of Rayfos	Antron Prize Girl	Mrs S. Tonkin	Breeder
Jenroy Pop My Cork to Walkon	D	B/W	17.12.84	Ch. Tyegarth Glenmorangie of Jenroy	Jenroy Whoopsie Daisy	Mrs J. Townsend	Mrs Y. Miller
1987							
Bailiga Rigoletto of Holwell	D	R/W	19.10.84	Ch. Faerdorn Pheasant Plucker	Tynesider Emanuelle of Bailiga	Mrs J. Price	Mr D. Carter
Wrencliffe Flying Scotchman of Winuwuk	D	B/W	9.3.84	Ch. Norwatch Brock Buster	Wrencliffe Let's Try Again	Mrs M. Best	Mr & Mrs Ward-Davies & Miss J. Brown

Name	Sex	Colour	Birth	Sire	Dam	Breeder	Owner
Slightly Sloshed of Sunhawk and Walkon	B	B/W	26.5.84	Ch. Tyegarth Famous Grouse	Norwatch Mustang Wine	Mrs H. Banks (formerly Watchorn)	Mrs Y. Miller
Investigator of Abythorn	D	B/W	20.2.85	Abythorn Secret Agent	Jeans Secret Suzy	Mrs J. Everitt	Mrs R. Tucker
Roxess Daze of Wine and Roses	B	R/W	10.7.85	Jenroy Knight and Daze	Ocean Breeze at Roxess	Mrs N. Todd	Breeder
Hey Good Lookin' at Marbelton	D	B/W	22.7.85	Dolf The Buhe Farm of Marbelton	Marbelton Green Goddess	Mr T. Jones and Mrs M. Hambleton	Mrs M. Hambleton
Marbelton Burley Chassis	B	B/W	11.12.85	Dolf The Buhe Farm of Marbelton	Marbelton Hustle Bustle	Mrs M. Hambleton	Breeder
Glenfall The Gladiator	D	B/W	4.7.85	Ch. Kinbra Uncle Sam of Winuwuk	Glenfall Amber Spirit	Mrs P. Broughton	Breeder
Jenroy Lot Less Bother	B	B/W	3.12.85	Ch. Norwatch Brock Buster	Ch. Bucksteps Bit 'O Bother at Jenroy	Mrs J. Townshend	Breeder
Rupik Bellringer of Seefeld	D	R/W	20.7.84	Braemerwood Proclamation of Seefeld	Rupik Jingle Belle	Mrs S. Bowman	Mesdames Heath & Bowman
Witherford Gay Jasmin	B	B/W	27.2.85	Witherford Parsley Pepper	Witherford Lime Wise	Mrs P. Withers & Mr T. Dahlstrom	Breeders
Sheffordian Ruby Tuesday of Norwatch	B	B/W	31.5.83	Ch. Norwatch Brock Buster	Sheffordian Sherry	Mrs D. Carter	Mr & Mrs E. Banks
Norwatch Sunhawk Raffles	D	B/W	27.6.86	Ch. Tyegarth Famous Grouse	Ch. Sheffordian Ruby Tuesday of Norwatch	Mr & Mrs E. Banks	Breeders

APPENDIX B

PEDIGREES OF KEY DOGS

Int. Ch. Dorian von Marienhof of Mazelaine

Parents	Grandparents	GG-parents	GGG-parents
Sire Ch. Xerxes v. Dom	Int. Ch. Sigurd v. Dom of Barmere	Iwein v. Dom	Buko v. Biederstein Zweibel v. Dom
		Belinde Hassia	Adi Hassia Anita v. d. Schillerstadt
	Dudel v. Pfarrhaus	Caesar v. Deutenkofen	Moritz v. Goldrain Liesel v. Deutenkofen
		Ossi v. Dom	Iwein v. Dom Dragga v. Schweizerland
Dam Saxonia's Andl	Ch. Check v. Hunnenstein	Caesar v. Deutenkofen	Moritz v. Goldrain Liesel v. Deutenkofen
		Dina v. Hunnenstein	Sgr. Drill v. Gum- bertusbrunnen Zitta v. Durrenberg
	Yvonne v. Marienhof	Lauser v. Frankenjura	Egen v. Gum- bertusbrunnen Adda v. d. Adelegg
		Fee. v. Marienhof	Agis v. Schonburg Sgrn. Beate v. Marienhof

Int. Ch. Lustig von Dom of Tulgey Wood

Parents	Grandparents	GG-parents	GGG-parents

Parents	Grandparents	GG-parents	GGG-parents
Sire Zorn v. Dom	Ch. Sigurd v. Dom	Iwein v. Dom	Buko v. Biederstein Zweibel v. Dom
		Belinde Hassia	Adi Hassia Anita v. d. Schillerstadt
	Dudel v. Pfarrhaus	Caesar v. Deutenkofen	Moritz v. Goldrain Liesel v. Deutenkofen
		Ossi v. Dom	Iwein v. Dom Dragga v. Schweizerland
Dam Esta v. d. Würm	Ch. Sigurd v. Dom	Iwein v. Dom	Buko v. Biederstein Zweibel v. Dom
		Belinde Hassia	Adi Hassia Anita v. d. Schillerstadt
	Siegerine Uni v. d. Würm	Edler v. Isarstrand	Ch. Egon Gumbertusbrunnen Belime v. Isarstrand
		Meta v. Rechenberg-Wehrspitz	Astor v. St Jakob Ch. Meta Birkenhain

Ch. Panfield Serenade

Parents	Grandparents	GG-parents	GGG-parents
		USA Ch. Stainburndorf Zunftig v. Dom	Int Ch. Lustig v. Dom Blanka v. Fohlnhöf
	Stainburndorf Zulu	Bessi v. Trauntal	Tanko v. Haïdhausen Sgrn. Fricka v. Berggeist
Sire Juniper of Bramblings		Panfield Adler	Ajax v. Mühlenberg Gretl v. d. Boxerstadt
	Panfield Dolla of Bramblings	Alma v. d. Frankenwarte	Int. Ch. Lustig v. Dom Alfa v. Wurz-burger-Glockli
		Zorn v. Dom	Ch. Sigurd v. Dom Dudel v. Pfarrhaus
	Int. Ch. Lustig v. Dom	Esta v. d. Würm	Ch. Sigurd v. Dom Uni v. d. Würm
Dam Alma v. d. Frankenwarte		Ch. Dux v. Marienhof	Ch. Xerxes v. Dom Saxonia's Andl
	Alfa v. Wurz-burger-Glockli	Arri v. Hetz-Gelder Giemanl	Ch. Aspirin v. Neu-Drosedow Waben v. Dom

Ch. Panfield Ringleader

Parents	Grandparents	GG-parents	GGG-parents
		Stainburndorf Zulu	USA Ch. Zunftig v. Dom / Bessi v. Trauntal
	Panfield Flak	Panfield Astra	Ajax v. Mühlenberg / Gretl v. d. Boxerstadt
Sire Ch. Panfield Tango	Alma v. d. Frankenwarte	Int. Ch. Lustig v. Dom	Zorn v. Dom / Esta v. d. Würm
		Alfa v. Wurz-burger Glockli	Ch. Dux v. Marienhof / Arri v. Hetzfelder Giemaul
		Stainburndorf Zulu	USA Ch. Zunftig v. Dom / Bessi v. Trauntal
	Juniper of Bramblings	Panfield Dolla	Panfield Adler / Alma v. d. Frankenwarte
Dam Ch. Panfield Serenade	Alma v. d. Frankenwarte	Int. Ch. Lustig v. Dom	Zorn v. Dom / Esta v. d. Würm
		Alfa v. Wurz-burger Glockli	Ch. Dux v. Marienhof / Arri v. Hetzfelder Giemaul

Dutch Ch. Faust vom Haus Germania and his full brother Breakstones Helios vom Haus Germania

Parents	Grandparents	GG-parents	GGG-parents
		Ch. Lump v. Menchendahl	Emir v. Schillerstein / Heidi v. Menchendahl
	Dutch Ch. Ceberus vom Haus Germania	Ch. Idella v. Pfarrkirchen	Ch. Lustig v. Dom / Dora v. Pfarrkirchen
Sire Dutch Ch. Leoncillo's Alf		Edler v. Bismarksaule	Hektor v. Menchendahl / Betty v. Bismarksaule
	Boekios Alma	Ceres v. Vlederinckhoven	Int. Ch. Lustig v. Dom / Adda Typolog
		Ch. Dolf v. Uracher Wasserfall	Zorn v. Dom / Seigerine Gretel v. Hohenneuffen
	Ch. Dolf v. Richtersblick	Cita vom Haus Germania	Ch. Lump v. Menchendahl / Ch. Idella v. Pfarrkirchen
Dam Diva vom Haus Germania		Int. Ch. Lustig v. Dom	Zorn v. Dom / Esta v. d. Würm
	Ch. Idella v. Pfarrkirchen	Dora v. Pfarrkirchen	Bummel v. Dom / Astra v. Pfarrkirchen

Ch. Winkinglight Justice

Parents	Grandparents	GG-parents	GGG-parents
Sire Winkinglight Jandan Jupiter	Winkinglight Vanquisher	Dutch Ch. Faust vom Haus Germania	Dutch Ch. Leoncillo's Alf
			Diva vom Haus Germania
		Ch. Orburn Kekeri	Ch. Holger v. Germania
			Margarethe of Maspound
	Juno of Robinhalt	Ch. Holger v. Germania	Rex v. Hoheneuffen
			Dutch Ch. Favorite vom Haus Germania
		Antigone of Quatrefoil	Champus v. d. Fischerhutte
			Akroma Khamsin
Dam Winkinglight Vesper	Ch. Gremlin Inxpot	Axel v. Bad Oeyn	Roon v. Waldenburg-Truchsess
			Stella v. Weissen Schloss
		Gremlin Moonbeam	Ch. Panfield Tango
			Gremlin Bossi v. Rhona
	Ch. Orburn Kekeri	Ch. Holger v. Germania	Rex v. Hoheneuffen
			Dutch Ch. Favorite vom Haus Germania
		Margarethe of Maspound	Maspound Amos of Field-Burcote
			Stainburndorf Franconia

Mazelaine's Texas Ranger

Parents	Grandparents	GG-parents	GGG-parents
		Ch. Duke Cronian	Int. Ch. Dorian v. Marienhof of Mazelaine
	Ch. Yobang of Sirrah Crest		Ch. Crona V. Zwergeck
Sire		Madeira of Sirrah Crest	Ch. Utz v. Dom
Int. Ch. Ursa Major of Sirrah Crest			Ouphe of Sirrah Crest
		Whirlaway of Mazelaine C.D.	Ch. Kavalier of Mazelaine
	Umbra of Sirrah Crest		Ch. Mazelaine Leocadia
		Ch. Oracle of Sirrah Crest	Ch. Duke Cronian
			Ouida of Mazelaine
		Nightcap of Sirrah Crest	Ch. Endymion of Mazelaine
	Ch. Xebony of Sirrah Crest		Ouinkle of Sirrah Crest
		Madcap of Sirrah Crest	Ch. Kobang of Sirrah Crest
Dam			Onyx of Sirrah Crest
Verily Verily of Sirrah Crest		Ch. Kobang of Sirrah Crest	Ch. Duke Cronian
	Ch. Questa of Sirrah Crest		Kantatrix of Mazelaine
		Ovation of Sirrah Crest	Ch. Kavalier of Mazelaine
			Ouida of Mazelaine

Ch. Marbelton Desperate Dan

Parents	Grandparents	GG-parents	GGG-parents

Sire
Ch. Marbelton Top Mark

- Ch. Witherford Dawn Sky
  - Ch. Witherford Crystal Clear
    - Winkinglight Jandan Jupiter
    - Witherford Cotten Candy
  - Witherford Sunwarm
    - German Import Xanti Von Don
    - Miss Tycoon
- Waylands Top Trick of Marbelton
  - Ch. Winking-light Justice
    - Winkinglight Jandan Jupiter
    - Winkinglight Vesper
  - Texas Flare of Jacinta
    - Finemere Makreen Gay Spark
    - Quick Trick of Jacinta

Dam
Marbelton Charnvyl Personality Girl

- Ch. Marbelton Double O Seven
  - Ch. Marbelton Top Mark
    - Waylands Top Trick of Marbelton
    - Felden Fickle Felden Flame Girl
  - Marbelton Red Sash
- Marbelton Rayfos Chatterbox
  - Ch. Summer-dale Walk Tall
    - Summerdale Knockout
    - Ch. Summerdale Shatter
  - Rayfos Desert Wanton
    - Sheafdon Madellist
    - Geronimo School For Scandal

Int. Ch. Seefeld Picasso

Parents	Grandparents	GG-parents	GGG-parents
		Felcign Faro	Rainey Lane's Raffles (USA)
	Seefeld Radden Rembrandt		Ch. Toplocks Welladay of Sheafdon
		Ch. Wardrobes Miss Sable	Ch. Winkinglight Justice
Sire Ch. Seefeld Holbein C.D. (Ex)			Wardrobes Silver Spurs
		Feldon Fohn	Gremlin Sirocco of Felden
	Mixonne Mitzi Moonbeam		Tania of Shangri-la
		Boxmoor Amanda	Gremlin Sirocco of Felden
			Tina of Avondale
		USA Ch. Jered's Spellbinder	USA Ch. Elixir of Rainey Lane's
	Wardrobes Delhart's Mack the Knife		Hot Copy of Gay Oaks
		USA Ch. Delhart's Diamond Lil	USA Ch. Barrage of Quality Hill
Dam Ch. Seefeld Musk Rose			Delhart's Candie Babe
		Ch. Wardrobes Red Sash	Ch. Winkinglight Justice
	Seefeld Radden Rosina		Wardrobes Silver Spurs
		Ch. Wardrobes Miss Sable	Ch. Winkinglight Justice
			Wardrobes Silver Spurs

Ch. Wardrobes Autumn Haze of Amerglow

Parents	Grandparents	GG-parents	GGG-parents
			Winkinglight Jandan Jupiter
		Ch. Winking-light Justice	Winkinglight Vesper
	Ch. Wardrobes Swinging Kilt		Wardrobes Starlight of Belfoyne
		Wardrobes Silver Spurs	Wardrobes Gay Taffeta
Sire Ch. Wardrobes Wild Mink			Winkinglight Jandan Jupiter
		Ch. Winking-light Justice	Winkinglight Vesper
	Ch. Wardrobes Miss Mink		Wardrobes Starlight of Belfoyne
		Wardrobes Silver Spurs	Wardrobes Gay Taffeta
			USA Ch. Yobang of Sirrah Crest
		USA Ch. Ursa Major of Sirrah Crest	Umbra of Sirrah Crest
	Mazelaine's Texas Ranger USA Import		USA Ch. Xebony of Sirrah Crest
		Verily Verily of Sirrah Crest	USA Ch. Questa of Sirrah Crest
Dam Merriveen Destiny			USA Ch. Dion of Rainey Lane's
		Felmoor Rainey Lane's Raffles	Mindy of Rainey Lane's
	Ch. Merri-veen Fascination		Cerne Combat Geronimo
		Merriveen Moussec	Gretel

Ch. Seefeld Goldsmith

Parents	Grandparents	GG-parents	GGG-parents
		Seefeld Radden Rembrandt	Felcign Faro Ch. Wardrobes Miss Sable
	Seefeld Ch. Holbein C. D. (Ex.)	Mixonne Mitzi Moonbeam	Felden Fohn Boxmore Amanda
Sire Ch. Seefeld Picasso		Wardrobes Delharts Mack The Knife	USA Ch. Jered Spellbinder USA Ch.Delha Diamond Lil
	Ch. Seefeld Musk Rose	Seefeld Radden Rosina	Ch. Wardrobes Red Sash Ch. Wardrobes Miss Sable
		Carfanlain Ibex of Beaverslodge	Ch. Wardrobes Autumn Haze of Amerglo Bush Baby of Beaverslodge
	Ch. Carfanlain Opus Too	Brynderi Bashful Queen	Thurgo Gay Lord Babs of Newport
Dam Cherryburton Fine Art		Cherryburton Magicion	Cherryburton Diplomat Cherryburton Enchantress
	Hildorf Honeypot	Hildorf Honey Dew	Ch. Wardrobes Wild Mink Stainburndorf Peachnut

Ch. Gremlin Summer Storm

Parents	Grandparents	GG-parents	GGG-parents
		Rainey Lane's Sirrocco	USA Ch. Dion of Rainey Lane's Lady Lita of Lennane
	Ch. Summerdale Shamus		
		Summerdale Selmus Debutante	Gremlin Signature Summerdale Sunglow
Sire Gremlin Famous Footsteps			
		Summerdale Knockout	Summerdale Southpaw Summerdale Radden Ragazza
	Gremlin Walk On		
		Ch. Summerdale Shatter	Rainey Lane Sirrocco Normlin Maxonia's Leprechaun
		Treceder's Catch Me Red	USA Ch. Treceder's Sequel USA Ch. Treceder's Calendar Girl
	Gremlin Catch Fire		
		Sheasum Gremlin Fantastique	Ch. Summerdale Shamus Gremlin Walk On
Dam Gremlin Mere Magic			
		Treceder's Catch Me Red	USA Ch. Treceder's Sequel USA Ch. Treceder's Calendar Girl
	Gremlin Catch the Dawn		
		Gremlin Walk On	Summerdale Knockout Ch. Summerdale Shatter

Winuwuk Milray's Red Baron of Valvay

Parents	Grandparents	GG-parents	GGG-parents
Sire Ch. Scher Khoun's Abednego	Ch. Scher Khoun's Shadrack	Ch. Millan's Fashion Hint	Ch. Salgray's Fashion Plate Ch. Gaymitz Jet Action
		Ch. Scher Khoun's Carousel	Ch. Standfast of Blossomlea Ch. Scher Khoun's Apricot Brandy
	Ch. Scher Khoun's Carousel	Ch. Standfast of Blossomlea	Ruda River's Happy Go Lucky Ch. Fireside Chat of Blossomlea
		Ch. Scher Khoun's Apricot Brandy	Ch. Standfast of Blossomlea Ch. Scher Khoun's Fire Imp
Dam Milray's Flame of Candelwood	Ch. Holly Lane's Winter Forecast	Ch. Scher Khoun's Meshack	Ch. Scher Khoun's Shadrack Ch. Scher Khoun's Syncopation
		Ch. Holly Lane's Windstorm	Ch. Brayshaw's Masquerader Ch. Holly Lane's Cookie
	Candelwood's Cinderella	Ch. Pinebrook's Radiation	Candelwood's Straight Shot Oliver's Happy Talk
		Candelwood's Cassandra	Ch. Treceder's Shine Boy Candelwood's Gina

Ch. Tyegarth Famous Grouse

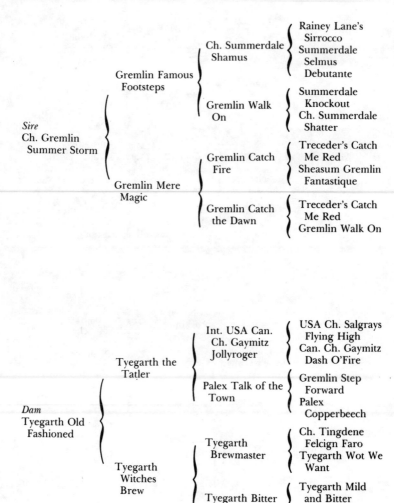

Parents	Grandparents	GG-parents	GGG-parents
		Ch. Summerdale Shamus	Rainey Lane's Sirrocco / Summerdale Selmus Debutante
	Gremlin Famous Footsteps	Gremlin Walk On	Summerdale Knockout / Ch. Summerdale Shatter
Sire Ch. Gremlin Summer Storm		Gremlin Catch Fire	Treceder's Catch Me Red / Sheasum Gremlin Fantastique
	Gremlin Mere Magic	Gremlin Catch the Dawn	Treceder's Catch Me Red / Gremlin Walk On
		Int. USA Can. Ch. Gaymitz Jollyroger	USA Ch. Salgrays Flying High / Can. Ch. Gaymitz Dash O'Fire
	Tyegarth the Tatler	Palex Talk of the Town	Gremlin Step Forward / Palex Copperbeech
Dam Tyegarth Old Fashioned		Tyegarth Brewmaster	Ch. Tingdene Felcign Faro / Tyegarth Wot We Want
	Tyegarth Witches Brew	Tyegarth Bitter Brew	Tyegarth Mild and Bitter / Tyegarth Bitter Lemon

Ch. Simoor Status Symbol

Parents	Grandparents	GG-parents	GGG-parents
		Ch. Seefeld Holbein C. D. (Ex.)	Seefeld Radden Rembrandt Mixonne Mitzi Moonbeam
	Int. Ch. Seefeld Picasso	Ch. Seefeld Musk Rose	Wardrobes Delharts Mack the Knife Seefeld Radden Rosina
Sire Ch. Simoor Status Quo		Seefeld Bailiff	Ch. Hazefield Barrister Seefeld Miss Cezanne
	Simoor Queen's Counsel	Simoor Barley Wine	Int. Ch. Seefeld Picasso Simoor Keyen Miss Brandy
		Kreyons Back In Town of Winuwuk	Int. Ch. Scher Khoun's Shadrack USA Ch. Kreyons Firebrand
	Ch. Kinbra Uncle Sam of Winuwuk	Kinbra Alice Blue Gown	Kitwe Blue Mink Kinbra Alice Springs
Dam Winuwuk Kissing Cousin of Simoor		Seefeld Roast Chestnut	Bockendon Beechnut Seefeld Miss Charcoal
	Ziggy Starlight of Winuwuk	Clifton Carousel	Keignton Kavalier Clifton Red Velvet

Ch. Steynmere Night Rider

Parents	*Grandparents*	*GG-parents*	*GGG-parents*
Sire Aust. Ch. That's Right of Panfield	Ch. Steynmere Summer Gold	Ch. Seefeld Goldsmith	Ch. Seefeld Picasso Cherryburton Fine Art
		Ch. Steynmere Ritzi Miss	Ch. Seefeld Picasso Black Rose of Cherokee Oaks
	Ch. Gold Bangle of Panfield	Ch. Seefeld Goldsmith	Ch. Seefeld Picasso Cherryburton Fine Art
		Ch. Faerdorn Truly Gorgeous	Ch. Seefeld Picasso Ch. Faerdorn Truly Scrumptious
Dam Ch. Kalendars Gold Mink of Steynmere	Ch. Steynmere Ritzi Link	Pirol Van Belcane	Int. Ch. Us-Ranus v.d. Rieterstadt Verden Weldek Fancy Free
		Ch. Steynmere Ritzi Miss	Ch. Seefeld Picasso Black Rose of Cherokee Oaks
	Kalendars Tartan Gold	Borderfame Tartan Gold	Ch. Wardrobes Rytonways Autumn Gold Borderfame Coastguards Tartan Ribbons
		Kitwe Bridget	Kitwe Blue Mink Kitwe Copper Belt

Ch. Norwatch Brock Buster

Parents	Grandparents	GG-parents	GGG-parents
Sire Ch. Steynmere Night Rider	Aust. Ch. That's Right of Panfield	Ch. Steynmere Summer Gold	Ch. Seefeld Goldsmith Ch. Steynmere Ritzi Miss
		Ch. Gold Bangle of Panfield	Ch. Seefeld Goldsmith Ch. Faerdorn Truly Gorgeous
	Ch. Kalendars Gold Mink of Steynmere	Ch. Steynmere Golden Link	Pirol van Belcane Ch. Steynmere Ritzi Miss
		Kalendars Tartan Gold	Borderfame Tartan Gold Kitwe Bridget
Dam Norwatch Mustang Wine	Liedeberge Ramsey	Kreyons Back In Town of Winuwuk	Int. Ch. Scher Khoun's Shadrack USA Ch. Kreyons Firebrand
		Liedeberge Chiamano Mimi	Gremlin Treceder's Catch Me Red Ch. Liedeberge Musetta
	Gremlin Soft Steps	Gremlin Famous Footsteps	Ch. Summerdale Shamus Gremlin Walk On
		Gremlin Semi-Sweet	Gremlin Famous Footsteps Gremlin Mere Magic

Ch. Faerdorn Pheasant Plucker

Parents	*Grandparents*	*GG-parents*	*GGG-parents*
Sire Ch. Tyegarth Famous Grouse	Ch. Gremlin Summer Storm	Gremlin Famous Footsteps	Ch. Summerdale Shamus Gremlin Walk On
		Gremlin Mere Magic	Gremlin Catch Fire Gremlin Catch the Dawn
	Tyegarth Old Fashioned	Tyegarth the Tatler	Int. Can. Ch. Gaymitz Jollyroger Palex Talk of the Town
		Tyegarth Witches Brew	Tyegarth Brewmaster Tyegarth Bitter Brew
Dam Faerdorn Ginger'n'Spice	Winuwuk Milray's Red Baron of Valvay	USA Ch. Scher Khoun's Abednego	USA Ch. Scher Khoun's Shadrack USA Ch. Scher Khoun's Carousel
		Milray's Flame of Candelwood	USA Ch. Holly Lanes Winter Forecast Candelwoods Cinderella
	Ch. Faerdorn Truly Gorgeous	Int. Ch. Seefeld Picasso	Ch. Seefeld Holbein Ch. Seefeld Musk Rose
		Ch. Faerdorn Truly Scrumptious	Ch. Summerdale Normlin Freelancer Faerdorn Gay Enchantment

Ch. Antron Prize Guy

Parents	Grandparents	GG-parents	GGG-parents
		Ch. Witherford Cool Mango	Ch. Witherford Stingray Ch. Witherford Cool Cat
	Ch. French Spice of Witherford	Lynpine Polly Parekins	Golden Baron of Klenco Witherford Wayout Red of Lynpine
Sire Ch. Ackendene Willy Wagtail		Faerdorn Firecrest	Ch. Summerdale Defender Faerdorn Surpise Packet
	Ackendene Flirtybird	Ackendene Poldice Pippaway	Ch. Ackendene Royal Fern Wardrobes Poldice Pendorra
		Yeovale Rural Craftsman	Int. Ch. Seefeld Picasso Yeovale Sherry
	Toro of Kenstaff	Yeovale Cool Miss	Yeovale Cool Customer Yeovale Dominoe
Dam Antron Arabian Knight		Ch. Ackendene Willy Wagtail	Ch. French Spice of Witherford Ackendene Flirtybird
	Ackendene's Raven's Wing	Ackendene Nutty Slack	Ch. Ackendene Royal St John Ackendene Royal. Glass

APPENDIX C

BOXER CLUBS IN THE UK

British Boxer Club
Cotswold Boxer Club
Gwent Boxer Club
Irish Boxer Dog Club
London and Home Counties Boxer Club
Mancunian Boxer Club
Merseyside Boxer Club
Midland Boxer Club
Northern Boxer Club
Scottish Boxer Club
South Wales Boxer Club
South Western Boxer Club
Tyne, Wear and Tees Boxer Club

The names and addresses of secretaries can be obtained on application to the Kennel Club, 1–4 Clarges Street, Piccadilly, London W1Y 8AB

INDEX